CAN'T FIGHT IT

KAYLEE RYAN
LACEY BLACK

Cover Design: Sommer Stein, Perfect Pear Creative Covers
Cover Photography: Sara Eirew
Editing: Hot Tree Editing
Proofreading: Kara Hildebrand & Deaton Author Services

CHAPTER 1

Colton

"Well, little man, it's just you and me," I tell my son, who is sleeping peacefully in my arms. I look around the sparse furnishings of our new home and sigh. I've been in the military since the day I graduated high school. I own nothing but the clothes that traveled with me. That's both a good thing and a bad thing at this point in my life. It's good because I have saved most of the money I've made. Bad, because here I am, a single father, with an infant son, in a house that's well... bare.

And I'm sure this is no surprise, but kids are expensive. Diapers, formula, co-pays, clothes that he grows out of overnight. Toys and car seats, and I could ramble on forever. Kids are expensive, and it's just me. His mother signed him over to me, and although I don't understand it, I'm grateful she did. I always thought my life would be spent in the military. One trip home changed all that. This little man snoozing away in my arms changed it all. Not to mention, I'm going to be an uncle. My little brother got married and is going to be a dad himself. My parents are getting older, and I realize that life is passing me by. I've done my duty, served my country with honor, now it's time to live for me, and Milo. Hence the reason it was time to man up and buy a place of my own.

This house is small but is set up with an in-law suite with a separate entrance. It's a two-bedroom, three if you count the in-law suite. Nothing lavish, it's actually perfect for Milo and me. The realtor convinced me that getting a tenant would be a good idea to offset some of the mortgage payment. The in-law suite is more like a tiny one-room apartment. There is a kitchenette, and a full bathroom, along with a small sitting area and room for a bed and dresser. Nothing huge, but definitely worth a couple of hundred bucks a month in rent.

I was starting to have second thoughts about the tenant. I don't know if I want some stranger living here with my son and me. I mean, I can afford this place on my own, but having some help is always nice. I want to be able to give Milo the best in life, family vacations, the cool new tennis shoes that are ridiculously expensive. I know that's all far away, but I'm a dad now. I have to think about these things.

Chase and Gabby were here last week after the closing, and Chase mentioned the door to the in-law suite could be locked both ways. Since it has its own entrance, I can lock the door from my side to prevent my new tenant from having access to our home. That sold me on the idea, and I posted an ad. Within hours, I had several inquiries, but one stood out. This guy named Hollis. His email was short and to the point. I don't need much space, and I just need a new start. Can pay first and last month's rent before moving in, and I'm willing to take any drug, alcohol, or background tests needed to be approved. He even attached a criminal background check from two years ago.

I messaged him back, we emailed back and forth a few times, and he sent me the first and last month's rent on Monday. Now, here we are, Saturday midday, and he should be here any minute. Chase and

Gabby are coming over too. Gabby is going to watch Milo, while Chase and I help the new guy move in. That's the least we can do. Then we'll probably invite him in for a beer after so we can get to know him.

"Knock, knock." My brother's voice echoes through the pretty much empty house.

"We've got company, buddy." I climb to my feet, my son none the wiser, and head toward the kitchen. "Hey," I greet Gabby and Chase.

"Aw, is my little guy sleeping?" Gabby asks, completely ignoring me. Not that I blame her. My son is handsome and hard to resist. He does get his good looks from his father. Just saying.

"He just conked out about fifteen minutes ago. What's all this?" I ask, nodding toward the bags on the island.

"Oh, just some housewarming stuff. We stopped at the store and got some spices and condiments. Some kitchen utensils, potholders, a pizza pan, and some other random stuff."

"And by stuff, she means, she filled the back of her SUV. Hand over my nephew and help me carry this stuff in." I carefully transfer Milo into Gabby's waiting arms.

"I can't help it. I was in the mood to clean and get our house settled."

"She's nesting. That's what the books say," my brother replies.

"Oh, hush," Gabby says, still staring at my son. "I'm not nesting. I'm just trying to go through my stuff that was stored in the garage before the baby gets here. I just want it off our plates."

"It's not hurting anything sitting in the garage."

"No, it's not. However, I feel better having gone through it."

"Nesting," Chase says again.

"Call it what you want. It's done, so that's all I care about."

"Happy wife, happy life." Chase winks at her, and she rolls her eyes.

"What time is this guy getting here? What's his name again? Harry?" Chase asks.

"Hollis. And he should be here anytime."

"Good, let's get busy unloading so we can help him." He leans down, places his hand on Gabby's protruding belly, and kisses her softly. "Love you," he whispers before disappearing out the door.

I follow along behind him with a twinge of jealousy. I never really thought much about settling down and having a family of my own. However, I assumed if I ever did, it would be in the right order. Never in my wildest imagination did I ever think I would be a single father to an infant, courtesy of a one-night stand.

"You weren't kidding," I tell Chase when we open the back of Gabby's SUV. "You guys didn't have to do all of this."

"It was all Gabs. It's expensive to start out on your own. We've both been there, and we didn't have a baby to take care of. Besides, some of this stuff is used. We combined our places, cleaned out the garage from when she moved in, and we have duplicates of a lot of things. We figured you wouldn't mind."

"No. I appreciate it, man. I was just thinking about how I have this house, but it's bare-bones."

"This should get you by. It's all in good shape. We just don't need it."

"Thank you. Not just for this, but for taking such good care of Milo. I don't even want to think about what could have happened if it had not been your doorstep she dropped him off on."

"Yeah, well, maybe think twice before you use my name again. I don't think my wife would appreciate that."

"Trust me, that's not going to happen. Those days are long gone. I have more than just myself to think about. Milo needs stability, and I'm going to make damn sure he has it."

"Great. Start by taking this." He places a large box in my arms.

"What's in here?"

"Dishes. Baking dishes, and honestly, I'm not really sure. What I do know is it's yours now, toss or keep it. We don't care either way."

I carry the box into the house and place it on the small kitchen island. "Thanks for all this, Gabby."

"It's nothing. We were going to get rid of it anyway. If you don't like it or need it, just pass it on or donate it. Whatever. I only brought the stuff I thought you might want or need."

I start unpacking the box and pull out some mixing bowls, a couple of glass baking dishes, and a full set of glasses. "Are you sure you don't need this stuff?"

"Positive. Between everything from my apartment and what Chase already had, we're overflowing."

"These are new." I point to the glasses.

"Yeah, I bought them on clearance right before I had to move. We like the ones that Chase had better so, there you go." She grins. "I'm going to lay him down and then start helping you wash and put all this away. Do you have a preference of where it goes?"

"No. The cabinets are clean and bare. You do what you think makes the most sense, and we'll go with that. Thank you, Gabby." My brother did damn good finding his forever.

"We're family." She leaves the room to place Milo in his Pack 'n Play and then reappears and gets right to work.

"I thought we were hauling all this shit in? As in, you and me, brother? Instead, I find you in here chatting up my wife."

"My sister," I counter, and he smiles despite his words. "And I was just taking the time to thank her for all of this."

"I'm taking it all back if you don't get your ass out here and help me."

"That means you have to load it all back up in your SUV," I counter, and he curses under his breath, making Gabby giggle. "Come on, you big baby." It takes us two more trips to get it all unloaded.

Once the bags and boxes are unpacked, my house doesn't feel so bare anymore. The kitchen is stocked. From baking dishes, glasses, to plates and bowls, even silverware. I have a stack of linens, a throw blanket, and an end table and a lamp that fits perfectly next to the new couch that was delivered earlier this week. There's now a rug lying in front of the front door, and there are two empty laundry baskets ready to be filled in the small laundry room.

"If you need me to watch Milo while you go out and grab whatever else you need, just let me know."

"Thanks. I need to get some paint for his room, and get it all fixed up."

"Oh, I can definitely help with that." She smiles, and her eyes light up at the possibility.

"How about you pick it all out? I'm not good with that stuff." I'm sure I could figure it out, but I know Gabby, and this is right up her alley.

"You have no idea what you just agreed to," Chase jokes. "She's been shopping online every night for our baby's nursery. Who knew there were so many options, and that a tiny little human would need so much?"

"Well, they don't really need to have all of it," Gabby chimes in. "But, it's cute, and you want them to have a place of their own, and babies need routine and security."

"I already told you. Tell me what you want, and it's yours." Chase leans in and presses his lips to hers.

"I knew I loved you for a reason," she quips.

"My baby-making skills," Chase offers with a smirk.

"Well, I mean, I guess there is that," Gabby says, barely able to contain her laughter.

"Woman." He slides his hand behind her neck and crushes his lips to hers. I have to look away. I don't need to see all that. Especially since I've been in a dry spell. So dry, in fact, the night Milo was conceived was the last time my baby-making skills were utilized.

"Keep it PG, brother," I chide Chase.

"Have you seen my wife?" he retorts, pulling away from her.

"Put us to work, babe," Chase tells her.

She doesn't hesitate as she points out dishes and which cabinet to put them in. I do as I'm told. Sure, this is my house, but it's overwhelming. Besides, Gabby loves this stuff. Might as well give her this, for as much as she's done for Milo and me.

"That's the last of it." Gabby wipes her hands on a hand towel that she must have brought with her as well. "At least you're set up for meals, and Milo has what he needs as well."

"Thanks to the two of you. I can't ever repay you for all you've done for me, and for Milo."

"You would have done the same thing," Chase tells me.

He's right, and I would have. I'm just about to tell him that when Milo's whimper stops me. "He didn't sleep long."

"It's a new place, and we weren't exactly quiet."

"You told me not to be quiet."

She nods. "You want him to get used to sleeping through everyday sounds. Keeping a serene quiet house is hard to do, and you and Milo are both going to be sleep-deprived if that's the path you try to take."

"I'm in over my head, aren't I?" I ask them. Milo's whimper turns into a full-on cry. Making my way toward the living room, I lift him in my arms, and I can smell immediately why he was crying. "We'll get you cleaned up, little man." His cries quiet once he's in my arms. "Phew, you stink," I tell him, and his cries quiet further.

The doorbell rings. "That must be him. Time to meet our new roomie." I pull open the door, just as I feel wetness seep through on my hand. Taking a better look, I see my hand is now covered in shit, and my son, well, let's just say his current situation gives new meaning to covered head to toe. "Come on in," I say, not bothering to look up. "I've kind of got a situation on my hands." I turn to head to the bathroom. That's the only solution to this mess.

"I can see that." A soft angelic voice greets my ears and has me stopping in my tracks.

I turn to look over my shoulder, and the most beautiful woman I've ever seen is standing just inside the doorway. Long brown hair, tan skin, and big green eyes that are regarding me with amusement.

"I'm sorry, do I know you?"

"You're Colton Callahan, right?"

"I'm Colton." My mind is going through every woman I've ever met, but I'm pretty sure I would remember her.

She takes a step forward and holds out her hand. "It's nice to meet you. I'm Hollis, your new roommate."

"Colt, everything okay?" Chase enters the room, but I don't look at him. I can't seem to pull my eyes from the goddess standing in front of me.

My new roommate.

Fuck me.

"Y-You're Hollis? You're a woman." A sexy as hell, mouthwatering temptation is more like it. To a man who's been in the desert a good portion of this last year, she's a tall, cold drink of water. I can hear Chase laughing, but my eyes remain on her.

"Is that a problem?" she asks, tilting her head to the side.

"Babe, wh— Oh, hi." Gabby offers her hand to Hollis. "I'm Gabby, Chase's wife."

"Hollis."

Gabby's mouth forms the perfect O. "You're Hollis?"

"I am." She turns to me and grins, then scrunches up her nose. "What on earth?" She moves toward me, and that's when I remember that not only is my hand covered in my son's shit, but he's covered as well.

"Right. I need to handle this." I turn on my heel and rush toward the bathroom. Once Milo and I are behind the locked door, for good measure, I take a deep breath. "This isn't what I was expecting, bud. We're going to have to tell her to leave, right? She can't live here with us. No way. Sleeping with our tenant is not a good idea. Daddy's just going to have to tell her there was a mix-up, and she needs to find a new place. Yeah, that's what I'll do."

I take my time getting my son cleaned up before wrapping him in one of his infant towels that I just folded and put away this morning. From the bathroom, I head down the hall to his room and quickly get him in a fresh diaper and clean clothes. He's smiling up at me, happy as can be.

"Your belly feeling better?" I ask. He coos and kicks his legs, which is a good enough answer for me. "All right, bud, time to do this." I lift him into my arms, and we head back toward the living room. I stop when I see Chase carrying two totes and Hollis behind him wheeling two suitcases.

"Thank you for your help, Chase."

"No problem. My nephew has bad timing."

"Maybe I should go see if he needs help," Gabby speaks up.

"He can handle it."

"All better," I state and the three of them turn to look at me.

"Come here, you little stinker." Gabby takes Milo from my arms and snuggles him close. "Aunt Gabby missed you."

"This is the last of it," Chase tells me.

"The room's great. Thank you," Hollis adds.

I open my mouth to tell her to leave, and nothing happens. It's like I forgot how to speak. I try again and still nothing. What the hell is wrong with me? She has to go. I can't live with her. Nope. I thought she was male. Someone I can have a few beers with, maybe watch the game. I can't with her. What if I want to bring someone home? How awkward would that be having a female roommate? Even as my mind ticks off reasons, I can't form the words. I can't tell her to leave.

"So, Hollis. We were just about to order some pizza. You in?" Chase asks.

"I don't want to impose."

"Not at all. That will give us all a chance to get to know one another. Chase and I are here a lot, or Colt and Milo are at our place, so I'm sure we'll be seeing a lot of each other."

"Sure. I'll eat anything. Give me a few minutes to freshen up from the drive, and I'll be right back." I watch her as she disappears through the small hallway off the living room that leads to her room. I don't take a full breath until I hear her bedroom door close.

I feel a hand on my shoulder, followed by a tight squeeze. "You all right, brother?" Chase laughs.

"Hollis. I thought she was a man."

"Did you not look at her background check?"

"I did. It was clear. I didn't read the gender section. I just wanted to make sure the guy wasn't a criminal."

"Woman," he corrects me.

"Fuck me."

His laughter rings in my ears. This should be interesting.

CHAPTER 2

Hollis

Deep breath.

And try not to stare at my new landlord's ass.

That's proving to be a much harder task the longer he's in my presence. I've been around plenty of guys in my life, but none that make my heart hammer in my chest like a steel drum and tempts me to spill all of my secrets. Heaven knows *that's* not happening. Not today. Not ever. My instant attraction to Colton Callahan is the exact reason why I should pack back up my measly belongings and head for another location.

Though, I've always heard about this town. Fair Lakes, in the heart of Missouri. With its humid summers and its blustery winters. My grandma grew up here, so I heard all about the small midwestern town that she called home for nearly two decades until she met my grandpa and moved with his military career. I've heard enough of her stories though. How this town was built around the large lakes. How everyone greets you when you pass on the sidewalk. How they host festivals in the town square. Of course, I'm certain the town has changed in the last five decades since she left.

I'm locked in my little studio apartment—in-law suite, I believe is what they call it—and trying to dig out a fresh sweatshirt to throw on. I could really use a shower, but my bath products are still packed away in one of my boxes, and that's not something I want to tackle right now. My stomach growls, reminding me it's been a while since I gave it food. That's probably why I actually said yes to their pizza offer. It was my stomach talking and not logical sense. The logical part of my brain would have declined their offer for food and would already be through the first box of belongings. But here I am, washing my hands and getting ready to share a pizza with my landlord, his brother, and sister-in-law, and apparently, his baby boy.

Of course I'd find the one guy who clearly has his hands full, right? Hell, he probably has a girlfriend, or worse, a wife. Then I'll meet her, like her, and feel guilty for staring at her husband's ass every chance I got. Though, this house clearly doesn't have a woman's touch—at least not yet. In fact, there's not much of a touch at all. The outside needs a little landscape help and a good grass trimming before the hard winter hits. The shutters are a faded green, and the wooden steps creaked a little with each step we took. I'd probably call it a fixer-upper, which isn't far off from his description in the ad I found.

Actually, this place is exactly how I envisioned it, which is how he described it. I was shocked, and maybe a little thankful, he answered my email so quickly. He just purchased this place and had the space to rent to a single occupant. The in-law suite features its own entrance, which will come in handy for maintaining privacy. I can keep to myself and come and go as I please. Of course, I'm already o-1 in the whole keep-to-myself bit. I'm sure enjoying pizza and maybe a few drinks don't fall under the loner category. How are you supposed to blend in and make everyone forget you when the first person you meet, your tongue is hanging out like a horny dog, and you jump at the opportunity to spend just a little more time with him?

You're doing a swell job there, Hollis.

Sighing, I wipe my wet hands on a paper towel by the sink and glance around my new space. It's small—*very* small—but practical. All I need is a little space to work from my laptop, a place to rest my head, and a kitchen to cook some food. I have all of that. Well, minus the resting of the head part. I have no furniture yet, which I hope to rectify in the morning with a trip to a local secondhand store I found in my online search of the area. Until then, I'll take my blankets and pillow and make a nice bed on the floor. It'll be like camping, only better. Fewer bugs and bears.

Laughter spills through the closed door. I'm sure the reason it echoes is that my place is empty, right? Add in a few pieces of practical furniture, and I'm sure I'll barely know I have roommates so close. The baby cries loudly, and I can't help but wonder what I got myself into. I've never been around a baby before. He didn't say anything about a baby in the ad, but I guess that's not a deal breaker. It's not like I'm here to care for the little guy, right?

That's right, Hollis. You're just renting a room. This isn't your family or problem to deal with.

Deciding I've been gone long enough, I open the door and step into Colton's space. My entrance is off the laundry room, right next to where the washer and dryer are positioned. The ad mentioned a communal laundry room for both him and myself, as well as the back exit. I take a quick peek at the backyard and am surprised by the size. It's large, with several old trees that will provide plenty of shade in the summer. It needs a good mowing and trim job, but I can see why a man with a young son would want a yard like this one.

I head to the kitchen and find Colton. His back is to me, and he's talking to the little boy perched against his shoulder. The little guy sees me and starts waving his arms around. "That's right, champ. We'll get your belly full and then finish getting the furniture set up in your room. You're gonna sleep in your big boy crib tonight in your new room. Are you excited?" he asks his son as he shakes up the fresh bottle he just made. Colton turns his head and places his mouth on the baby's side, blowing a raspberry kiss through his onesie outfit. Milo wiggles and yells, but not in the pissed off way he yelled when I first arrived. No, this one is a happy yell, one that makes me smile.

"Oh, sorry. I didn't know you were standing there."

I glance up from the baby and find Colton's blue eyes watching me. "Sorry, I didn't want to interrupt," I say, glancing down at my shoes.

"You weren't interrupting," he insists, maneuvering Milo to the crook of his arm and plopping the bottle into his awaiting mouth. "It's his dinner time," he adds, glancing down and smiling at the boy in his arms.

"I'll let you get to that. I can wait in my room," I insist, starting to turn back the way I came.

"No, let's take a quick tour. I don't mind feeding him on the go. In fact, I'm pretty much becoming a professional at it," he adds with a chuckle. The deep timbre of his voice can be felt clear down to my toes.

"Are you sure?" I ask.

He waves me to follow him as he heads toward the front of the house. "This is my living room," he says, stepping into a wide, open space. It has a couch and large television, but that's about it. Well, besides the playpen set up in the corner of the room. The walls are painted the same taupe color as my walls, and the carpet is the same tan plush. Whoever decorated didn't enjoy too much of a color palette.

"Back here are our bedrooms. This one is Milo's," he says, pushing open the door and revealing his sister-in-law.

"Oh, hey! I'm just getting some of Milo's things put away," she says to me before looking at Colton. "As soon as Chase gets back, he'll help you get all this stuff put together," she adds, pointing to the disassembled crib and changing table.

"Okay. Pizza should be here soon. Hopefully, my little brother doesn't take his sweet-ass time at the hardware store," Colton says, making Gabby roll her eyes.

"You know him. He'll check out every single locking mechanism they have in stock before he makes a final decision."

Colton snorts. "No shit. He's worse than a woman." Then he looks at me and nods toward the hallway. "Let's finish this tour."

I follow him across the hall and stop in the doorway. Colton's room. It's practically empty except a small mattress on the floor and a stack of boxes with some clothes piled on top of them. "This is my room. Or at least it will be when I get some furniture," he adds with a sheepish grin.

"Well, you've already got more than I do," I tell him with a laugh. My intention was a joke, but I can tell the moment my comment registers in his brain.

Colton looks at me, his blue eyes watching me closely. "You don't have any furniture?"

I shrug. "I'm going to Second Street Treasures tomorrow to get a few things," I tell him casually, praying he doesn't bring up the fact that I moved here without having much of anything in tow.

He nods. "I was thinking of stopping in there too for some of the little things. My bed and dresser will be here Monday, and while my mom offered to let me have my set from my old room, I'm not really interested in a twin-sized bed and dresser with GI Joe stickers all over it. Nothing about that screams responsible adult."

I laugh at the thought. "No, you're probably right."

"Come on, let's finish up the tour before Milo needs burping."

I follow Colton out the front door. The walkway leads to both the sidewalk out front and the driveway beside the house. There's a two-car garage, with a wide driveway to allow two vehicles to park easily. "You're welcome to take one of the garage bays. I'll move my truck into the garage in a little bit and free up the space."

"No problem. I'm parked in the street right now. I don't mind keeping it up there," I tell him, thinking about my older Honda Accord. It's a few years old and has more dents and dings than a race car. Whoever owned my baby before me, definitely was rough on her.

"No need. I don't need both spaces. You might as well utilize one," he says, heading toward the back of the property. "Your entrance is here. I've got the keys on the counter inside. You're welcome to use the backyard anytime you want. I'm hoping to put a few chairs back here, maybe a firepit or something like that too. Someday, probably a swing set," he adds, glancing down and smiling at Milo, who's going to town on the bottle of formula.

The yard is even bigger than it looked through the window. There's a small lot between Colton's place and his neighbor's, and the whole thing is fenced in with a basic wooden privacy fence. "It's a great yard."

"It is. It's part of the reason I bought it. I wanted this little guy to have plenty of running room."

We head to the back door, and I hold it open for Colton. I catch a whiff of something woodsy as he passes, either his soap or his detergent, and the fumes go straight to my dormant lady parts. Suddenly, they're alive and raring to go, as if waking from a long, deep hibernation. It was one thing to steal a few appreciative glances at his very nice rear, but smelling him is on a whole different playing field. Whatever it is short circuits my brain and makes my nipples tingle. I'm definitely out of my league here with this one.

I didn't sign up for intoxicating sexy man scent.

"Back here is the laundry room, which you know. You're welcome to use it anytime you want. Store anything you need in the cabinets to the left. I'll take the cabinet above the washer since it's so high up."

I glance around, taking in my new home. "Thank you, Colton. I want you to know how much I appreciate you putting your faith in me as your tenant. I'm sure it's not easy, with a son and all, but I promise not to be a bother or a nuisance. In fact, you won't even know I'm here," I reassure him.

"I doubt it," he mumbles, glancing off to the right. In fact, I'm not really sure he meant to say it aloud.

I know I wasn't what he was expecting when he opened the door earlier. In my defense, I never once tried to hide it from him that I was a woman. If he didn't read my background check, well, that's on him. But I need this place, which is why I'm determined to be the best tenant and roommate he could ask for. I'll be as quiet as a mouse and make sure to be respectful of his property. I'll keep to myself, so he never regrets renting his place to me.

"Got a lock," his brother, Chase, hollers as he walks in the front door. "Oh, hey," he adds when he sees us standing in the kitchen. "I come bearing pizza gifts." Chase sets two pizza boxes down on the counter.

"Thanks. I'll give you some money in a bit," Colton says, setting the empty bottle aside and moving his son to his shoulder.

"Don't worry about it. I got ya covered. Consider it a house-warming gift. For both of you," Chase says, giving me a warm smile. It's actually a quite nice smile. Sexy, even. I imagine that smile gets him out of any trouble he may find himself in, especially with his wife.

She enters the kitchen. "Food. I smell food," she says as she lifts the first pizza box lid and inhales the cheesy goodness. "Oh my God, that smells so freaking good." Then, she pulls a slice of mushroom pizza out of the box and shovels a third of it into her mouth. "Mmm-grrrmm," she mumbles while chewing.

"What's that, baby? I couldn't hear you over your pizza inhalation. Did you even taste that?" Chase teases, coming over and placing his big hand on her small belly.

"Fuck off, Callahan. Baby needs pizza," she says, drawing out that last word, before taking another massive bite.

"Come on, Hollis, let's get you a slice or two of pizza before the pregnant lady eats it all," Colton says, humor in every word.

"Watch it, older Callahan. Be nice, or I'll eat *you*," Gabby chastises, finishing off her first piece.

Colton grabs me a paper plate and waves me on, all while extracting a loud burp from his son. "That's my boy," Chase says proudly, then seems to stop. Something passes between the brothers that I can't decipher, but the moment passes quickly. Chase grabs a plate of pizza and goes to sit next to his wife on the couch.

I follow and take the floor, trying to stay off to the side and out of the way. Not that I'm really *in* the way, but you know what I mean. I'm the outcast here, the outsider who doesn't know any of the people in her company. A few minutes later, Colton comes into the living room and lays Milo down on a blanket he stretched out in the middle of the floor. The little guy starts kicking and waving his arms, wiggling from side to side and kicking his leg to the side.

"You know, it won't be long until he's rolling over," Gabby says between bites.

Colton, who returned to the kitchen to grab a plate of food, says, "Hard to believe we're already approaching that milestone. Seems like just yesterday he was getting up every two hours and making sure I never had a moment's alone time to shower."

Chase snorts. "No shit. He was damn good at pulling the 'scream until you picked him up' card."

"It's better now though, right?" Gabby asks.

"Much better. He's getting up once, maybe twice a night now. And he loves that stupid singing bear, so as long as my shower is under ten minutes, I can usually get it done before the bear shuts off and he vocalizes his disappointment," Colton says, taking a seat on the floor beside his son.

Nibbling on my slice of pizza, I have to concentrate on not inhaling my food. It's been a long day on the road, and since I spent a big part of my travel money on gas, I kept my food to a bare minimum. I have the basic furniture to get yet, and with paying first and last month's rent and only two jobs on the horizon, I need to make sure I stick to my budget.

"So, Hollis, what do you do?" Gabby asks, starting on her second piece.

I glance up and find three sets of eyes on me. I shift in my place on the floor, hating having all the attention on me. "Umm, I design websites mostly, but also some graphic design like logos and business graphics."

"Oh, cool," she says, leaning forward. "Websites, huh? Interesting..."

Chase looks at his wife and smiles. "I already know what you're thinking."

"Didn't I just tell Harrison he needed an updated website?" She turns back my way and says, "The one we have now is not user-friendly. I'd really like to have a page we can keep updated with our calendar. We've been adding all sorts of special classes, and it would be nice to have them all displayed in one place. You know?"

"Absolutely. A good website can be a very effective marketing tool. If you constantly keep it updated, you will train your customers to look there for information."

Gabby's already nodding. "Totally. And you do logo design? We have four locations now, and I'd love to incorporate each location with the image."

"What kind of business is this?" I ask, my design brain already starting to sort and file ideas.

"Oh, sorry. So, my brother-in-law, Harrison, and my sister, Gwen, own All Fit, a local fitness center, which specializes in personal training and fitness classes. Chase is the manager and his right hand. They started the first location together several years ago."

"Cool. I designed a website for a national chain gym last year. You could always check that out for a reference," I tell her, feeling a little weird about pimping a job mere hours after meeting these people. But hey, a girl's gotta eat, right?

"Which gym?" Chase asks, hanging on our every word.

"Family Fitness."

Chase whistles low and gives an appreciative nod. "They're everywhere. That's a pretty big corporation. You must be pretty good."

I just shrug. I've done a lot of websites for a lot of companies. I love creating, giving them their own unique space to sell their product or services, to tell a story about their business, or even create a place of togetherness and solace, and many of them have come back for updates or redesigns. I've come a long way in the last few years, slowly but surely building a name for myself, site by site.

"I'm the office manager, and I'd like to talk to you soon about a possible design," Gabby says. "Do you have a card or something? I mean, it's not like I don't know where you live or anything, but it might be easier to give you a quick buzz than just stopping by unannounced."

"Yeah, I'll leave you my card. It has my cell and email on it."

"Awesome," Gabby says, a wide smile on her face. She turns to Colton and adds, "This might be a great way to start promoting your new classes."

Colton lifts his shoulders. "Whatever you think, Gabs."

She rolls her eyes and turns back my way. "Colton is our newest trainer, and he's starting a self-defense class for women. We've already had about ten ladies sign up at the gym."

"That's probably because he's a Callahan," Chase adds with a smile. "It's a curse."

Gabby snorts and rolls her eyes. "Be careful or you'll trip over that ego."

"The only thing I trip over is my large—"

"Stop talking right now, Callahan," Gabby interrupts, holding her hand up in the universal stop sign.

"No shit, Teeny," Colton mumbles, eating a little food, while still entertaining his son.

"Teeny? What the f—hell? I was defending you, and now you're jumping on her side?" he says to his brother. I can't help but smile at their goodhearted banter. You can tell the brothers are close.

"First off, she writes my paycheck," Colton replies.

"So? I never told Dad about the *Penthouse* magazine I found hidden in your room when you were thirteen," Chase says, crossing his arms over his broad chest.

Now it's Colton's turn to roll his eyes. "That's because you were looking too. Don't pretend you weren't."

"True. But... bro code."

"Which brings me to my second reason as to why I'm on her side," Colton says, kicking back and leaning against the wall, his legs extended in front of him and crossed at the ankles.

"Which is?"

"She's way hotter than you are."

Chase growls at his brother and throws a balled-up napkin. "Whatever, dude. I mean, yes, she is totally hot. The hottest. Right, Milo? Auntie Gabrielle is a fucking knock-out and gets Uncle Chase's pee-pee hard all the time," Chase says as he crouches down and swipes his nephew off the floor. Milo kicks happily and nestles into Chase's arm, his little eyes hanging on his uncle's every word.

"Don't talk about your pee-pee in front of my son, Teeny."

Chase, ignoring the comment from his brother, looks down at the baby and says, "Daddy knows it's not teeny. In fact, it's pretty big. Right, Aunt Gabby?"

"You two are too much. Hollis, you want to join me in the kitchen and get away from all this testosterone? We can discuss the website a little more," Gabby says, standing up and heading to the kitchen space. The moment we're away from the guys, she turns and says, "Sorry about that. They get a little silly sometimes. Colton was in the military for a long time, and I think they've missed each other. Now they're back together, it's like they have to catch up on all their brotherly jabs and tormenting. It's comical, but I don't want to encourage them," she says with a smile.

Tossing my plate in the trash, I ask, "So, he was in the military?"

"Like twelve years. He only recently took an honorable discharge because he found out about Milo."

I yawn and glance at the clock. It's still fairly early, but I've been driving most of the day. My body is starting to scream for a shower and a soft place to crash. Though, thinking about the blankets on the floor, I might have to ease up on what constitutes as soft. "He didn't know about him before he was born?" I ask, yawning a second time.

Gabby shakes her head. "Nope. It's a big dramatic mess. One-night stand shows up at Chase's doorstep and leaves a baby, assuming Chase is the one she slept with. Turns out, a paternity test proves he's not Chase's, but Colton's. Colt happened to be home for a visit after we found out, so Chase told him the truth. Colt didn't reenlist. The moment he found out Milo was his son, he quit the Army to take care of him."

"Wow, that's good. And the mom?"

Gabby rolls her eyes. "She was young. I might not understand her position, but I appreciate her doing the right thing. She signed over her rights and gave Colt full custody."

"That's crazy," I reply through another yawn. "I'm so sorry. It's been a long day for me."

"Why don't you go get some sleep? It's about time for Milo's bedtime anyway, so we should head out. I'll let you get settled and give you a call mid-week if that's okay with you? I really want to redo our website, and I think you're just the girl to get the job done."

I preen a little at the compliment. "Thank you. I'd love to work with you."

"Good, because I'm sure we're going to be seeing each other a lot," she adds with a smile. "I'll get your number from Colton, okay? Nice to meet you, Hollis."

"Nice to meet you too. Thank you for the pizza."

"You're very welcome. I look forward to getting to know you," she says as she heads back to the living room.

I'm not really sure if I should go back in and say goodnight or just head back to my room. I guess I could pop my head in the doorway and wave. Then, I'm still being friendly and considerate while not completely engaging in their conversation.

Before I make it to the doorway, Colton comes around the corner and almost runs into me. "Oh, shit. Sorry," he says, reaching out and steadying me.

The moment his fingers graze my skin, electrical current soars through my body. "It's okay," I mumble, taking a step back and out of his grasp. His eyes seem almost... disappointed when I break our connection. "I was just going to bed."

He nods, shoving his hands in his pockets. "Okay. I'll install that lock on the door tomorrow. It's not that I don't trust you with my house," he starts, but I cut him off.

"It's fine. You don't know me," I reiterate. "I'd do the same if I were in your shoes. I mean, you have a son to think about."

He nods. "Yeah. I was going to put a lock on this side of the laundry room door. This way, it gives me privacy when I'm in here. I checked out the lock on the inside of the in-law suite before you got here. It's a good lock, so you'll be able to keep your privacy there when I'm in the laundry room."

"It creates boundaries. I get it."

"Okay," he says, staring down at me. At five three, I've always been on the shorter side of average, but when I'm standing in front of Colton, I feel tiny. He's easily six one or six two, with big broad shoulders and a tattoo on his left arm that peeks out beneath his shirt sleeve. I can't tell what it is, and I have to keep my hands to myself, so I don't grab the shirt and take a look. "Well, goodnight."

"Night, Colton," I say, heading to my door. "Oh, and thank you again for renting this place to me. I know you were expecting a man, but I appreciate you giving me a chance."

His blue eyes follow my movement. "You're welcome. Everything happens for a reason, right?"

I nod, throw him a quick wave, and disappear into my new mini apartment, locking the door behind me. I know I'm not exactly in the big city anymore, but it's a habit to lock the doors the moment you securely close them. I can't imagine there's much crime here, not after the Mayberry-like stories my grandma used to share, but it's better to be safe than sorry.

I quickly find my box with bedding and throw two blankets and my comforter onto the floor. In the bathroom, I'm able to locate the box with toiletries, and quickly wash my face and take out my contacts. After I brush my teeth, I turn off the light and head back to the living area. After finding a change of clothes, I take in my new place. It's definitely small, but I think it'll work just fine. It's homey and cozy, just what I've been looking for.

I toss my pillow into the pile of blankets and lie under the comforter. Even in the heat of summer, I always have to have my comforter. I sleep cold, so the more blankets, the better. I snuggle into my makeshift bed, the familiar scent of laundry detergent filling my senses. The light is still on in the kitchenette, and I make no move to shut it off. Maybe someday, I'll be able to sleep in the dark again. Today isn't that day, however.

And tomorrow probably won't be either.

As I lie here, I hear Chase and Gabby leave. It's not super loud, but I can hear their movements on the opposite side of the walls. I'm hoping when both places have furniture, maybe it won't be so echoey. Colton moves around in Milo's bedroom. His back wall butts up against one of my walls, so it's just a little noisier than before. I close my eyes and listen to the low hum of Colton's voice as he talks to his son. No, I can't make out what he's saying, thankfully, but I can tell when his talking turns to something more.

With my eyes shut, I let the silence of the night lull me to sleep as the soft sounds of Colton singing to his son rocks me to sleep.

CHAPTER 3

Colton

When Milo begins to fuss at around six, I know my chance at sleep is no more. When my boy is hungry, he's not afraid to let you know it. Typically, it wouldn't be so bad. I'm a morning person. I have many years in the military to thank for that. However, I barely slept a wink last night.

My sexy new tenant is already keeping me up.

It's not just because she's hands down the most beautiful woman I've ever laid my eyes on. But the fact that I know she's sleeping on the hard floor. I went around and around in my head, fighting the urge to let her sleep in my bed. I could take the floor, but in the end, I stayed put. I'm an asshole. I should have offered her the bed, but see there was a dilemma with that. Every time I pictured me going to knock on her door, offering her my mattress, we ended up in it together.

So, instead, I spent the night watching shadows dance across the ceiling as I chastised myself for being an inconsiderate asshole. Sometime around three, I decided I'd make her breakfast. Milo and I went to the store a few days ago and got the basics, and then with what Gabby brought over, I can find something better than cold cereal to offer her, surely.

My boy decides to exercise his lungs as he wails. Quickly, I toss back the covers and shuffle down the hall to his room. "Hey, buddy," I coo as I lift him into my arms. Quickly, I feel around in his bed for his binky and pop it back in his mouth. "Daddy's got you." I rub my hand up and down his back, trying to soothe him. "You know, before we get breakfast, we have to take care of your diaper." His cries turn into a whimper, and then one shuddering breath later he's calm, nestled in my arms.

I love these moments.

When I'm the person he needs.

Carefully, I lay him on the changing table, and start unbuttoning his pajamas. His little arms and legs are flopping all over the place, and from the sound of the suckling, he's going to town on that binky. My time of calm is limited. So, I opt to leave him in his jammies for now. A quick swap of the diaper that weighs thirty pounds for a clean one, and I button him back up.

"All set," I say, lifting him into my arms and kissing his chubby cheek. "Now we get some breakfast."

In the kitchen, I make his bottle one-handed with ease. I'm becoming a pro at this dad gig, if I do say so myself. My feet pad across the hardwood floor to the living room and settle on the couch. I stretch out, and through the early morning light, watch my son as he eats. As usual, he gets pissed off when I take the bottle from him to burp him. "I know," I tell him. "Daddy's just trying to keep you from a belly ache. Aunt Gabby said that was important. Come on, buddy, you can do it." A few more pats on the back and he belches, and it's one for the history books. "There it is." I place the bottle back in his mouth, and he goes to town.

Ten minutes later, the bottle is empty, and he has a blissed-out look in his eyes. His belly is full, and he's a happy baby. I move to put him in his swing, crank it up and go to the kitchen to see what I can scrounge up to make Hollis and me for breakfast. That's another selling point of what sold me on this house. I love the open concept and to know that I can be cooking and still keep an eye on Milo.

I have some eggs, some cheese, and some ham lunch meat. Omelets it is. Pulling out everything I need, I search through the cabinets for a pan. I know I saw Gabby washing one yesterday. I finally find it on the third try. I'm not much of a cook, but omelets I can do.

Ten minutes later, I have two omelets plated, and I'm popping some toast in the toaster. Glancing in the living room, Milo is still just swinging away, taking in his new surroundings. "I hope you like it, little man. This is home." Nothing left to do except finish up the toast, I find myself in front of her door, raising my hand to knock. I'm just getting ready to knock again when the door slowly opens.

I swallow back the urge to tell her she's beautiful. Her hair is pulled up into a ponytail haphazardly as tendrils that have come loose in the night frame her face. She blinks those big green eyes at me. "Colton?" she asks, clearing her throat.

That's the moment I realize I've woken her up. It was just a little after six when Milo woke me up. "I'm so sorry. I forgot not everyone is on my son's timeline. I made us breakfast but go back to sleep. I'm so sorry." I say it again. I feel like an ass. That's the second time I've done wrong by her. Hell, I don't have to worry about her being a distraction; she's going to get tired of my shit and move out.

"You made breakfast?" she asks, placing her hand over her mouth, covering a yawn.

"I did. I forgot what time it was, and I felt bad for not giving you my mattress, and I wanted to make it up to you, so I cooked, and then here I am waking you up. I'm sorry. Go back to sleep." I turn to walk away when she calls my name.

"Colton." I turn to face her once again. "Give me a few minutes, and I'll meet you in the kitchen?"

I nod. "Okay." Turning back around, I go to check on Milo, who is still just swinging away and then finish the toast just in time for Hollis to appear.

Her hair is now smoothed back in a knot on top of her head, and she looks more alert. "Thank you, Colton. You didn't have to do this."

"I did. Tonight, you take my bed."

"That's not necessary. I plan to go shopping today and get some things for my room. A bed and mattress are at the top of the list. It's not your responsibility to worry about me."

Then why does it feel like it? "You're welcome to take my truck," I offer. I have no idea why I just offered the use of my only means of transportation to a complete stranger, one who is living in my house, I might add. However, my gut tells me that even though I don't know her, she's trustworthy. It's something in the depths of those green eyes of hers. It also helps I've already seen her background check. I know she's not a criminal.

"Thank you. I think I'll just venture out and see what I can find. If I need your truck, I can always come back and get it."

"I'll be home all day. I have some class schedules I need to nail down for work for next month. Dig in." I push her plate toward her, and she smiles.

"Thank you."

I nod, and we dig in. I finish a few minutes before her, so I start washing the dishes. She brings her plate to me, just as Milo lets out a screech.

"I can get him if you want?" she offers.

"That's all right. You didn't move here to babysit," I say, trying to quickly rinse the soap off my hands and dry them to go see what's up with my son.

"Colton." Her hand on my arm, against my bare skin, stops my movements. "I don't mind. I love babies. Let me help. That's the least I can do for you making me breakfast."

"I woke you up," I say as Milo's screeches have turned into all-out wails. "He never cries, not unless he needs something." I reach for the kitchen towel, but she's already on the move to the swing and has him in her arms.

"What's the matter?" she coos softly to Milo. His cries instantly stop as he stares up at her. "Oh, I think I know," she says, wrinkling up her nose. "Daddy, I think we have a dirty-diaper situation."

He's mesmerized by her. I guess what they say is true, like father like son. "Come here, buddy," I say, taking him from her arms. My hand brushes hers and a current sparks between us. I pretend like I don't feel it and keep my attention on Milo. "Let's get you cleaned up," I tell him before looking up at Hollis. "Thank you. I'm just going to go change him."

"Thank you for breakfast."

"Anytime," I call over my shoulder. I don't stick around to stare into those green eyes of hers. I could easily get lost, and that has bad idea written all over it. A quick diaper change that has me gagging and a change of clothes, and Milo is ready for his day. I had planned on staying home, but I need to get out. Maybe we'll go visit Mom and Dad, or Chase and Gabby. Hell, I don't know, just a stroll to the park?

"Hey," Hollis says, smiling. "All better?" she asks as she closes the cabinet door.

"You didn't have to do that," I tell her when I see that she has dried and put away all the dishes. "The dishwasher is broken, so that's on my list to fix or replace."

"You cooked. That's the least that I could do."

"Hey, I'm thinking about running to my parents' place. You have my number, right? In case you need me to haul anything for you?" I definitely need to get out of the house. It will do Milo and me both some good.

She nods. "Yes, but I don't think I'll need you."

Why does the thought of her not needing me, bother me? "Well, if you do, don't hesitate." I look down at my son. "I'm going to grab his swing and try to grab a quick shower."

"Colton?"

I turn to look at her. "Yeah?"

"I can watch him for you. I don't mind."

"Thank you, but that's not necessary."

"It's early on Sunday. None of the stores are open for a couple of hours. I'm up. Let me help you. I can't imagine how hard it is caring for an infant all on your own."

"He makes my life better." I'm not just blowing smoke up her ass. I can't imagine my life without my son. He's given me something to come home for, a reason to stay.

Her eyes soften at my words. "He's a sweet baby. Now, hand him over." She holds out her arms, and I hesitate. Already, I'm crossing the lines, and they're starting to blur. She was supposed to be a male tenant who I never saw or heard. She's anything but, and when I can't see her, I can still feel her presence. I should see if Mom and Dad can keep him next weekend. I need to go out. I need to get laid. That's what this is. It's what it has to be. It's been too long.

"Colton, hand me the bundle of cuteness." She wiggles her fingers as she holds her arms out, still waiting for my son.

"I'll be fast." I take one small step and then another, and another until I'm standing close enough to transfer Milo into her arms.

"Take your time. I'm sure a long shower is a rarity for you these days."

"It is. Thanks, Hollis." She settles on the couch and sits Milo on her lap, facing her. She makes faces at him and talks softly. Seeing he's in good hands, I rush down the hall to my room. I strip out of my clothes and step into the shower before the water has even had a chance to heat up. It's a jolt to my system but does nothing to quell the ache in my balls as my cock grows hard.

Hollis.

Bracing my hands on the wall, I tilt my head forward, letting the now steaming hot water rain down on me. I close my eyes, and hers are all I see. Green eyes, dark hair, and a body made for a man's hands. My hands. My mind wanders to what it would feel like to trace every curve, to palm her breasts, testing their weight.

My hand slides between my legs as I grip my cock. I know this is wrong, but it feels all kinds of right. With each stroke, it's her that I imagine. I can't fight it. Not the need for relief, not that my mind only sees her when I close my eyes or the orgasm that blazes through me, like fire in my veins. Peeling open my eyes, I watch as the proof of my desire for her washes down the drain.

Fuck, I'm in so much trouble.

* * *

After my shower, I threw on some clothes, packed up the diaper bag, and fled. I started to go to Chase's, but he knows me too well, and he's met Hollis. He would be able to see right through me. Hell, I'm terrible at hiding it. I could barely look her in the eye this morning as I rushed out the door. I did give her a reminder that if she needed my truck to let me know, and then fled.

That's how I ended up at my parents', and I've been here the entire day. Mom has had Milo while Dad and I have worked on replacing the steps to the back deck. It's been good to stay busy and keep my mind off life and my sexy new tenant.

"What gives?" Dad asks as we're packing up the tools.

"What do you mean?"

He chuckles. "You're my son, Colt. I know when something's up. A father knows things."

"Is this what I have to look forward to? Reading my son, and drilling him to let me into his life?"

"Yes. When he's a teenager, hell even preteen. Yes. And then when he's a grown man and living on his own, you still have that right." He gives me a pointed look.

"Fine," I concede. "My new tenant moved in yesterday."

"Oh, that's right, I forgot about that. How'd that go?"

"He's a she."

"What?"

"Hollis is a she. Not a he."

His reply is to throw his head back in laughter. "I'm not even going to ask you what she looks like. That pained expression on your face says it all."

"Funny," I say, deadpan. "Seriously, I can't let her stay, right? I have to ask her to find a new place?"

"Depends. Is she going against the initial agreement the two of you had?"

"No."

"Do you feel as though it's not safe to have her around Milo?"

"No."

"Then, what would be your reason to ask her to go?" He smirks because he already fucking knows what my reason is.

"You're going to make me say it, aren't you?"

"Yes." He nods with a self-satisfied grin pulling at his lips.

"Fine. She's a fucking knock-out. There, I said it."

"So, get to know her, and who knows, maybe she's the one."

"She's my tenant."

"Technically, she's your roommate."

"That's even worse, Dad. Come on, and you have to see that this is a bad idea."

"I don't see it that way at all. What I do see is my son. A man who has fought for his country. Dedicated his life to his country. I see him not as a soldier but as a man. A man who has been thrust into fatherhood and has risen to that challenge better than anyone could have expected. I know I've told you this before, but I'm going to say it again. Son, I appreciate your service to this country, but as your father, I'm glad you're home. I'm glad you're home to stay. I want nothing more than to see you and Milo find a nice woman to bring into your lives. I want you to be happy and live a full life, one I wasn't sure I would ever see you have."

I swallow the lump in my throat. My parents knew that life in the military was my plan. I got to see the world, and I had a job, a career I was damn proud of. I miss my brothers-in-arms, but no way could I leave my son. His mother might not be in the picture, but I want him to know that I, his father, loves him more than anything. Not a day will go by that my boy won't know I'm there for him, just like my father was there for Chase and me.

"I see those wheels turning." Dad chuckles. "Just take it one day at a time, Colt. I would advise you to keep it in your pants until you know for sure she's someone you want to stick around. However, with that being said, you are the only one who can determine that. There are no rules and no set time limit. Go with your gut. It's brought you home to us many times in the past. It's not going to fail you on this either."

Leave it to my father to be able to bring things into perspective for me. I wonder how he would feel about the timeline, considering I've already jerked off with the gorgeous brunette on my mind? Yeah, what he doesn't know won't hurt him. We're close and all, but not that close.

"You two about ready to eat?" Mom opens the patio door and asks.

"Be right there," Dad tells her.

Quickly, we finish putting away the tools and head into the house to wash up. "Look at you, sitting in the high chair like a big boy." I bend down and press a kiss to the top of Milo's head.

"He's not old enough to eat what we're having, but he can get used to it," Mom explains.

"I think that's a great idea." I take a seat next to the high chair and dig in. Mom made her homemade chicken enchiladas. It's my favorite, and every time I was home on leave in the last ten years, this is the one meal she would make for me. "You spoil me," I tell her, taking a heaping bite.

"Of course I do. I've made your brother's favorite every few weeks for years, having him over for dinner. I have some dinners to make up for."

"This is perfect, Mom. Thank you."

"How's the new tenant? Hollis is his name, right? Did he get moved in okay?"

Dad chuckles under his breath as I heave a heavy sigh. "Yes. She got moved in okay."

"She?" Mom raises her eyebrows in question.

"Yeah, apparently, Hollis is a unisex name. Who knew?" I shrug.

"Well, how is she?"

Hot as fuck. "She's... nice. I haven't really spent much time with her. Chase and Gabs were at the house last night. They went through her things from her apartment they had stored in the garage and brought me what they didn't need or want."

"That was sweet of them."

"Yeah, it helped out a lot. There is so much I need starting from scratch."

"What can we do to help? Do you need money? Or a sitter?"

"No, I'm good on cash. I didn't spend much being deployed all the time. The sitter, though, I might take you up on that one."

"You just tell me when. I'd love to watch him. In fact, he can stay here tonight. I'll keep him tomorrow."

"Gwen is expecting him. Besides, it will help them with extra cash since she quit her job, and you didn't retire just to watch Milo."

"She kind of did," Dad chimes in.

"With Chase and Gabby with one on the way and little Milo here, it was time. Your dad's been trying to get me to for years."

"That will help when Gwen goes on maternity leave for sure. I don't want to take that income, even though she barely charges me anything for watching him. Not just out of the blue."

"Well, I'm here when you need me, and you can let her know that I'll gladly watch that sweet Sophia if she ever needs a break."

"I'll be sure to tell her."

"Good, now eat up. I made a double batch."

I look down at the heaping plate in front of me. "No way, I'll be lucky to get this down."

"I knew you would say that, so you can take the rest home with you. Maybe share it with Hollis. Get to know her a little better."

If I didn't know that my mother loves to feed anyone and everyone, I might think that she and Dad are on some kind of mission to marry me off. I agree to take home the leftovers, but keep quiet on her comment to share them with Hollis. It's not that I don't want to share, but steering clear of her is the better option for me.

I help Mom clean up, change Milo's diaper, and head home. I make two trips—the first with the diaper bag, and the leftovers, the second with my boy. The entire drive home, I think about what my dad said. I need to just get to know her and see what happens. Maybe once I spend more time with her, she'll annoy the hell out of me, and wanting her will no longer be an issue. Even as I think it, I know that's not going to be the case.

Parking my truck in the driveway, I see Hollis's car. Somehow, I manage to carry Milo in his seat, the diaper bag, and the leftovers without dropping any of it. With my arms carefully unloaded, I remove Milo from his seat and place him in the swing. He's snoozing away from our drive, and I hope he stays that way for at least another twenty minutes because as soon as we got into the house, I remembered that I need to install the lock on Hollis's door.

Grabbing the lock from the drawer in the kitchen, and the small toolkit from the counter, I head through the laundry room and knock on her door. She opens immediately, wearing a kind smile.

"Hi, Colton."

"Hey, I need to install your lock. Is now a good time?" I hold up the lock like an idiot as if I need to prove to her, that's why I'm knocking on her door.

"Sure. I was just lounging." She pulls open the door, and I see one of those fold-up lawn chairs, you know, the kind that you can shove into a bag and sling over your shoulder, and some kind of tablet sitting on a blanket on the floor.

I don't know what it is, but something primal pulls inside me. "You can lounge in the living room."

"This is fine, Colton."

"It's not fine. You can lounge on the couch," I say again. "In fact, you should take my bed tonight, and I'll take the couch."

"No. No way am I taking your bed. I have lots of blankets. It's fine. I ordered a mattress today and found a cheap frame at the secondhand store. I should have them here in a week."

"What? You can't sleep on the floor for a week."

"I can, and I will."

I shake my head and turn my back to her. Instead of focusing on how to get her to see things my way, I get busy installing the lock. I'm almost finished when Milo lets out a cry. "Dammit," I mutter.

"Do you mind if I get him?"

"Thank you. He's probably hungry."

"Time for a bottle?" she asks.

"Yeah. I'm almost done," I say, but it's to her back. She's already headed to the living room to take care of my son. For the second time today.

Finishing with the lock, I test it to make sure it works properly. Picking up my trash and my tools, I make my way back to the kitchen. Looking toward the couch, I see Hollis, sitting with Milo in her arms, while she feeds him a bottle.

"It was in the diaper bag."

"Thank you." My mind keeps telling me I'm letting this strange woman handle and now feed my son. However, my gut tells me she would never do him any harm. As long as I'm here with her until I get to know her better, it's fine.

"I don't mind. He's such a good baby."

"That's what they tell me. I mean, I think he's perfect, but I'm biased. I have nothing to go off of. I've never really spent much time around kids. Life in the military will do that to you."

"Well, he's an angel," she says softly, not taking her eyes off my son.

"Have you had dinner?"

"Not yet."

"My mom sent leftovers. I'll heat you up a plate." I need something to do besides stare at her holding my baby boy.

"You don't have to do that."

"Trust me, and you'll be thanking me once you taste it." I busy myself heating her up a plate and set it on the table. "I can take him so you can eat."

"You sure?"

I smile at her. "Yes. I'm sure. Thank you for helping with him."

"It's selfish, really. I get my baby fix."

"You love kids, huh?"

"Yeah." She smiles down at Milo, then transfers him to my arms. When she touches me, that same spark I felt earlier is present.

"You want any of your own?" I ask. Something passes in her eyes, but it's gone before I can name it.

"Maybe one day."

I want to pry, but it's not my place. "Go eat. Enjoy."

"Thank you, Colton."

I force myself to watch Milo eat instead of watching her ass as it sways on her way to the kitchen. "One day at a time, little man. One day at a time," I whisper, keeping my words a secret between father and son.

CHAPTER 4

Hollis

I should head back to my own side of the wall. I started a new design for a small finance company in Dallas and have plenty of work to do. Plus, there are a few of my own things to put away in my new place, including some secondhand dishes I picked up today. Not to mention the little bit of cleaning I want to do before my new bed arrives. So I have plenty to do and shouldn't monopolize anymore of Colton's time.

Yet, here I am, straightening up his dirty dishes and wiping down the countertop.

"You don't have to do that." He startles me, making me jump a mile high. "Sorry," he adds with a chuckle. "Didn't mean to scare you."

I turn around, my hand covering my heart. "No problem. I didn't hear you come in."

He takes a step closer and looks down at Milo. "Habit, I guess. I'm used to moving silently."

"What branch of the military again?" I ask, even though I remember. I just like hearing the sound of his voice. It's weird, considering I barely know him, but I find it soothing. Not to mention sexy as hell, but I'm ignoring that reason.

"Army. Enlisted when I was eighteen," he says, bouncing his son on his hip. "Thought I was going to be in for life until this one came along."

I smile down at the baby who's trying to eat his hand. "He's a pretty good reason to leave."

"The best reason," he agrees. "So, about what I mentioned earlier."

I cross my arms and notice when his eyes drop to my chest. They divert quickly, but it was there nonetheless. That glance and the slight flare of his eyes. "You were saying?" I hedge, even though I know where this conversation is going.

Colton clears his throat. "Right. So, uh, anyway, I want you to take my bed. I'll sleep on the couch. I insist."

I stare across the kitchen at the man before me. He's tall, muscular, and has a body built for your wildest dreams. A few years ago, I'd have taken him up on his offer to take the bed, and maybe even asked him to join me, but not now. Not since I gained my independence back. This is my life, to live the way I see fit, and if that means I sleep on the hard floor with only a few blankets to pad me, then so be it. I can do this my way, and don't need his charity, despite it being appreciated. He's clearly a gentleman, but I already know I have to turn him down.

Swallowing over the lump in my throat, I shake my head. "I appreciate the offer, Colton, but I can't accept it. I won't. I'll be just fine until my bed comes."

"Hollis, I can't let you sleep on the floor."

I take a step forward. "Let me ask you this. If I was a male roommate, would you be offering your bed to me?" He swallows hard. "That's what I thought. I truly do appreciate it, but I'll be okay. I've slept on the floor before, and it's only temporary."

He's silent for a few seconds. "I don't like it."

Shrugging, I reply, "I guess it's not really for you to like or dislike."

Those blue eyes watch me. "I guess you're right, but please know the offer stands." Colton takes a step forward, almost invading my personal space.

Needing to break the tension, sexual and otherwise, I reach forward and slip my finger inside Milo's hand. He tries to bring it to his mouth and gnaw on it, but I keep him from doing so by tickling his little Buddha belly. "Thank you. I do know the offer stands, and I appreciate it."

Colton exhales and looks like he wants to argue with me, but instead, glances down at the boy in his arms. "I was just about to get Milo here in his bathtub. For someone so small, he sure makes a big mess," he says, pointing to the big wet spot on his chest. I'm guessing formula... or possibly spit-up. Either way, I smile.

"I'm going to head back to my place. I have a site I'm working on," I tell him. As I pry my fingers from Milo's grasp, I throw his dad a wave and head to my door. "Thank you for dinner. Tell your mom they were the best enchiladas I've ever had," I add, glancing at him over my shoulder.

"I'll tell her," he says with a small grin.

"Goodnight, Colton."

"Night, Hollis."

I shut the door behind me, flipping the lock into place. I double-check the outside door as well, though I did that earlier. Call it a habit, I guess. Flipping open the notepad on the counter, I check my list of upcoming purchases. Curtains to cover the miniblinds on the windows, a small bookshelf, a couch, and chair, though both may not fit. I add waffle maker and Crock-Pot to the list, two things I'd love to own again since I enjoy cooking. I cross off *lamp* as it was one of the few things I picked up today at the secondhand store, and toss the list back onto the counter. I have a long way to go before this place has that homey vibe, but I know I'll get there. With each job I take, I'll earn more money to buy the things on the list. It'll take time, but that's okay. The end result will be worth it.

In the bathroom, I get ready for bed. I pop out my contacts and place them carefully in the case. I don't have that many pairs left, so I need to be cautious with the ones I have. After washing my face and moisturizing, I slip on warm, comfy pajamas, pull my hair up in a high ponytail, and return to my makeshift bed. I add an extra blanket to the padding and slip under the covers.

It's still early, and I'm not quite ready to sleep, so I grab my laptop and pull up the site I've been working on. I immerse myself in my work, adding the stock market widget to the main page, and grain and livestock on another. I scroll through the landing pages and make sure the images are right, based on specifics the company provided me. When I'm certain those are good, I click through a few other pages, working on the text and adding buttons for social media. I spend a good hour reading every line, looking for spelling errors and missing punctuation. Before the site goes live, I always send it to my client for a final set of eyes.

The only sound is the occasional clicking of my laptop keys, which is why, when I hear a loud wail, followed by that deep sexy timbre echoed through the wall, my entire body takes notice. They sound close, which means they're in Milo's bedroom again. I can picture them, Milo snuggled in one of those fuzzy animal towels with the hood attached, as Colton tries to wrestle a fresh diaper on him. Of course, Colton's shirt is probably soaking wet too. Milo seems like the kind of kid who'd appreciate bath time.

Shaking my head, I try to push all thoughts of my landlord and the way his T-shirt would mold to his chest if it were wet—I bet it would be a magnificent sight—and finish up my work for the night. Tomorrow, I'll comb the site one last time and send it to the customer for review. I know there will be changes, but I'd like to know if I'm on the right track.

Before I shut down my laptop for the night, I pull up my Facebook account. I have a few notifications, but most of them pertain to pages I follow, like authors and cute boutiques. My cursor hovers over the search bar, and before I stop myself, I type a name and click enter. Seven matches pop up with the name Colton Callahan, but it's the first one that I find myself clicking.

The profile picture is of a slightly younger version of my landlord, with his arms around two others. Their hair is buzzed super short, and the trio sport wide grins and army green. Even though the picture is a few years old, I can see the resemblance in Milo and even Chase. The Callahans must have strong genes.

I scroll down, scanning his page. He hasn't posted recently, but there are a few tags. More army pictures, usually featuring the same small group of guys, and more recently, All Fit Gym. They took to social media to promote his hiring, as well as push a few of the classes he's starting. I end up checking out the descriptions of each one, noting one particular I wouldn't mind checking into. It's a self-defense class for women, as well as one-on-one personal defense lessons, which includes kickboxing and karate introductions.

Redirecting my browser to the All Fit website, I can see why Gabby thinks an overhaul is necessary. Their current site is plain and lacks any recent news. All of those classes they're starting with Colton should be promoted on their website, with a direct link to sign up. A blog might also be a great addition to their site, where trainers and coaches can make weekly posts to engage their audience. Eating healthy, time management at the gym, personalized workouts, and classes. All things they could promote to their targeted audience.

My wheels are still spinning as I close out of their site and exit social media. A quick scan of my online bank account reveals a dangerously low amount of money, and even though I anticipated that number, it's still alarmingly shocking. After paying first and last month's rent, as well as my moving expenses and covering the purchases I made today at the store, I'm in desperate need of a little incoming cash. Hopefully, I can finish up this site and get paid sooner, rather than later, and then move on to the next one waiting in the wings. My business is successful, but the recent move took a hit to my finances.

After logging out, I notice the email icon lit up, so I hop over to check it out. I always get excited when I see a contact via my website because I know it's someone looking for my services. If I'm lucky, they'll sign on for a design soon, so I can get my checking account back up to where I prefer to keep it.

The message fills my screen, and my blood runs cold. My eyes fill with tears as I look at the seven words written, each one of them a reminder of the truth I'm running from. A truth that has followed me halfway across the United States. One that will continue to haunt my dreams, leaving me looking over my shoulder.

Contact: iwillfindyou@gmail.com
Message: You can run, but you can't hide.

With a shaky hand, I log out of my email and shut down the laptop. I turn off my new lamp, a sliver of light from the streetlight outside filters through the blinds and dances across the floor. I snuggle under the blanket for warmth. A chill sweeps through my body, though it has nothing to do with the temperature outside.

He doesn't know where I am.

I know it.

If he did, he'd already be here.

I'm safe.

I just wish I believed it.

A voice filters through the wall, steady and sure. Even though tears soak my pillow, I smile. Colton is singing again to his son. My heartbeat starts to slow, and my body starts to relax, as I reach out and grasp that little sliver of comfort he doesn't even realize he's providing.

. . .

******

By Tuesday evening, I feel a proud sense of accomplishment sweep through me. Glancing around my apartment, I smile. My cabinets are stocked with new-to-me kitchenware, and my oversized chair and ottoman are positioned in the tiny nook by the window. There's a floor lamp behind it and an empty bookshelf just under the window, and the small refrigerator has a little more food than it did the past few days.

The company I was working on the website for approved the model design yesterday, suggesting just a few minor tweaks. I should have the final product ready to go live by the end of the week, and the best part is they already paid their entire bill, including a ten percent tip. When that hit my account this morning, I went and purchased a few of the items I've had on my list, and still have cash in my account, a big thanks to the secondhand stores I've found in town.

The only thing I'm still needing is my bed, which should be delivered tomorrow. The furniture store called and said their shipment was arriving early, and while I hate to spend the fifty extra dollars for delivery, I don't exactly have a way to get a full-sized mattress and box spring to my new place.

You could borrow Colton's truck.

But that's not going to happen. I've done well at avoiding him since Sunday evening. I've heard him come and go, and yes, heard him singing to Milo every night at bedtime, but that's the extent of it. I've kept to myself, utilizing the laundry room during the day and working on my sites during the evening. So far, so good, especially when I have my earplugs in to block the sound of father and son bonding that makes my ovaries want to explode from my body.

I look over at the mountain view paintings I found at the secondhand store and smile at the serene story they tell. I've always lived in the city, but there's something about that picturesque mountain landscape that calls to me. The trees, the streams, and the snow-capped peaks. I think that's part of what beckoned me to Fair Lakes. I'd heard the stories, and while there are no mountains, it still gives that same charming and small-town feel.

Heading into the kitchen, I pull a Lean Cuisine from the small freezer and stick it in the microwave—another find at the resale shop. One thing I'm going to have to learn is what can and cannot fit in my small fridge. For as small as that part is, the freezer portion is even worse. I was able to stuff four Lean Cuisines, a pint of chocolate cherry ice cream, and a package of microwavable soft pretzels. Anything else isn't going to make the cut.

When the microwave dings, I grab a hand towel and retrieve my dinner without burning my hand. I pull a glass from the cabinet and fill it with tap water, taking it over to the bookshelf beside my new chair. As I grab my chicken parmesan entrée, a knock sounds on the door that separates my place and Colton's.

I head over and disengage the new lock he installed. When I open the door, my heart gallops in my chest. Colton stands there, holding a happy Milo, who gives me a toothless, drooly grin. The older man's eyes do a quick scan before returning to my face, and I can't help but wonder what he sees. I'm wearing a pair of jeans and a basic fitted T-shirt in an aqua color. My feet are stuffed in cozy socks, because no matter what time of year, my feet are always cold.

"Hey," I say, running a hand over the top of my head, hoping like hell I don't have crazy flyaways with my messy bun.

"Uh, hey." He glances over my shoulder and smiles. "This place looks great."

Stepping back, I give him a better view of the work I've put into my space today. "It's getting there."

He walks in and looks around, a small smile on his lips. "Love the chair," he says, pointing to the tan-colored, oversized chair and ottoman.

"Thanks. I found some good deals today," I tell him, trying to look around the room through his eyes. The curtains are a tan and navy chevron stripe, so I added navy rugs in the kitchen. My bedding is a blue, green, and tan floral print and will really tie the colors together when my bed arrives tomorrow.

"How did you get all of this in here?" he asks, noticing the small four-drawer dresser I have in the closet.

"Well, everything but the dresser, bookshelf, and chair and ottoman all fit in my car, and the owner of the resale shop volunteered her husband to deliver the furniture this afternoon for free."

"Herb and Jeanette? They're pretty awesome. I grew up with their daughter Kaitlyn," he says, his blue eyes returning to mine.

"I tried to give him some money for his time, but he refused."

Colton chuckles. "That sounds like Herb. I'm glad he helped you get it all in here."

I shrug and wait him out, wondering why he dropped by tonight. I'm saved from asking when Milo lets out a holler for attention. "Oh, that's right. Milo's hungry. He had a big day this afternoon, didn't you, Milo?" he asks, holding his son up and giving him a small bounce. "Little man here had his four-month doctor's appointment, and while we had to get two shots, his doctor agreed that it's time to start him on baby food. We're starting with green beans tonight, aren't we, buddy?" His blue eyes meet mine once more. "He's very excited about this."

I laugh as I watch Milo try to shove his entire fist in his mouth, drool hanging from his chin and dripping on his shirt. "His mouth is already watering at the thought."

Colton glances down and wipes away the drool. "Yeah, I should probably start putting a bib on him during the day. He's like a faucet with this drool."

"He's probably going to start teething soon," I tell him.

Colton shakes his head. "Doesn't seem possible yet. It feels like yesterday I was told I was a father to an infant." Again, the room falls silent. "So anyway, the reason I stopped by was I thought you'd like to witness the amazing feat of feeding Milo yummy green beans for the first time. It's sure to be a photo-worthy affair," he says with a burst of pride. "I picked up some fried chicken and mashed potatoes and gravy from the deli and thought you'd like to join me."

"Oh," I say, glancing over at my now-cold Lean Cuisine. Honestly, it doesn't really look as appetizing as the fried chicken he's proposing, but my budget is pretty tight, and I don't want to waste a meal just because I'm offered something that sounds better.

He looks over at my food, and as if he can read my mind, he suggests, "You could probably throw that in the fridge and eat it tomorrow." When I still don't reply, he adds, "Or not. You probably already have plans tonight."

He's giving me an out, but I instantly realize I don't want it. I'd actually much rather eat chicken and watch Milo try to eat green beans for the first time, than to be here alone, reading, and eating my Lean Cuisine.

That's probably the exact reason I should decline his offer, but I don't. I can't. "Umm, okay. Let me wrap this up and put it in the fridge."

His smile could melt the glaciers in Alaska—it's that hot. "Great! I'll just get Milo ready in his high chair. Come over when you're ready," he says, heading for the door. "Oh, Hollis? Those mountain paintings are amazing. They make me want to move to some small mountainside town."

I smile broadly. "Thanks. I thought so too."

Colton nods. "Don't worry about knocking. Just come in when you're ready," he says, and then he's gone.

I wrap up my forgotten meal and try not to dissect the excitement I feel at heading over to Colton's. I've done so well at avoiding him— forty-eight hours strong—and suddenly, I'm throwing all my hard work out the window the moment he offers me chicken. Going over there is just going to make it more difficult to separate the attraction I feel toward him and the fact he's my landlord and shouldn't be ogled over. Yet, here I am, heading over to ogle.

I'm a mess.

But every reason to stay away doesn't stop me from opening the door and stepping into his living space. As soon as I do, a smile stretches wide across my face. Milo is seated in his high chair, a large bib wrapped around his neck. The little boy is banging his hand on the tray as if telling his dad to hurry up.

"Grab a plate," Colton says without turning my way. He walks carefully to the table and takes a seat beside his son. Milo reaches for what his dad has in his hands, but isn't able to reach it. He goes ahead and lets his dad know exactly what he thinks about that and lets out a screech. "Settle down, little man."

I watch as Colton carefully scoops a tiny bite of the green goop from the container and moves it to his son's mouth. Milo opens wide and closes it on the spoon. When Colton pulls it back, I'm holding my breath to see what the little boy will do. He chews and chews, spitting out just as much as was put in his mouth, and opens his mouth for more. When it doesn't happen fast enough for his liking, Milo hollers loud.

"Okay, okay, little man. Give me a second here," he says as he drags the spoon across Milo's chin and moves it back to his mouth. The little guy's eyes are wide as he eats, his arms and legs both pumping with excitement.

I grab my phone from my back pocket and snap a few pictures of this moment. Colton laughs as he tries to drag the food off Milo's chin, but the second it's clean, more oozes from the baby's mouth.

Then Milo opens his mouth and blows.

And green slime sprays all over Colton.

My eyes are wide as a bubble of laughter spills from my lips. I try to cover it with a cough, but Colton looks my way, totally busting me on my laughter. He looks equally shocked at his son and my reaction to it. "You think this is funny?" The quiver in his lips tells me he agrees.

With my phone camera in hand, I nod and snap another picture.

Colton turns and looks at his son. "You just sprayed me with green shit, and the pretty girl is laughing about it," he says. My heartbeat jumps at his comment, and even though he doesn't elaborate anymore, I'll never forget the way he said I was pretty. That touch of midwestern accent, his tone all deep and husky. It does inappropriate things to my lady bits.

Milo reaches for the food, so Colton shovels a few more bites in his mouth. I grab the paper towels off the counter and hand him a few. Between feeding his son bites, he wipes at his face and blots at his T-shirt. "You might as well eat," he says, pointing to the containers of food.

Feeling relaxed, I go ahead and help myself to a chicken drumstick and a small pile of mashed potatoes and gravy. I join them at the table, staying as far away from Milo as possible. There's not much time for chitchat, as Colton spends a big part of his time focusing on feeding his son. When he makes it about halfway through the container, Milo appears to be done, refusing to open his mouth for another bite. Colton jumps up and grabs a warm washcloth and goes to town on clearing the food from his son's face. Upon closer inspection, however, he finds that green slime... everywhere.

"He's going to need a bath," he says, almost dejectedly.

"He'll get better at eating," I reassure him.

"But will I get better at feeding him, so he's not wearing half of his dinner?"

I smile over at him. "Yes, you'll get better too."

Colton sighs. "Well, I better grab a bite to eat quickly and then throw him in the bath. Sorry I'm not very good company," he says as he fills a plate with food.

"You're fine," I state, finishing up my mashed potatoes and gravy. "Oh, I have a few pictures of dinner. Would you like me to send them to you?" I ask, retrieving my phone and pulling up my photo app. Leaning over, I hold up the phone, so Colton can see the pictures I snapped of him and Milo. He leans in as well, smiling at the phone display. I catch another whiff of his woodsy, earthy scent mixed with green beans and pull back a little so I don't do something silly like lick his neck.

"Yeah, I'd love for you to send me those. I'll forward them to my mom and Gabby," he says with a smile.

We chat a little while he eats, mostly about Milo's doctor's appointment. Apparently, he's notorious for peeing the moment his diaper is removed, and today was no different. The moment the doctor pulled it open to check him out, Milo let a steady stream of pee fly, barely missing the good doctor's chest.

Milo starts to fuss. "It's getting close to his bedtime. I should get him cleaned up," Colton says as he stands up and takes his plate to the trash.

"Go ahead. I'll put the food away and head back to my side of the wall," I tell him, already standing up and moving.

"Oh. Okay."

There's something in the way he says those words. It's as if he's slightly... dejected that I'm leaving.

Or maybe it's just me and my wishful thinking.

"Come on, buddy. Let's get you cleaned up and ready for bed," he says, taking Milo out of the high chair.

When I turn, I spy a glob of green goo on Milo's pants that smears all over Colton's shirt and have to fight my grin. I'm sure Colton wouldn't appreciate me laughing again at his mess. "Thank you for dinner," I tell him, reaching over and shaking Milo's little fist. "Goodnight, Mr. Milo. Sweet dreams."

Colton is standing directly in front of me, his gaze burning into me. I feel it so strongly, and when I glance up and my hand brushes against his arm, an electric current charges through my blood. I pull back quickly and move to finish cleaning up the food mess.

"You're welcome," Colton says behind me. "Goodnight, Hollis."

"Night," I reply brightly, barely glancing over my shoulder as I close the mashed potato container.

The moment he heads down the hall, I exhale the breath I was holding. *Jeez, Hollis, get yourself together. You can't act like a crazy, lovesick teenager every time he's near.*

I finish closing the containers and seal the chicken in a baggie.

After a quick rinse of the washcloth, I wipe down the messy high chair, grinning at the smears of pureed green beans on the top of the tray, and the bottom. I find the dirty bib and toss it in the washer. Once I clean off the table, I take the soiled washcloth and throw it in the washing machine.

I remember the green food all over both Milo and Colton's shirts and know it won't be long before it stains the material. Before I can even give it a second thought, I head through the kitchen and down the short hall.

"Hey, Colton, if you want, I can throw the dirty clothes in the—" I stop dead in my tracks, the words evaporate from my lips.

Colton steps out of Milo's room, standing directly in front of me, wearing nothing but a pair of basketball shorts. The baby is naked too, wearing only a diaper, but my eyes... oh, my eyes are glued to his chest. His wonderfully magnificent, perfect chest. It's hard and muscular, with definition that only comes from hard work and labor.

My God, this man is... wow.

"Hollis?"

I blink. And blink again.

Is he speaking?

"What?"

I can't stop staring at his chest.

"Did you need something?" he asks, the humor very evident in his voice.

When I glance up, I find his eyes dancing with laughter. Suddenly, it hits me. I'm standing in the middle of my landlord's hallway, ogling his bare chest as if it were my job. Milo slaps me out of it with a hand to his dad's face.

"Oh, God," I gasp, my eyes wide with shock. "I'm so sorry!"

"It's okay." He takes a step forward, invading my personal space. I can't think when he stands this close to me. "Hollis, did you need me?"

Yes, yes, I do. So many things I could use you for....

"I'm so sorry just to barge in," I reply, averting my eyes. "I'll just...

go," I add, pointing behind me as I backtrack down the hallway. "Bye!" I holler as I turn and practically run back to my place.

The moment I'm on my side of the door, I slam it closed and engage the lock. I'm panting, my mind reeling with embarrassment and disbelief. I can't believe I just walked into his house like I owned the place and stumbled on him in his... nearly nakedness. Sure, glorious, but inappropriate. I had no business wandering around, even if it was under the guise of helping him.

I close my eyes and try to not picture Colton's chest, but it doesn't work. There's no doubt I'll be thinking about that marvelous display of man long after I should have fallen asleep.

CHAPTER 5

Colton

It's been a week. Seven days. One hundred and sixty-eight hours since Hollis moved in. It's been... that exact amount of time that I haven't been able to stop thinking about her. It's wrong, and I know that, but that doesn't stop my cock from rising to the occasion anytime she's near. I can still see her eyes and the way they raked over me the night she caught me without a shirt on. I've been shirtless in front of women countless amounts of times. Never in my life have I ever felt more naked yet alive, than I did when her eyes were on me. It's as if I could feel the heat from her gaze.

Not only do I think about her, but I also find myself thinking about ways to invite her over. Reasons to knock on her door and ask her a question. Anything that gets me access to her. What's worse is that I can't pinpoint any one thing that makes me feel this way. Sure, she's beautiful, but I've met many beautiful women in my lifetime. Is it her kind yet shy demeanor? She's not out to seduce me, although her eyes tell a different story. Is it because she's so good with my son?

The way she holds him and talks to him as if he's precious to her... is that it? I wish I knew. I wish I could say it's X, Y, or Z that makes me think about her all the damn time.

I've got nothing.

Zero.

Zilch.

Nada.

No explanation. Just the want and the need to be around her. That's why I'm standing outside her door, hand raised to knock. Mom called and invited Milo and me over for dinner. She insisted I pass the invitation on to Hollis as well. I half-heartedly put up a fight before giving in and promising I would invite her.

Taking a deep breath, I rap my knuckles lightly on her door. One, two, three, four heartbeats pass before she pulls the door open to greet me.

"Hey, Colton."

"Hey, uh, do you have any plans tonight?" I manage to get the words out without swallowing my tongue. She's wearing a pair of those tight leggings things that all the women are into, and that all men appreciate. And a sweater that hangs off her shoulder, with some kind of other shirt, looks like a tank top with really thin straps underneath. Her face is void of makeup, and her hair is pulled back in a ponytail. To sum her up in a word, fucking beautiful. Okay, that was two words, but you get the idea.

"No. I was just going to do some laundry."

"Well, my parents are having dinner. Chase and Gabby will be there. They've invited you to come." I want you to come. In more ways than one.

"I don't want to impose."

"You won't be. In fact, my mother insisted I not show up unless you're with me. They want to meet you."

Her brow furrows. "I don't know."

"Milo wants you to come." I'm aware of how desperate I sound right now.

She smiles, and it sets my world on fire. "Oh, Milo wants me to come?" She crosses her arms over her chest and leans against the doorframe.

"That's what he said. Told me not to come back to the living room unless you had agreed to go."

She shakes her head in amusement. "What time?"

"We're leaving here at five." She turns her head. I'm assuming to look at the clock. It's four now, so that gives her an hour to get ready.

"What should I wear?" The crack in her voice tells me she's nervous.

"You look perfect. What you have on is fine," I rush to add.

"Are you sure? This is just for lounging."

Lounging is sexy on you. "Yes. It's informal. In fact, I'm almost positive Gabby will be wearing something similar." I don't know that, but I've seen her in similar items in the past. I want Hollis to feel comfortable.

"Are you sure they won't mind?"

"Positive. Besides, my parents would never tell Milo no." I wink, and she chuckles.

"Okay. Do you want to give me the address?"

"Why?"

"I thought I could meet you there."

No. That won't do. "We leave at five. I'm driving." I take a step back from her door. "I'm going to get Milo's bag packed."

"You sure about this, Colton?"

I don't know why she's so worried, but I give her my most charming smile to try and ease her fears. "Trust me, you're doing me a favor. My mom would complain all night that I didn't do enough to make you feel welcome. She wants to meet you. I'm guessing because you're a stranger living with her son and grandson."

"Technically, I'm renting."

"You know what I mean."

She nods. "I'll be ready."

"Just come on over when you are. Don't bother knocking or whatever."

Another nod. "Okay."

"Okay," I repeat, because I'm not ready to leave her yet. I realize I'm standing here looking like a creeper, so I give her an awkward wave and flee to the kitchen. Has my time in the service really hurt my game that much? Is it because I'm a father now? I don't know what the fuck is wrong with me. Never in my life has a woman made me tongue-tied or nervous. I have an hour to get my head in the game. Otherwise, there will be no hiding this attraction I have for my new tenant.

An hour later, I have the diaper bag packed to the gills, with everything extra that Milo might need. He's strapped into his car seat and smiling up at me as I rock it back and forth on the kitchen table.

"Hey." The sweet sound of Hollis's voice greets me.

"Hi." I smile, looking over my shoulder at her. "You ready?"

She looks down at herself then back up at me. "Yes." She's still wearing the leggings, but instead of the off-the-shoulder sweater showing her soft creamy skin, she's wearing another sweater that covers her. It's probably for the best. I would have spent the entire night in a trance. Thinking about tracing that bare shoulder with my tongue. Then again, I still might.

"All right, I think we're good. You ready, buddy?" I ask my son. He smiles up at me and kicks his legs. "Let's get you covered up." I grab the soft baby blue blanket and place it over him, making sure his face and head are covered. His little hands and legs squirm as he tries to pull it off. This is a game I play with him, hiding behind the blanket, peekaboo of sorts. I might want to rethink that now the weather is getting colder.

I pull the blanket off and say boo in my non-scary, silly dad's voice, and he laughs. His little laugh warms my heart. "You have to keep this on, you little stinker. It's getting cold outside, and Daddy doesn't want you to get sick." I place the blanket back on him, tucking it in around him, and lift his seat into my arms. I throw the diaper bag over my shoulder and check to make sure I have my phone. Good to go, I look up to find Hollis watching me intently.

"You have this single-dad thing down."

"It's all an act," I tell her as we make our way out to my truck. "It's more of a 'fake it until you make it' kind of situation."

"I don't see that at all."

"No? I'm a better actor than I thought."

"Stop."

I load Milo into the truck and pull the blanket back from over his head, his eyes are already getting droopy. My boy can't resist a ride, puts him to sleep every time. "Really," I say once I'm behind the wheel of my truck. "I'm constantly worrying if I'm doing enough, taking good enough care of him. I don't want to mess him up, you know?"

"First of all, that's absurd. Do you love him?"

"Of course I do. What kind of question is that?"

"Sorry, it wasn't meant to sound bad. What I mean is that you love him. It shows through with everything that you do. The way you hold him, the way you talk to him, the way you take care of him. No one is perfect, Colton. But at the end of the day, if you've done your best and you can say without a shadow of a doubt that he knows you love him, I'd say, you, sir, will have passed with flying colors as a father." My chest inflates from her praise. I'm learning as I go, going at this mostly on my own, and it's nice to know that someone outside my family can see that I'm trying and that I love my son with everything in me.

"I hope you're right. It's not just being a single father, but it's molding back into civilian life. I graduated and enlisted. That's been my life. Short visits home, then back into the barracks, or the field. I feel so... out of place. That's really the best way that I can explain it."

"I can imagine that would be hard for you."

I nod. "Yeah, my brothers, those not by blood, but by duty, they were my closest allies. They're all still enlisted, fighting and standing tall without me. Sorry, I don't mean to drop all of this on you."

"You have to talk to someone. It might as well be a stranger."

"I'd hardly call us strangers." She's consumed my life for the last week that she feels like anything but a stranger to me at this point.

"We're more strangers than friends, maybe acquaintances."

Glancing over, I see she's staring out the passenger-side window. She looks sad, lost in her own thoughts. I reach over and place my hand on her arm, returning my eyes back to the road. "We should fix that." Sure, it's selfish of me to offer an olive branch of friendship, but something tells me she needs it just as much, if not more than I do.

She glances over and offers me a shy smile. "Yeah. I think I'd like that," she agrees as we pull into my parents' driveway. "I'll help," she says once the truck is parked. She climbs out and opens the back door, reaching in to grab the diaper bag.

I make sure the blanket is tucked in close around Milo as he slumbers in his seat, and we head inside. I don't bother knocking. I grew up here, and Mom would give me all kinds of hell for knocking. She and Dad have always made sure we know that this is our home, no matter how old we are. I want Milo to have that same reassurance.

"There's my nephew," Chase greets, reaching for the car seat and taking off toward the living room.

"He seems really attached to him. That's great that he's so involved."

"Yeah, but there's a story there."

"Oh, I'd love to hear more of it sometime."

I nod. "I'll give you all the gory details. Actually, it's pretty cut and dried, but I don't want to get into it right now."

"I didn't mean to pry."

"You didn't. However, my mom and Gabby are about two point five seconds from stealing you away from me. We can talk later?"

"Hollis. It's good to see you," Gabby says, walking into the foyer.

She leans in and hugs Hollis, and then me. "Come on." She grabs Hollis's hand. "I'll introduce you to Connie and Wes."

"He's snoozing," Chase says when I join him and Dad in the living room. He has Milo resting on his chest with his blanket snuggled around him.

"He took a pretty good nap earlier this afternoon, so he shouldn't sleep long. In fact, don't let him, that way he will sleep tonight."

"Is he still sleeping all night?"

"For the most part. There's a night here or there that he'll wake up hungry. I give him a bottle, and then he goes right back to sleep."

"You're welcome." Chase gives me a cheesy grin.

"Thank you, Chase." He's kidding, but I've never been more serious. I don't know what I would have done if Chase and Gabby had not looked after my son when they did.

"I'm going to need a sitter one day soon." He winks.

"How about you leave both of the crumb snatchers with me and your mother, and you boys have a good time?" Dad offers.

"Mine's not here yet. I can't wait until we find out what we're having."

"Did Gabby finally decide to not keep us all in suspense?" I ask him.

"Yeah, she said she could wait, but nine months is a long damn time to wonder."

"But it's one of the true miracle surprises in life," Dad comments.

"Did you know we were both going to be boys?" Chase asks.

"Yep." Dad chuckles.

"Come and get it!" Mom calls out.

"Want me to take him?" I ask Chase.

"No. My time is limited. Once Grandma and Aunt Gabby get their hands on him, my time will be over."

"You're not getting out of this house until we've all had a turn," Dad says, pointing at me. "This one," he points at Chase, "is a baby hog."

"Soon, there will be another, so more baby love to go around," I remind him.

"Right. Like that's going to make a difference. Until we have one for each of us, it's going to be a battle."

"Hold up, old man. You're rushing that a little, don't you think? Milo and I are flying solo."

"Are you?" he asks, giving me a knowing look.

"Yes. Now let's go eat before Mom comes in here and hits us all over the head with a frying pan."

"I heard that." Mom laughs as we enter the kitchen. "Make your plates and give me that baby." She walks over to Chase with her arms out, ready to steal Milo.

"Fine," he grumbles, kissing my son's fuzzy head before passing him over. "Hollis, good to see you," he greets her.

"Hi, Chase." She gives him a kind smile.

"Colt, can you show Hollis the refrigerator in the garage where all the drinks are?"

"Follow me," I tell Hollis. "Sorry about that. I know my family can be overwhelming."

"Not at all. It's obvious how close you all are."

"It was like this all the time growing up. I was a little worried about the dynamic when I decided to leave the service. However, I should have known better. It was always fine when I was home on leave, but that's a week or so, not permanent."

"I can see how you would worry, but not with your family. They're great, Colton, really."

"What about your family? Do you have any local?"

"No. Just me." As she says this, something flashes in her eyes. Her body language tells me she doesn't want to talk about it. I'll leave it alone. For now.

"What would you like to drink?" I open the refrigerator door, and as always, Mom has it stocked with anything and everything you could imagine.

"Is that bottled root beer?" She leans in to get a better look, and I get a whiff of her perfume. I can't place it, but it smells damn good.

"Yes. Chase and I loved drinking these when we were kids. I didn't even know they made it anymore. Want one?" I ask her, grabbing one for myself.

"Yes, please."

I reach in and grab another before shutting the door. "After you," I say, nodding toward the door. Everyone is standing around the island, filling their plates with Mom's pot roast. The conversation is flowing, and it's taking a lot of effort to keep my cool when it comes to Hollis.

"What? You didn't get us drinks?" Chase asks.

"You're a big boy. Besides, Mom told me to show Hollis, not to wait on you."

"I tell you. It doesn't matter how old they get, they still bicker like ten-year olds." Mom smiles fondly, shaking her head.

"He started it." Chase points to me and sticks out his tongue, making us all laugh.

"Is this what I have to look forward to?" Gabby asks.

"If you have more than one, yes," Mom answers.

"Let's see how we do with this one." Gabby rubs her small baby bump, wearing a smile.

"So, Hollis, tell us about you. What do you do?" Dad asks her.

"Here we go," I mutter. "You don't have to answer."

"I don't mind. I'm in graphic design. I do websites and company branding mostly. I work independently since it's all electronic."

"You kids and these computers, I tell you. I can't keep up."

"Mom, you sound like you're eighty," Chase jokes.

"I can do what needs to be done, but that design stuff, I don't know how you do it."

"You're not supposed to, dear. We'll leave all that high-tech stuff to the offspring. We just need to worry about spoiling those grandbabies of ours," Dad says.

The night couldn't be better. Hollis fits right in as if she's been a member of my family for a lifetime. I admit as I sit here, listening to her and Gabby talk to Mom about Gabby's baby shower, I wonder what it would be like if she were mine. What if she was more than just a tenant or a friend? I can see us here for Mom's monthly dinners and at home together with Milo. I can see it all, and I confess, it's enticing.

* * *

"Thank you for tonight," Hollis says when we are in my truck and heading home. "Your family is great."

I glance over and catch her watching me. The cab of the truck is dark, but from the glow of the dash, I can see her smile. I can't seem to keep my own from pulling at my lips just because she's happy. "I told you that you had nothing to worry about."

"You were right."

"Wait, can you write that down for me? I might need it for future reference."

"Oh, hush." She pushes on my arm, and we both laugh. "Truly, you have a great family. You're lucky to have them."

"I couldn't agree with you more. When you're ready to talk about yours, I'm all ears."

"Thank you, but there's not really much to tell." Her reply is soft, and from my glance to the passenger seat, I know her smile has faded. Luckily, we're at home. So I do the mature thing and pretend like I never brought it up.

"I need to get him in bed. Stick around?" I ask. "I have some beer in the fridge. I can tell you about his mom."

"Colton, you don't have to do that. I shouldn't have asked."

"I know I don't have to. I want to. I think you're right. It will do me some good to talk about it with someone who's not family." I also hope that by opening up to her, not only does she get to know me better, but maybe, just maybe, she'll feel comfortable enough to open up to me. When she's ready.

I grab Milo, and she takes the diaper bag. I can't help but think that this is how life would be if I had done things in the right order. Or even had a baby momma who wanted to be a momma. I don't hold that against Laura. In fact, I'm glad she did what she did. She got Milo to family. I don't agree with her just leaving him on the doorstep and then driving off. How did she know Chase—or, more specifically, I—would take care of him? That part still bothers me, but the fact that she gave him up? Well, I commend her for that. If she knew without a doubt that motherhood was not for her, I think what she did was brave and selfless. It gave Milo the chance to grow up in a home where all he knows is love. I'll make damn sure that happens.

"I'm just going to change him into some pajamas and give him a bottle. Help yourself to whatever."

"I think I'm going to go change."

"Okay." I lift Milo from his seat and head to his room. In my mind, I'm picturing her stripping out of her clothes, with my help. I have to stop this. I can't think about her getting naked, just down the hall. I also hope that whatever she decides to change into covers her. I don't know if I have the willpower to sit next to her in some kind of skimpy lingerie. In fact, I know that I don't.

"All right, buddy. Time for a new diaper, some jammies, and a nice big bottle. We should really take a bath tonight, but Daddy's going to skip that." I lay him on the changing table and get to work. "What do you think of Hollis? She's nice, right?" He coos. "I know, and she's beautiful." I manage to wrangle a clean diaper on him and some pajamas. I even get them buttoned correctly on the first try. "Look at that. Daddy's getting the hang of this," I tell him, picking him up and kissing his cheek. "Now, time for a bottle and then lights out for you."

"Need any help?" Hollis asks.

I look up to find her in a pair of flannel pajama pants, a long-sleeve T-shirt, and her hair is in a knot on the top of her head. No makeup, no fanfare, and I was so unbelievably wrong. She's just as sexy in this get-up as she would be in lingerie.

I'm fucked.

"I think I'm good. Help yourself to a beer, or whatever you want. I'm just going to mix him up a bottle."

"Do you mind if I hold him while you do that?"

"Sure." She holds out her arms, and I pass Milo to her. His eyes are wide open as he takes her in. I can only imagine what's going through his mind. It's not the first time I've wondered if my son can understand the crazy shit I tell him each day. Only today, not so crazy, I spoke the truth. From the way he's staring up at her, the way she's captured his attention, I'd say it's safe to say that my son is just as enthralled with the lovely Hollis as I am.

Like father, like son.

Quickly, I mix up a bottle, grab a bib, and a blanket. "Thanks," I say, reaching for my son.

"I can do it." She reaches for the bottle.

"You don't have to do that."

"I know, but I want to. Go do... dad things." She chuckles. "Fold some laundry or take a long hot shower, or just sit and watch. I don't mind. He's such a cutie." She coos that last part down to my son. He gives her a toothless grin. My boy knows how to turn on the charm.

She reaches for the bottle, bib, and blanket, and I let her take them. I watch in fascination as she heads to the couch and gets settled with Milo on her lap. She's a natural and looks as though she's done this countless times.

"You look like you've had some practice," I say, both hands braced on the island as I look toward where she's sitting in the living.

"A little. I did some babysitting in high school."

"Thank you." I nod toward her and my son.

"Go. Find something to do that you don't usually have time to do or sit down. You're making me nervous. I promise he's in good hands."

"Right. I'm going. I do have about three loads of laundry to fold and put away."

"Good. Go. We're just fine."

I watch them for a little while longer before heading to my room to fold the mountain of laundry I've not gotten around to folding. Once that's done, I change the sheets on my bed and decide to do the same to Milo's. That's where Hollis finds me.

"Hey," she whispers.

"Hi. Looks like you have the magic touch."

"He's in a food coma." She laughs softly.

"I'm almost done putting a new sheet on his bed." I finish what I'm doing and turn to face her.

"Just lay him down?"

"Yes." Carefully, she places my son in his crib. Then, she does something that knocks the wind from my chest. I watch her as she kisses her index and middle fingers, then softly presses them to his forehead.

"Sweet dreams, sweet boy," she says, her voice soft and gentle.

I have to push my hands into the pockets of my jeans to keep from kissing her. The urge is strong, but I fight it. Instead, I step up to the crib and lean over, placing a kiss on his forehead. "Love you, son." When I stand back up, she's there. Right there. We stare at each other, a current passing between us. Neither of us willing to move in fear of breaking the connection.

"I think I'll take that beer now," she says and rushes from the room.

I count to ten, and then twenty, then thirty before I leave the room and follow after her. I find her in the kitchen with two beers, one in each hand. She hands me one and takes a long pull from the other. She grimaces.

"I'm not much of a beer drinker," she confesses.

"No? What's your drink of choice?" I ask, taking a sip of my own. I move to the living room, hoping she'll follow me. I'm not disappointed when she takes the seat on the opposite end of the couch. Not close enough, but she's not hidden behind her door either, so I'll take what I can get.

"Fruity. I prefer to not taste the alcohol."

"Got it." She smiles, and I don't want things to grow awkward, so I begin. "I enlisted in the Army when I was eighteen. I was young and had no idea what I wanted to do with my life. I knew that I didn't want to go to college, that just wasn't for me. So, when a recruiter came to my high school and talked to my senior class, it just felt right. I enlisted. My parents, although worried, supported me. Turns out, I loved it. I was good at it, and I met my brothers-in-arms. Those are relationships I will never forget."

"That had to be hard being away from your family."

"It was, but as time went on, it became my normal. I found out that I loved the Army. It gave me a sense of pride fighting for my country."

"It's very honorable."

I nod. Her praise warms something inside me. "Anyway, I would come home on leave. Most of the time, for a couple of weeks, max. My last leave of absence, Chase and I met up, and we pretty much got hammered. I lost track of the number of shots and drinks we had. It wasn't something we often did, but I was going away for at least nine months, so we made the best of our last night together."

"No judgment zone, Colton. We've all done things we regret."

"Yeah, but I can't regret that night. It gave me Milo."

Her eyes widen. "Oh."

I go on to tell her how I told Laura that my name was Chase. I don't stop until we get to the present. Me being a single father to a little boy whose mother signed her rights away to him.

"Wow."

"Yeah, so now you know."

"You're a good man, Colton Callahan."

"He's my son. There is no other option but for me to try and be both mom and dad for him, and love him unconditionally."

"Thank you for telling me. For trusting me with your past."

"I'm not going to push you, but I want you to know that you can trust me."

She gives me a weak smile. "It's late. I should get to bed." She stands, and downs the rest of her beer, with yet another grimace. "That is truly awful."

"You didn't have to finish it."

"Isn't that alcohol abuse?" she asks with a hint of mischief in her eyes.

"That it is, Hollis. That it is. Thank you for tonight. For putting up with my crazy family, your help with Milo, and listening."

"Anytime. Goodnight, Colton." She stops in the kitchen and tosses her bottle in the trash, then disappears into the laundry room.

I stare after her long after she's gone. I'm disappointed our night was cut short. I could have spent the entire night talking to her. I don't want to push her, but I want to know her. It's more of a need at this point. I want to know what makes her who she is. I spent my entire adult life in the Army. We strive for discipline and patience. Let's just hope I still have that skill set in me. No matter how hard I try, I just can't fight it.

Hollis Taylor is quickly becoming my addiction.

CHAPTER 6

Hollis

I keep myself busy, submerging myself in my work throughout the next few days, even though I can hear Colton and Milo move around on the other side of the wall. The rest of his furniture was delivered Monday, and he stayed home that morning to oversee the job. His place is now equipped with a complete living room, kitchen, and bedroom furniture, as well as a few more things for Milo. This place is really starting to look like a home.

Even though we're two separate homes.

The temperatures are starting to dip, and now I see the disadvantage of moving to the Midwest. Southern California left my skin tanned and thin to the elements, not really prepared for what November in Missouri brings.

First stop today: the strip mall for some warmer clothes.

I hop into my car, noting Colton is already gone for the day. He usually takes off around seven, dropping Milo off at Gabby's sister's house before heading to work. I've heard a lot about the gym in the last week, especially from Gabby. She talked to her boss, Harrison, who's married to her sister, Gwen, and he's agreed to update the website. I sent him a mock-up of a new site yesterday but haven't heard back yet. The wait is killing me.

The first place I stop is a boutique for women. The lady behind the counter greets me the second I walk through the door, asking if she can be of any assistance. "I'm just looking," I tell her as I glance around the store.

I'm not really a big fan of shopping. I never have been one of those girls who likes to browse and try on everything and anything. I'm more practical. Come in, get what you need, and get out before the credit card starts to smoke. Fortunately, I don't need much today. A few sweaters to go with my leggings and jeans, a coat and gloves, and maybe a pair of warmer boots since my ballet flats probably aren't going to cut it in the Missouri winter.

I head over to a display of sweaters and check the price. They're a little higher than I'd like to spend, but this is a small, locally owned boutique. I decide I can spend a little extra on a sweater here and find one in a soft blue and gray. The material is thick, promising to keep me toasty this winter, so I find my size and decide to buy it. I glance around a little more, finding all sorts of cute items that would look great paired with skinny jeans or leggings. I promise myself I'll come back when the budget allows a little more wiggle room for clothing expenses. Right now, I need to stick to the basics until another job or two comes my way.

As I head to the register, I come across a display of gloves and scarves. My eyes immediately fall on a set of black and gray mittens, hat, and scarf. A smile falls on my lips as I think about my grandma and all the times I found her knitting or crocheting. Of course, when I was younger, I didn't find it cool to wear a handmade hat or scarf, but now? I'd give anything to have something handmade with her love in every stitch.

"Those are made by Estelle Brown. She spends all of her time knitting those items and even infant hats that she donates to the local hospital maternity ward," the lady states as I gaze at the big display of warmth.

When I spy the price tag, I gasp. "These are really underpriced," I tell her, shocked by the low number on the tag.

The lady laughs. "Tell me about it. I've tried to get her to raise her prices, but she refuses. Estelle says everyone who needs them shouldn't have to pay an arm and a leg to get them. She doesn't charge for her time to make them. That covers the material and what little markup we have to sell them on her behalf."

Another smile spreads across my lips as I add the hat, gloves, and scarf set to my small stack of purchases, as well as a second pair of red and navy gloves. Placing my items on the counter, I grab my wallet and pull out some cash. I don't use my debit card unless I have to. I've found that having a set amount of cash is a great way to keep me on task and on budget.

"Forty-five sixteen," she says as I hand her a few bills to cover my total. Today's purchases definitely took a chunk out of my planned spending, but that's okay. It was worth it. "Thank you," she adds as she hands me my bag. "Stop by again soon!"

"I will," I tell her and know that it's the truth. This boutique is definitely a place I'd love to shop at again in the near future. "Thank you," I reply before slipping out the door and heading to my car.

My plan to visit a few of the other stores in the strip mall proceeds, but I don't spend any money there. Instead, I find myself heading over to that secondhand store I found a lot of my great furniture pieces at. There was a huge clothing section too, and I'm anxious to see what sorts of treasures I find there.

The moment I walk through the door, the owner greets me by name and offers me a smile. It's one of the best parts about living in a small town. Back in California, no one took the time to remember your name, let alone your shopping style.

"I'm so glad you're here! I just took in a new consignment, and there is this great aged lantern. I instantly thought of you and the bookshelf," she says as she retrieves the medium-sized wooden and glass piece from behind the counter. "I was just pricing it to put on the shelf."

My eyes are glued to the rustic piece, and I know she's right. This decoration would look fabulous sitting on my bookcase, maybe with some ivy and a battery-operated candle inside. "I love it," I whisper, reaching for the lantern when she sets it in front of me.

"I was going to put six ninety-five on it," she says.

"That's a great price," I reply with a smile.

"I'm so glad my husband, Herb, here last time," she says. "He got you all set at home with your new things, right?"

Nodding frantically, I reply, "He did. I offered to pay him for his time, but he refused to take it. I'm willing to pay for any delivery fee," I insist.

She waves her hand in dismissal. "No, dear, that's not necessary. Herb is always willing to help out, especially delivering some furniture to a young woman who doesn't have a truck to haul it."

"Well, I definitely appreciate it." I look back down at the lantern, wishing it was something I could get today, but if I'm going to be successful in my new home, I need to stick to my lists and allowance.

"Are you looking for anything special today?" she asks, sorting through a few more items and adding price tags.

"I was going to check out your selection of winter coats and sweaters."

"There's several over on the far wall, and I'm sure there's a few in your size. Do you want help?"

"No, thank you. I'll just go take a look."

"Let me know if you need anything. Oh, and there's a changing room in the back if you need it," she says before turning her attention back to her task.

I make my way through the shop, eventually coming across the women's clothes section. The first thing I find is a rack of jeans and slacks. Beside it, a rack of sweaters and long-sleeved shirts in all colors and sizes. Zeroing in on my size, I find several I like, but ultimately decide to try on four. Before I head back to the dressing room, I find her display of coats. There's a few leather ones, but I'm not really a leather kinda girl. So I pick a navy blue Columbia puffer coat that's marked at only fourteen ninety-five and make my way to the back.

Each sweater I try on fits well enough to buy, and at only about seven dollars each, it's almost a crime not to get them. The coat is a tad on the big side, but by the time I layer for the winter, I'm sure it'll be a perfect fit.

Happy with my purchases, I head to the front with my four new sweaters and coat. "I'm loving that coat," Jeanette says, ringing up my new-to-me clothes. "Oh, and the deal of the week is buy one, get one half off. So, two of the sweaters are fifty percent off," she adds with a smile.

"Can't beat that deal," I reply, digging out a few more bills.

"It's mix or match. If you want something else, you get it half off, since you're getting the coat," she adds, folding the sweaters and setting them aside.

I glance around, wondering if there's anything else I should purchase. When my eyes fall back on the lantern, a grin spreads across my lips. "I'll take the lantern," I tell her.

"Excellent choice," she replies, grabbing the lantern and some newspaper.

We chitchat about the predicted cold front coming in before the Thanksgiving holiday, while Jeanette wraps up the lantern to protect it. When she gives me my total, which is considerably less than I expected to pay, I hand her some cash to cover the amount and take my two bags of goodies from the counter.

"It was a pleasure seeing you again, Hollis. Stop by anytime. I run different deals all the time to keep inventory moving, so if you're ever looking for anything in particular, come here first," Jeanette boasts with a wave.

"I will, thanks," I tell her as I head to the door.

Outside, the mid-November air is brisk and dry, so I speed-walk to my car and fire it up as soon as I'm inside. I also pull my new coat from the bag and slip it on, instantly appreciating the warmth that wraps around me. I sit for a few minutes, wondering where my next stop will be. I still have a little money left and want to grab some boots, so I guess I'll head out toward the supercenter to see what they have in stock.

Just before I go to pull from my parking spot, my cell phone rings. I dig it from my purse and find a local number I don't recognize. "Hello?"

"Hey, is this Hollis?"

"This is," I reply, already recognizing the voice on the other end.

"It's Gabby," she says.

"Hi, how are you?"

"I'm good. Listen, I'm at the gym and just had a meeting with Harrison about the website. Are you available soon for a quick meeting?"

My heart starts to dance in my chest with excitement. Past experiences tell me, a meeting request is usually a very good thing. "Yeah, sure, anytime. I'm just running a few errands now."

"Yeah? Well, would you want to stop by after your errands? I don't want to rush you, but Harrison's afternoon schedule is open so he can go to a doctor's appointment with my sister. He's got a little time before he leaves," she tells me.

"Yeah, sure! I can come right now, actually," I reply, feeling that familiar anticipation of potential work bubbling up inside me.

"Really? I mean, if you're sure," she says, the smile evident in her voice.

"I'm sure. I'll be there in about ten minutes."

"Okay, I'll meet you at the front desk. See you in a few," she replies before hanging up.

"Yes!" I holler in the confines of my car, my palms hitting my steering wheel a few times in celebration. Giving myself a few seconds to enjoy the prospect of another new job, I finally pull from my parking spot and head toward the gym, boot shopping forgotten for the time being.

It only takes me a few minutes to get there, and when I pull into the lot beside the building, I spy Colton's familiar truck in the back. My heart starts to beat a little faster in my chest, and I can't help but wonder if I'll see him, but then I think about how stupid that line of thinking is. It doesn't matter if I see him or not, right? I'm here for a job, nothing more, and that job doesn't involve ogling my landlord while he's at work.

I get out of the car and head to the front door, thankful for the extra layer of warmth. Inside, I instantly find Gabby, who's smiling widely, her hands resting on her slight baby bump. "I'm so glad you're here," she says, pulling me into a hug.

"Me too," I tell her.

"Let's go. We're meeting in his office."

I fall in step beside her as we make our way through the massive gym. Even for the time of day, there are a bunch of people walking or running on treadmills and ellipticals. They're using rowing machines and free weights. There's even a handful of older gentlemen standing around the water cooler and pointing to the football game muted on the television.

"We've been crazy busy," she says, walking swiftly down a short hallway. When she rounds the corner, we're in a small room where what I assume is her desk is positioned. Gabby heads over to the open door and knocks as she walks in, me tagging along behind her.

"You must be Hollis. I've heard a lot about your work," the man behind the desk says with a smile. "I'm Harrison Drake, owner of All Fit."

I'm going to be honest with you. Harrison is hot. Like walking on the sun barefoot kinda hot. He's tall and muscular, with a tight All Fit T-shirt and dark glasses perched on his nose. Actually, he reminds me a little of Chase. No, there isn't much of a resemblance outside their physical bulk, but there's just something about their charming smiles and bad boy demeanor.

But as good-looking as they both are, neither of them are Colton Callahan.

Funny, Chase and Colton are brothers, yet I don't feel the

slightest attraction toward the younger brother. Colton, on the other hand, has this way of constantly keeping my heart pounding and my panties wet, and he doesn't even realize it. At least, I hope he doesn't realize it. Otherwise, things are going to get awkward real fast.

"Pleasure to meet you," I tell him, shaking his extended hand.

"Have a seat. Gabby has been raving about your work for the last week or so, and we were finally able to sit down and review the information you emailed her," he starts, steepling his fingers at his lips. "I'm definitely ready to improve our online presence. I think it's a logical step in marketing the company, but I'm honestly a little hesitant to do this now."

My heart skids to a stop, and I just pray my eyes don't bug out of my head in shock. "Oh."

Not exactly how I expected this meeting to go. He couldn't decline my business via the phone? No, he just had to bring me to his office and fire me face-to-face.

Well, not fire, really. You can't be fired from a job you didn't have.

The letdown is real as I feel myself sag in my chair.

"Don't be an ass, Harrison. Tell her the rest," Gabby demands, opening up his candy dish and taking a mint from the jar.

Harrison chuckles and glances my way, a small smile on his face. "My assistant loves to point out when I'm being an ass. Anyway, here's my concern," he starts, sitting up straight and looking across the desk at me. "Gabby is going to be taking maternity leave in a few months. I'm afraid to start this project, train our clients to check it for updated classes and such, and then her be off for six to eight weeks post-baby. What I'd like is to have someone maintain the site for us. Someone who can make the adjustments quickly online in a timely manner. I want this person to show Gabby how to do it, but then take the reins and maintain the site for a period of up to six months. You interested?"

I find myself staring back at him, listening to his words, but not truly hearing them.

"I'm sorry, you want me to maintain your site?" I ask, stuttering and stammering around like an idiot.

Harrison smiles. "I do. I'd pay you, of course, for your time."

My own grin breaks out as I think about his offer. "I could do that," I tell him without even really considering it. The thing is, I know my websites. No one can navigate them as quickly and as easily as I can. It does seem logical to have me do it.

"Umm, yeah, I think that can be arranged," I tell him.

He grins again and stands up. "Perfect. I'd also like you to design a branding package. Gabby says she's already mentioned it to you, so go ahead and come up with a design or two and send them my way."

I blink once, twice. I can't seem to find my words.

"Are you okay?" he asks, a concerned look crossing his face.

"Hollis?" Gabby asks, moving her head into my line of sight.

"Oh! Yes! Sorry, I was just..."

Embarrassing myself.

"Does that sound okay?" he asks, taking his glasses off and watching me closely.

"Yes, that sounds amazing, actually. I'm definitely interested in designing your site and logo and am more than willing to help maintain the site while Gabby's gone," I assure him, elation bubbling up in my chest.

"I'm glad," he says, smiling across at me. When he stands up, I do the same. "Work with Gabby on the project, okay? When she's happy with it, I'll sign off on final approval."

"Sounds good, Mr. Drake," I tell him, unable to stop the grin on my lips.

"Please, call me Harrison," he replies with yet another smile.

I nod. "Harrison. I'll be in touch with Gabby by the end of the week," I tell him, reaching down for my handbag.

"Good. Now, if you'll excuse me, I'm going to meet Winnie and the kids for lunch before the appointment."

And just like that, Harrison Drake is gone.

"Wow," I whisper, forgetting I'm not alone in the room.

"Yeah, he's something. Pisses me off more often than not, but he makes my sister happy, so I try not to bust his balls too much," Gabby says.

"Whose balls are you busting now?" Chase asks, entering the way Harrison just left.

"Yours, if you're not careful," she sasses, crossing the room to where her husband stands.

Chase wraps his arms around his wife. "I love it when you do anything to my balls."

I snicker a laugh because even I saw that comment coming a mile away.

"Oh, hey, Hollis. You talk to H about the website?"

I nod as Gabby replies, "She did. She took the job and is going to knock this site out of the park."

"Well, I appreciate the vote of confidence. I guess I should probably head home and get to work. I'll have a few more ideas to you by Friday," I tell her, heading toward the doorway.

"I'll see you out," she says, her arms wrapped around Chase's waist.

"No need. I can find my way," I tell her.

Chase winks at me and gives a knowing grin. "Thanks, Hollis," he replies, confirming my suspicion that he's going to take advantage of a few minutes of alone time with his wife.

Waving goodbye, I head out the way I came. As I reach the end of the little hallway, a wall moves into my path, hard and unforgiving. I practically bounce off it, no doubt heading toward the floor until two arms reach out and wrap around me. I'd know that scent anywhere. It's a touch of woodsy, mixed with spice and sweat.

Colton.

"Hey, sorry about that. I wasn't watching— Oh, Hollis."

"Hi," I reply, my voice sounding dangerously high-pitched for a late twenties woman. "I didn't mean to run into you." I'm flustered and probably flushed with embarrassment, my body suddenly sparked to life.

"My fault," he says, those blue eyes gazing down at me. I swear he can read me like a book. "I was headed to find Chase. Was he in the office?"

I glance back the way I came, and it's the first time I realize his arms are still wrapped around me. He must notice too because he suddenly straightens and drops those strong arms from around my body. "Oh, uh... yeah. But you may want to give him a few minutes. He had that look in his eyes that said he was about to do something to Gabby that you can't unsee if you were to walk in there."

He chuckles that deep, sexy sound that makes my lady parts tingle. "Thanks for the warning. It's been a while since we were kids, and seeing my brother's naked ass isn't something I care to see again anytime soon. Not to mention my sister-in-law..."

"Yeah," I reply, glancing down at the floor to where a few sheets of paper lie at his feet. Bending down, I gather the flyers and look at the headline. "Self-defense for beginners?"

He nods. "We've been talking about starting a class, and I was finally able to nail down a schedule. We'll meet Wednesday evenings for four weeks." He seems to study my face for a few long seconds, and I can't help but wonder if he sees the curiosity and hesitation I feel as he talks about it. Curiosity because I'm seriously considering taking this class, but hesitation because I'm not sure I can be around the instructor without embarrassing myself further.

"Are you interested in taking the class?" he asks, clearly able to read my body language and my facial expressions better than I'd like.

"Umm... maybe?"

"Is that a question?" he asks with a smile.

Oh, that sexy smile.

"No?"

He laughs.

Fuck, that sexy smile.

"Well, how about you join me tonight and give it a try? I won't even charge you. If you don't like it, no harm, no foul."

"Oh, no, I couldn't do that. If I come tonight, I insist on paying," I tell him, but my mind zeroes in on that one word.

Come.

There's no denying the way his man-brain homes in on it as well. His eyes dilate dark and fierce, and his breath catches in his throat. His Adam's apple bobs as he swallows, and suddenly all I can think about is that dark dusting of stubble on his jaw and neck. I bet it would feel amazing rubbing against my—

"So what do you say, Hollis? Join me tonight? We can just ride together. Mom is coming over to watch Milo."

Milo. Right. His son. The reason I need to stay away from my landlord and not imagine all the... stuff I was just imagining. He has priorities that don't involve giving me a whisker burn on my thighs.

"Um, okay, that sounds good. What time should I be ready?"

"Class starts at seven, but I'd like to be here by six thirty. Be ready at six fifteen?" His arms cross over his broad chest, the shirt pulled tautly over his arms. Arms that were just wrapped around me a few minutes ago.

The words just don't come, so I nod in agreement.

Colton flashes me a warm smile. "Great. Just knock on the door when you're ready," he says, taking the flyers and moving toward the hallway. "Oh, Hollis?" I glance over my shoulder to where he stands. "Can't wait."

I open my mouth, but nothing comes out. My brain officially stops working, just like it did in high school when the star basketball player stopped by my locker after school to chat. I turned into a stumbling, bumbling idiot then too, barely able to form sentences.

Cooper Miller didn't have anything on the man standing behind me right now.

"Bye," I mutter, throwing him a wave and practically hightailing it for the front door.

My heart hammers in my chest, and my palms are a little sweaty as I reach my car and lock myself inside. "Holy shit," I whisper as I turn on the ignition and crank up the heat.

That man is doing a number on me. I can't seem to think straight, let alone speak. All I can think about are his shoulders and his chest and his stubbly jaw. Not to mention those lips that are full and perfect for kissing.

No, Hollis. You will not think about kissing him!

Oh, but I do. I think about the lingering graze of his lips to mine and the caress of his hands on my neck. I picture the burn of that stubble and the taste of his tongue. I envision the way he deepens the kiss, taking me on a ride I'll never forget, all-dominating and consuming.

My body hums. A warm tingle of anticipation spreads through my veins. I can't even close my eyes without suddenly picturing his large body hovering over mine, those lips so close to mine. I can practically taste his skin.

But it's just a daydream, Hollis. A fantasy. It's not real.

Tell that to my soaked panties.

CHAPTER 7

Colton

I got home a little after five. Since I'm going back to the gym tonight, I left early to spend a little time with my son before returning to All Fit. I'm excited about tonight's class for a multitude of reasons. The first being I feel as though I'm actually bringing something to the table for All Fit. I'm not just Chase's older brother, who didn't know what to do with his life after the Army. Even though that's true.

When I found out about Milo, I knew reenlisting wasn't an option and that my savings would hold us over for a while, but I needed to find a way to support myself and my son. To give him what he needs. When Chase suggested All Fit, I first thought of it as a handout. One I was willing to take in order to get out of the newly-weds' hair and into my own place. However, with each passing day, it feels more like home. I know that going to a nine-to-five job, dressing up every day is not my thing. Not when I spent my days in Army greens in the desert. No, I need a job that allows me to blend in as I try to find my footing back on American soil.

Teaching self-defense classes is perfect. I get to use the training from the Army to help others protect themselves if the need ever arises. I served my country in the Army, and these classes, they give me the ability to serve my community as well. Not to mention, I'm getting paid to do it. I couldn't imagine a better outcome.

And then there's Hollis. My running into her today and inviting her to class was impulsive and out of my lane as far as being her landlord goes. However, as a man, a man who's extremely attracted to her, it's perfect. So much so I can't stop thinking about her. If I've looked at the clock once, I've looked at it a thousand times. Milo has had his dinner and his bath, and now we're playing. Well, he's playing. He's lying on the floor under the activity mat that my parents bought him. He loves this thing. It has a lot of toys that hang down and a little mirror so he can see himself. He'll lie under it for hours, his little arms and legs just swinging away.

A knock on the door tells me it's almost time. That has to be my parents here to watch Milo. "Come on, buddy. That's Grandma." I climb to my feet and lift him into my arms before going to answer the door. Sure enough, it's my parents. "Hey, come on in."

"Colt, this place looks great. It's really coming along," Mom says, examining the house while Dad takes Milo from my arms.

"Thanks. I think so too," I admit.

"We were thinking the roads are supposed to get bad with this snow rolling in. How about we keep this little guy at our place for the night?" Dad offers.

"I don't know." There's an ache in my chest. An actual physical ache at just the thought of being away from him for a night.

"Come on," Mom says. "We raised you and your brother. He'll be just fine."

"But what if he needs me?"

"Colton," my mom whispers. "I'm so proud of you. You're such a good daddy, but even daddies need a break. You've been working on the house, working long hours at the gym. Chase said you've been working on planning your classes at home at night. We don't want you to burn out."

"He's my son. I could never," I say, my voice louder and obviously defensive. I know they mean well, but after the way his mother just left him, it's important to me that he knows I'll always be there.

"Son, I know what you're thinking," Dad says. "He knows you love him. It's okay for you to take time for yourself. When you and Chase were little, Grandma and Grandpa did that for us too. We're going to do it for you and for Chase and Gabby. Let us have this time with him."

"That means I don't see him until tomorrow sometime." That's seems like forever away from my son.

"And you'll both live," Mom says before leaning down to kiss Milo on the back of his hand.

Before I can answer, I hear her soft voice. "Oh, sorry to interrupt. Colton, just let me know when you're ready," Hollis says from behind me.

"Hollis, it's nice to see you," Mom tells her. "You're not interrupting a thing. In fact, maybe you can help me. We're trying to convince Colt to let us take Milo for the night so he can have a break."

"I don't need a break from my son," I tell anyone who will listen.

"I've been trying to get you to let us keep him so you can go out and have some fun. That's not working, so at least give us this. If your class runs over, you don't have to worry about rushing home so we can get home. I promise if we need you, we'll call you."

"We won't need you," Dad chimes in.

"Help me out here, Hollis." I turn to look at her.

She shrugs. "He's their grandson, and it's good for all parents to take a step back now and then. Ask anyone who has kids. Your time is important."

"How do you know that?" I ask her.

"Women's intuition," Mom speaks up, answering for her.

Hollis steps up and places her hand on my forearm. "He'll be okay, Colton. They love him as much as you do." Her words are softly spoken, and they calm me instantly.

"You're right." I nod. "Let me go pack him a bag."

"No need. We have everything he needs. Diapers, formula, bottles, clothes, all that stuff. We will take the diaper bag just in case we need something between here and home," Mom says.

"He needs his blue blanket. He likes to snuggle with it when he takes his nighttime bottle. He keeps it up close to his face and falls right to sleep."

Dad nods. "We're going to need that then." He chuckles. "Aren't we, buddy? You excited to stay with Grandma and Grandpa?" he asks my son. Not that Milo can answer him.

"I'll be right back." I rush to Milo's room and grab his favorite blanket. I stop on my way out the door and turn and look at his empty bed. I don't know why I'm having such a hard time with this. He's in good hands, and I know that. I just want those hands to be mine. Always.

In the living room, I find my parents, Hollis, and Milo, all laughing. Hollis leans into Milo, who is still in my dad's arms and says, "Boo," and the little bugger gives her a toothy grin. "He likes you," I say, startling her—if the way she whirls around to look at me is any indication.

"He's a cutie, Colton. You should be proud."

"I am. Aren't I, little man? You get your good looks from Daddy, right?" I ask playfully. Not that his mother wasn't pretty, she was, but I'm not much on talking about the woman who threw her son away. I still have mixed feelings about her. I'm grateful she got him to my family, but still can't understand how she could just give him up. He's the best thing that's ever happened to me.

"We should get going so you can be on your way." Dad hands Milo to me, and I kiss him, all over his tiny little face.

"I'm going to miss you. Don't be giving Grandma and Grandpa a hard time." I put him up to my shoulder and give him a gentle squeeze. His baby scent wraps around me, and I feel as though I could cry. In fact, if Hollis were not standing right here with us, I just might have. "Why is this so hard?" I ask, my voice gravelly with emotion.

"Because he's a part of you," Mom replies softly. "Just wait until he tells you he wants to join the Army. Wait until he's gone for months at a time and can't tell you where he is. This is nothing," she says, wiping the corner of her eye.

With my hand firmly on Milo's back, holding him close, I snake the other arm around Mom's waist and pull her into my chest. "Love you, Mom," I say, my voice low and just for her. I get it now. The worry, the tears. I get it.

"Enough of that," she says, pulling away. "Call and check on him anytime, but I assure he's going to be just fine."

"Thanks, guys." I give Milo one more hug before putting his coat on him and strapping him into his car seat. I walk them to the door and watch as they grab the base of the car seat out of my truck to place in the back of Mom's SUV. And then, just like that, they're gone.

"You okay?" Hollis asks from behind me.

I close the door, realizing I was just standing there, letting all the cold air inside, and turn to face her. "I'm good. It's just... hard to know I'm not going to be with him for so long. It's the longest I've gone since I found out he was mine."

"He's lucky to have you." Something passes in her eyes, but she masks it before I can figure it out.

"Are you ready to learn how to kick some ass?" I ask, giving her a wide grin.

"Definitely." She returns my smile. "Are you nervous?" she asks once we're in my truck and headed to All Fit.

"About the class? No. This is what I've been trained to do."

"Do you miss it? The Army?" she asks, then quickly adds. "I'm sorry I'm being nosey. It's none of my business."

"No. It's fine. I miss my brothers-in-arms. Their life was in my hands, and mine in theirs. That's a bond that runs deep."

"Are they all still enlisted?"

"Yes, some are, some are honorably discharged, some just did it on their own."

"Maybe you should reach out to them. Introduce them to your son."

"You know, that's not a bad idea. I just might do that."

"That's my one good idea for the day. I'm all tapped out."

I glance over in time to see her tap her index finger against her temple as she flashes a grin. "Just one?" I tease. "I think there are more good ideas bouncing around up there."

"Nope." She pops the P, making me smile.

"Here we are." I pull my truck into the lot and turn off the engine. "Thanks for coming early. I just wanted to be here when everyone started showing up." I look through the front window of my truck at the snow that started falling on our way here. "Then again, this looks like it's sticking. Class might be small."

"Should you cancel?" She leans forward to look out the window, getting a closer look.

"Nah, it'll be fine."

"Can we get home?"

"This machine," I pat the dash of my truck, "is four-wheel drive. We'll make it home," I assure her.

"Okay, then. I guess we have a class to get to." She reaches for her handle and climbs out of the truck, and I scurry to catch up with her. Luckily my legs are a hell of a lot longer than hers, and I'm by her side in no time.

"Hey, Colton," Mary, one of the nightshift receptionists, greets me. "I have a few cancelations for tonight." She hands me a list.

"How many do we have left?" I ask her.

"Four." She looks up at Hollis. "Are you taking the class?" she asks her.

"Yes."

"Then, five." Mary grins.

"Thanks, Mary. Keep me updated. I'm going to go make sure the room is set up." With a wave, I settle my hand on the small of Hollis's back and lead her to the room where the class is going to be held. I guide us into the room, and to the back corner where the storage closet is. Punching in the code on the keyless entry, I open the door wide, turn on the light, and step in. "You can put your coat and purse here. This will stay locked so no one will mess with it."

"Are you sure? I can get a locker."

"Positive. Just lay it on the desk over there." I shrug out of my coat and lay it across the desk. "I'm going to start getting the mats out and organized."

"Need any help?"

"Nah, just chill until class starts. Unless you want to go hit some of the machines or something?"

"Do I need to?" she asks. My eyes peruse her body. Tight long-sleeve T-shirt and skin-tight work out pants. "I mean, am I in the way?" she adds.

"N-No." I shake my head. "You're not in the way." Needing to get busy, to fight off this attraction I have for her, I start dragging mats out and setting them up so that each person will have their own work-space. From the research I've done, most women who sign up for self-defense classes are usually too late. It's usually as a result of some type of violence, often an ex or current lover they are trying to defend themselves from. This also means that most of them are not comfort-able with having their personal space invaded. So, I set up six large mats, giving each person coming to class tonight their very own personal space. I want them to feel safe and confident while they're here and, eventually, leave here with that same confidence and carry it with them every day.

"Colton." Mary sticks her head in the door. "Everyone has canceled. It's really starting to get bad out there."

"Thanks, Mary. Why don't you go ahead and go home? I'll be here to close up."

"Everyone's gone, and I don't think anyone is going to be coming in tonight anyway. I'll just put a note on the door that due to inclement weather, we're closed. I'll update all of our social media sites, and then head home."

"Thanks, Mary."

"Should we go?" Hollis asks.

"Nah, we can stay a little longer. Besides, I promised you a self-defense class, and we're already here. Hell, we have the place to ourselves." That part worries me just a little. No, it will be just like it is at home. I'm going to keep it completely professional.

She nods. "Let's do it."

"Perfect. Okay. Take a mat. You can have your pick," I say with a chuckle.

"Where are you going to be?"

Wherever you are. "I'll take the one in front so you can see me." She chooses a mat in the center of the room, and I take the one directly in front of her. "Okay, the first move we're going to practice is the hammer strike. Anytime you're walking alone, you should have your keys in your fist like this." I rush to the storage closet, grab my keys, then back to the mat. "Since I drove, you're going to need these." I show her how to hold the keys in her hand.

"Like this?" she asks, taking my keys and doing as I demonstrated.

"Just like that. Now, should someone approach you aggressively, you swing your arm like this as if it were a hammer." I demonstrate with my hand to show her. She copies me and nails it. Not that this one is complicated, which is why I started with it.

"Do you feel comfortable with me moving in on you so that you can practice?" I ask her.

She swallows hard but nods her agreement. "Okay, so I'm going to go walk around the room. You keep your head pointed forward. I'm not going to hurt you, or grab you, but I want you to be on alert for when I present in front of you."

"Got it." She looks at her hand, makes sure the key is still positioned correctly and lowers her hand to her side.

I walk away from her, keeping my steps light as they carry me around the room. Then I'm coming at her. I'm in her face, and she doesn't hesitate to lift her arm and strike. I barely miss getting stabbed with my own key as I jump out of the way.

"Oh my God." The keys fall from her hands as they move to cover her mouth. Her eyes are wide and filled with worry.

"It's fine, Hollis. You did exactly as you were supposed to do."

"No." She drops her hands and shakes her head. "I wasn't supposed to attack you. You could have been hurt."

"Trust me, I'm perfectly fine. This is all a part of your training. It has to be as real as possible so you can imitate being in that exact situation. You did great," I praise.

"This was a bad idea."

"No, it wasn't." I step in close to her. Bending my knees so we're eye to eye, I try to capture her attention, but her gaze is glued to our feet. With a gentle hand, I place my index finger under her chin and gently lift until I have her eyes. "This is what's supposed to happen. I promise. You did perfectly." I stand back to my full height and clap my hands together. "Now, you ready for another move?"

"You sure?" She's hesitant, and her beautiful green eyes are shining with uncertainty.

"Positive. This next move is escaping from a bear hug attack." I usually go over the easier moves, but this one is the most common for attacks. Women getting assaulted from behind before they even realize what's going on. My gut tells me I need her to be prepared to be safe. She might have just come into my life, but I know I need that much. I need to know I've given her the skills to protect herself. Sure, it's not going to all happen tonight, but this move, knowing it's the most common attack, it will help to ease my mind that I've taught her this one.

"Okay." Her agreement is weak, but she stands tall, well as tall as she can at five foot three and gives me all of her focus and attention.

"This one is better if I demonstrate so you know what I'm talking about. In order to do that, I need you to step behind me and wrap your arms around my waist, clasping your hands together. I'll talk you through the process, we'll go through the motions, and then switch places."

"Got it." She moves to step behind me, and I'm assaulted with her scent, something lavender, as her arms wrap around my waist just as I've instructed.

I can't help but run my hands over hers. I tell myself it's to make sure her grip is good and tight when the reality is that I just want to touch her. Her skin is so damn soft, and this is just her hands. I can only imagine how it would be if my hands got to roam all over her body. "Good," I croak. I cough to clear my throat. "Now, when in this situation, you want to shift your weight forward. You do that by bending forward at the waist. This makes it more difficult for your attacker to lift you from the ground, and it gives you a better angle to throw an elbow or two." I bend over at the waist and turn with my elbow poised to demonstrate. "You want to switch from arm to arm counter-attacking to throw the attacker off. This should lead to you being able to turn fully and getting a good groin shot or heel palm strike, which we haven't gone over yet. However, from a man's perspective, always go for the groin. That pain, when delivered precisely, will drop him to his knees." I turn to face her and then step back. Her arms drop to her sides, and her eyes stay locked with mine. "You ready to try it?"

"What if I hurt you?"

"First of all, I'm a big guy, I can take it. Don't use all of your power, just walk through the steps. If you make contact, you make contact. It's not the roughest thing I've been through. Trust me on that." My mind flashes to being in the trenches in the desert. An elbow is nothing compared to the things I've been through.

"Okay." She nods, and I can see a little of her hesitation start to drift away.

"Turn around." My voice is gruff. I move in behind her, clasping my arms around her waist. My cock is nestled next to her ass and twitches. I don't even fight it because there is no use. No way can I hide what she does to me. As I feel myself harden from being this close to her, she gasps.

"I can't apologize for that. That's what you do to me," I whisper in her ear. It's bold, and I'm so far out of line. However, when I'm holding her close like this, I can't seem to find it in me to care. No, in fact, I pull her a little closer. I want her to feel my body's reaction to hers.

"W-What next?" she asks.

My lips are still next to her ear, so I keep my voice low. "Bend over, push your weight forward at the waist." She bends over, and on instinct, my hands go to her hips, holding her to me. "Fuck," I murmur. There are so many wildly inappropriate things running through my head right now.

"Colton?" She says my name, and it sounds like a plea.

"Elbows," I grind out. "Alternate elbows." I try to focus on what this is supposed to be about. Her safety. Hollis learning how to defend herself should the need arise.

Lifting her right arm, she turns to mimic elbowing me, but turns all the way around and her hands land on my shoulders. My hands still on her hips, pull her close. Looking down at her, her gaze is focused on my lips. I lick them, the anticipation of what I think is about to happen overwhelms me. When her tongue peeks out, and she wets her own, I know I'm about to cross another invisible line.

"Hollis," I murmur, and her eyes dart to mine. I lean in just a little. "Tell me to stop. Tell me I'm not allowed to kiss you."

"I-I can't do that, Colt."

Colt. The familiarity in the way she shortens my name only fuels my desire for her. I want that with her. Not just so I can learn every inch of her. I want to know what makes her who she is. I can't explain it, and frankly, I'm done trying. I just want her. I can't fight it, and honestly, I don't want to.

She rises up on her tiptoes, and I meet her halfway. At first, it's just a soft press of my lips against hers. It's delicate as we both take the time to savor one another. Needing more of her, I nip at her bottom lip, and she opens for me. My tongue lazily strokes her bottom lip soothing the ache, before I slide between her lips, and get my first real taste of her. She whimpers, a sound that's released from the back of her throat, and it fuels me. Needing a better angle, needing to be closer to her, I bend and lift her into my arms. We never break our kiss as she locks her legs around my waist and her arms around my neck, holding on while I devour her mouth.

My hands grip her ass as I deepen the kiss. My feet carry us to the far wall, and I'm just about to push her into it when my phone rings from the storage closet. Fuck. I peel my lips away, resting my forehead against hers while I catch my breath. "I'm sorry. It could be my parents about Milo."

She nods. Her chest is rapidly rising as she struggles for breath. I'm glad the kiss had the same effect on her as it did on me. Changing directions, I head for the closet.

"You can put me down." Her voice is winded, and it makes me want to beat on my chest, screaming to the world that I did that. I made Hollis Taylor breathless.

"I'm not ready to let you go," I murmur as we enter the small room. I move to the front of the small desk and set her on top of our coats. Reaching for my phone, I see that I missed a call from Chase. With one arm around her, holding her close, I hit his contact to call him back.

"Hey. You still at the gym?" he asks.

"Yes. What's wrong?"

"Nothing. I just know you can't see outside. It's really starting to get bad. You should send everyone home and head out yourself."

"Already ahead of you. It's just me and Hollis left."

"Oh. Okay. Well, you two should get going. Wait, did Hollis take the class?"

"Yep."

Chase laughs a deep throaty laugh. "That's a story I can't wait to hear, brother."

"Thanks for the heads-up." I end the call, not waiting for a reply.

Sliding my phone in my back pocket, I place my hands on either side of her face and press my lips to hers once more. "That was Chase," I say, forcing myself to pull away. "He said it's really getting bad out. We should head home." She nods her agreement, and I lean in to kiss her again. "I don't know if I can stop," I say softly.

"Maybe... maybe we can pick up when we get home? I mean—"

I cut her off with another kiss. "Best fucking idea ever." She giggles when I pull away. "Let me go start the truck." I rush out of the room, pick my keys up off the floor, and race outside to start my truck. Good thing Chase called when he did; it's really getting bad. I clean off the front windshield, cursing that I didn't grab my coat, before hurrying back inside. "It's nasty out there."

"You think we can get home okay?"

I love that my home is her home. That we're going to the same place. And although she might not end up in my bed tonight, I'll still know she's in my home. That she's there with me is enough. "Yeah. We'll just have to take it slow."

Quickly, we bundle up and lock up the gym. I hold the door open for her, before running around to the passenger side of my truck. I'm suddenly cursing the fact that I don't have a bench seat. Making sure the truck is in four-wheel drive, I put my flashers on and pull out onto the road. Reaching over, I lace her fingers with mine and rest our combined hands on my lap.

"Don't you need to have both hands on the wheel?" she asks. I can hear the tension in her voice.

"Will you keep yours right here?" I ask her.

"Yes." No hesitation.

I bring our joined hands to my lips, kissing the back of hers, before placing it on my thigh. I release my grip and place both hands on the wheel. This is going to be a long drive. I just hope that by the time we make it home, she's still willing to pick up where we left off. Regardless, I plan to steal a goodnight kiss. Anything more is just a bonus.

CHAPTER 8

Hollis

I'm a box of nerves and anticipation as we head back home. Well, to Colton's place. The house I'm staying at. Renting.

Whatever.

Part of it is the hum of sexual tension filling the vehicle. My hand is still tucked on his thigh, and it takes everything I have not to slide it along the cotton of his Nike joggers. Maybe even angle it upward until my fingers brush up against the very cock that was pressed against my ass just a bit ago.

The other part is because of the weather. I can barely see where we're headed. My entire body is tense, but Colton just seems as cool as a cucumber. He threw it in four-wheel drive before we pulled from the parking spot and has been expertly driving the snow-covered streets back home.

"You're really good at this," I whisper, my eyes riveted on the roadway in front of us.

"Good at what?" he asks, glancing my way for a second.

"Driving in snow. I'd be a terrified wreck right now," I confess, realizing that moving to the Midwest may not have been my brightest idea.

Colton shrugs. "I grew up here, so the snow doesn't bother me. But I will admit, I haven't really driven in it in a while. It's kinda fun," he says, glancing my way again with a boyish grin. One full of mischief and excitement.

"Kinda fun?" I'm slightly stunned by his statement.

I'm even more stunned when he pulls into the superstore parking lot and stops the truck just off the deserted roadway. He pushes down the lever that controls the four-wheel drive and gives me another one of those ornery grins. Then, without so much as a word of warning, he guns the gas and turns the wheel sharply to the right.

We spin, and a piercing scream rips through the truck cab. One hand reaches up and grabs the handle over the door, while the other grabs the dash in front of me so hard, I'm sure there might be nail marks. At this point, I'm just praying to God and anyone who'll listen I make it out of this truck alive.

When the truck comes to a sudden stop, I realize the scream is ripping from my own mouth, and I clasp it closed. Well, as tightly as I can, considering I'm panting like a dog in July. "What the hell was that?" I holler, my eyes wide as they meet his playful ones.

"*That* was fun, Hollis. Admit it."

The fear I felt mere moments ago is quickly swept to the side by something that feels a lot like joy. Suddenly, I find myself smiling back at him from across the truck. "Can we... do it again?" I ask, not sure why I'm so nervous.

"Damn right, we can," he says before throwing the shifter back into Drive. "Hang on."

And just like that, we're spinning in the empty parking lot, doing donuts in the freshly fallen snow. I'm still hollering, but this time, it's more out of enjoyment than fear. I realize quickly that I trust him. I trust Colton to not wreck and kill me while spinning circles in the empty lot.

When he stops, my smile matches the ear-to-ear one on his gorgeous face. We're having fun. Something that's both as surprising as it is comforting. "Okay, your turn," he says, throwing the truck back into Park.

Wait. What?

He just smiles and unbuckles his seat belt. Before I know it, he's already throwing the console up and sliding my way. "Yep, you heard me. You've never driven in the snow, right? Your information when you filled out the rental application said you were from California, so something tells me playing in the snow isn't exactly a regular activity for you in the winter. Am I right?"

Wide-eyed, I just stare at him as he moves to sit right beside me.

"This is the perfect place for you to practice for a bit. I can teach you how to drive in snow with and without four-wheel drive."

"But... what about your truck?" I ask.

Again, he just smiles. "As long as you don't wrap it around a light pole, it'll be fine, Hollis. My girl is used to getting down and dirty in the winter weather," he states, tapping the dashboard with his palm.

I swallow through my anxiety and unbuckle my seat belt. "Are you sure?" I croak over my too-dry throat.

"Positive. I'll just show you the basics since it let up for just a few minutes. Then, we'll get back home," he says, his eyes boring into mine, "and finish what we started."

Oh, boy.

My heart is pounding, and my palms are sweating. I'm not sure if it's because of the driving in the snow bit or the *after* with Colton.

Carefully, I move, trying to stand up and shift myself over his body. He slides under, while I move over, and there's no denying the bulge in his pants that rubs against my ass. When I finally get to the driver's seat, I buckle up, pulling it as tightly as I can. There's a slight tremble to my hands as I reach up and place both hands on the wheel. Ten and two. I'm gripping that wheel like it were my first day of driver's education.

"Okay, let's leave it in two-wheel for now. I want you to get a feel of the roadway and how the truck handles. Each vehicle is different, Hollis, so just remember to go slow and take your time. Only drive as fast as you feel comfortable going."

I nod, staring out at the lazily falling snow and the unplowed lot.

"Go ahead and put it in drive."

I reach over and slide the shifter into gear.

"Now, gently press on the gas."

I do as instructed, my hands death-gripping the wheel, as I let the truck slowly crawl forward like a turtle. I'm not even sure the speedometer is moving.

"You do know the gas is on the right, right?"

"Don't use your sexy charms right now, Colton. I'm concentrating," I tell him, my eyes locked ahead.

"Sexy charms, huh?" he asks, the humor evident in his voice.

And then, he leans over and moves my way. "Hey! You're not buckled in!"

"You're not going fast enough to register speed. I think I'm in the clear from potential accidental injury," he says as he reaches over and swipes a strand of hair off my forehead. I look his way—Jesus, he's gorgeous—and then focus back on the path in front of me.

"Stop trying to distract me," I chastise.

Why is it suddenly so hot in here?

"You've been distracting me since the moment I first laid eyes on you," he whispers, just before his lips graze across my jaw. A shiver slips through my body, though I don't think it has much to do with the temperature.

Pressing the brake, I turn and look his way. His full lips are so close, close enough that I could move just a hint forward, and they'd touch mine. But I don't. I stay right where I am, barely breathing. Our eyes remain locked, and so much passes in just a few moment's time. I can see his desire, his lust for me. I can see his playful side and a hint of danger. But most of all, I see the man I want to get naked with, a long-forgotten hunger hitting deep in my gut for the first time in longer than I care to admit.

He's been a craving I can't seem to fight.

His throat bobs as he swallows hard. "You ready?" His voice is husky like it was raked over gravel.

"Ready?" I ask, not really sure what he's talking about.

Suddenly, a smile so devastatingly handsome spreads across his face that my panties practically explode. I'm so distracted, so lost in the depths of his blue eyes and the familiarity and comfort in that very smile that I almost miss his movement. I almost mistake the touch of his boot against mine as something sexual.

Only, it's not.

Oh, no.

That touch hurtles my blood pressure into stroke level and my heart rate toward another medical emergency as he hammers down the gas pedal, catapulting us forward into the gray dark of night. He spins us to the right, his laughter drowning out by my bloodcurdling screams. Colton reaches for my hand and moves it under his, the warmth of his touch only offering slight relief in this traumatic situation.

When we stop, he looks at me eagerly, like a kid on Christmas morning. "See? Isn't that fun?"

"You and I have way different ideas of fun, buddy."

"Ehhh, come on, Hollis. Live a little." There's something in the way he says it. It makes me want to throw caution to the wind and do just that: live a little. I've been so worried lately, glancing over my shoulder and trying to remain in the shadows, that I haven't exactly been living much. Only existing.

Deciding it is time to take the bull by the horns—and I'm not talking about Colton and that very impressive bulge in his pants... *yet* —I shove his hands off the steering wheel. I kick at his boots to get them away from the pedals and sit up straight in the seat.

I got this.

Just as Colton did moments ago, I push on the gas pedal, ignoring that need to slow down that tingles at the back of my neck. Instead, I go. I launch forward, our wheels spinning and the bed wanting to come around to the front. I overcorrect, sending us into a spin, but keep us moving and my eyes on the roadway. I maneuver the truck through the building snow, angling it toward a drift. When we hit that drift, the truck stops, a small gasp rasping from my throat.

"Shit!" I holler, pressing on the gas even harder, yet only spinning the tires.

Colton laughs. "Okay, hold up on the gas. This is a perfect time to talk about four-wheel drive since you've managed to get yourself stuck in a drift."

He goes through the process of engaging four-wheel drive in the truck and tells me to slowly drive forward. I'm shocked at how easily the truck moves through the snow, thanks to four-wheel drive. When we get through the drift, I stop and turn to face him. Colton's smiling, leaning back in the seat casually, his arm extended toward me on the seat back.

Suddenly, the desire to kiss him is overwhelming, and it takes everything I have not to climb over the seat and sit on his lap.

"You did well today," he tells me as I put the truck in park. We both look out at the snow, which is starting to fall heavily again, the only sound our mixed breathing.

"I have a long way to go."

He shrugs. "Maybe, but that's a great start. At least you know what it feels like to drive in these kinds of conditions, and when to engage the four-wheel drive."

I glance out again, barely able to see the tracks we made earlier. "We should probably get out of here."

"Yeah," he says, starting to slide my way.

After I unbuckle, I shift so my butt is pressed against the dash and try to step over Colton's legs. His catch on mine, though, and my weight shifts. Suddenly, I'm falling forward, into his arms. The moment his hands touch my face, I'm straddling his lap, and our lips meet in a frenzy of pent-up desire.

His hands slide down my sides and move beneath my coat. Even without his skin touching mine, the heat of his hands sears my flesh. His tongue begs for entrance, one which I readily grant. I rotate my hips, my core grinding against that delicious erection in his pants.

A groan tears from his throat, his head falling back and lying on the headrest. Seeing him so close to losing control has my hips automatically rocking again, my body seeking out the relief only he can provide. Colton grips my hips as he simultaneously tries to still my movements and help guide them to where he craves the touch.

"Hollis," he whispers, his voice barely a whisper.

I'm so close to losing my own mind, I can barely think straight. All I can think about is the way he feels, the way we feel grinding against each other, desperately looking for release. Feeling more daring than ever before, I slide my hands under his coat, under the T-shirt he's wearing underneath, and graze my fingers along those very abs I've been picturing for days. Weeks, really. Ever since I saw him walk out of his room in nothing but shorts, I've imagined touching him. It's what I think about as I touch myself late at night when he is asleep.

His hands slide up my neck once more and dive into my hair. He moves me forward, our lips meeting once more in a tidal wave of lust. He trails open-mouthed kisses across my jaw and down my throat as he rocks his hips upward, hitting my clit like a bull's-eye. "Colt," I gasp, the sensations almost too much.

As his hand glides down the column of my neck, my heart knocks hard against my chest. It's so loud, I swear Colton can hear it too. He stills, his eyes wide. My heart pounds again, and suddenly it hits me.

That's not my heart.

Someone is knocking.

On the window.

On the very foggy window of Colton's truck.

"Fuck," he whispers as I practically leap from his lap like a hurdle jumper.

Colton adjusts his tight pants and moves into the driver's seat. I've never been so grateful for leaving my clothes on as I am right now. Thank God, we're both wearing coats, or who knows what state of naked we'd be in right now.

He hits the window button, and the foggy glass of the driver's window starts to fall. Instantly, snow starts to blow in, and I snuggle into my coat a little more.

"Everything all right here?" And then the cop pauses. "Jesus, Colton Callahan, is that you?"

"Hey, Rusty, yeah, it's me," he says to the police officer standing at his window.

Rusty looks over Colton's shoulder at me and gives a knowing grin. "I just stopped to make sure everything was okay here. There's no traffic out, and when I saw a running truck in the lot, I was afraid something was wrong." His smile tells a different story. One that lets me know he hasn't missed my rosy cheeks and disheveled hair. Nor the way the truck windows were fogged up. Yeah, the cop knows exactly what we were doing in this deserted parking lot.

"All good, man. Hey, it's good to see you," Colton says, changing the subject.

"Yeah, it's been a few years. I heard you were back in town. For good now?" he asks.

"Yeah, for good."

"Well, happy to hear it, buddy." Again, he glances over his shoulder my way. "The weather's getting pretty bad. You may want to think about taking this back home."

And cue the flaming blush.

"Headed that way now. Thanks, Rusty. Good to see you again," Colton says as he rolls up his window and shakes the snow off his arm. "Well, that was unexpected." He glances my way, and we both burst into fits of laughter.

"I can't believe that just happened."

He gives me a smirk and buckles up. "Rusty was a classmate. I'm sure half the town will hear all about this by morning," he says as he puts the truck in Drive.

I buckle up and sit back to enjoy the rest of our drive. As he pulls out of the lot, Colton reaches over and takes my hand, resting it on his thigh once more. I can't help but smile as he returns his hands to the wheel. I'm more aware of his driving, but not because I don't trust him. It's because I'm taking it all in and really paying attention to how he drives and responds to the road conditions. I imagine myself in the driver's seat, moving us through the snow to get us safely back home.

When he pulls into the driveway, I notice my car is completely unrecognizable. It's so covered with snow, you can't even tell what color it is. "Stay there. I'll help you out," he says before shutting off the truck. He grabs his duffel bag from the back seat before meeting me around to the passenger side. I take his offered hand and carefully hop out of the truck, wishing like hell I had purchased a pair of snow boots today. The cold, wet snow quickly seeps into my tennis shoes as we scramble for the back door.

Colton lets us in, and we both stomp our feet and shake off the snow. I toe off my wet shoes and set them on the mat by the door to dry. My fingers find my coat zipper as I start to remove my layers of warmth. When I glance at Colton, I find him standing there, his own boots off and his coat in his hand. Without breaking eye contact, he tosses his coat onto the dryer and reaches for mine, throwing it on top of his. Then, he moves, pressing his body against mine, pinning me to the washing machine.

His lips are eager and firm, his hands roaming my back and sliding down to cup my ass. He lifts me easily, my legs wrapping around his waist. Colton wastes no time in moving us through the house to his bedroom.

The moment we cross the threshold, I'm assaulted by his familiar scent. It wraps around me warmly, and full of familiarity, the same as his body is with me in his arms. He continues to move until I'm lying on the comforter, his body pressed into mine. That recognizable ache bubbles to life as he rocks into me, his erection firmly between us.

When he slows the kiss, I use the opportunity to pull my lips from his and slide them across his jaw. The bite of his stubble is like a bucket of gasoline to an already raging inferno. I have no control over my body, over my mouth, which is why it's so shocking when I say, "We're wearing too many clothes."

I'm never the bold one.

His blue eyes burn even darker. "I do believe you're right."

He stands up beside the bed and lifts his shirt up and over his head in that crazy, sexy one-handed way that men can do. His chest is chiseled to perfection with a smattering of dark blond hair. I get an unobstructed view of the tattoo on his left arm. It's some sort of military design with two names underneath.

"Franks and Tonner," he says, tapping just below the bold names. "My brothers who were killed eight years ago in a roadside bomb." He swallows hard. "The moment we got back to the US, we all went together and got them in memory of our brothers."

"That's beautiful," I whisper through my tight throat.

Colton pushes his workout pants down to his ankles, revealing tight black boxer briefs that make my mouth water. I sit up and pull my long-sleeved workout shirt up and over my own head, tossing it onto the floor. I wore my best bra that's somewhat supportive, yet isn't a sports bra, and I'm glad I did. Nothing's sexy about a flat chest in a workout bra.

Just as I reach down to slide out of my pants, a text message notification fills the room. At first, Colton pays it no attention. His eyes are greedily drinking their fill on my exposed chest, following the delicate curves of my breasts against the light blue satin. But when it chimes a second time, he startles and reaches for his pants.

"Shit," he says when he pulls his phone from the pocket. "It's my mom. She wanted to give me a quick update on Milo."

I give him a smile and nod as he dials the phone. "I'll just slip in the bathroom quickly," I tell him, pointing to the hallway.

"Hey, Mom. How's my little guy doing?" I hear him say as I step behind the door and turn on the light.

Inside, I glance at my reflection in the mirror over the sink. My cheeks are rosy and my lips swollen. There's the slightest hint of redness on my neck from where he dragged his scruffy jaw along the column of my neck. I can't stop smiling as I gaze at the woman in the mirror. She's come a long way since she was in California. She relocated and started over in a new city, a new house. She's stronger than she thinks she is, that's for sure.

I slip off my pants and wet socks and set them on the counter. When I turn around, I see the toddler seat in the tub and the yellow rubber ducky on the ledge. There's a small blue washcloth with Superman on it sitting beside men's shampoo. Axe bodywash sits beside a bottle of Johnson's Baby Wash. A wide smile breaks out on my face as I think of that little boy who is quickly worming his way right into my heart. And his father?

Let's not even go there.

I wait long enough to ensure he's either finished with his conversation, or it'll be ending soon. Quietly, I slip out of the bathroom and listen. There's silence coming from his bedroom. In the doorway, I stop and just stare at the incredible man in front of me. He's still wearing those tight boxer briefs and standing in the middle of the room, watching me. I can feel the caress of his eyes as they trace every square inch of my nearly naked body.

"Come here," he rasps, extending his hand toward me.

Stepping into his room, I slowly make my way to him and stop when I'm directly in front of him. His hand grips my hip as he pulls me against him, his other hand gliding along my ass cheek.

"If I had known you were wearing this beneath your clothes, we wouldn't have made it out of the house to go to class." He moves one hand up my side and around to the front, trailing a finger down the center of my chest. Air catches in my throat as he caresses my skin. This man is playing my body like a violin, and we've only just begun.

My mind spins as desire courses through my veins. "I love the way you touch me," I confess, my eyes closed as I savor the feel of his skin against mine.

"Honey, we've only just begun."

And then the lights go out.

Literally.

We're standing in the dark, almost naked, and we lose power. The wind howls outside the eerily quiet house. Neither of us moves as we wait to see if the power comes back on, but after several long seconds, we're still bathed in total darkness.

"Well, this wasn't exactly what I had in mind."

I can't help it, I laugh. "Talk about a mood killer," I mumble, glancing around for any sign of light.

"Stay here," Colton says. I feel his hands leave my body, and instantly miss them. He takes a few steps and then cries out when he walks into his nightstand. "Shit! I didn't realize I was that close."

"Oh, God, are you okay?"

"I'm fine," he grumbles, moments before the light from his phone illuminates the room. He points it around the room and toward the window. "There must be a massive outage. I can't see any streetlights either."

"You should check on Milo," I find myself saying, taking a step his way.

"Good idea," he replies as he pulls up one of his call list favorites. "Hey, Mom. Yeah, everything's okay. Sorry to call again. We just lost power and wanted to check on you guys." He listens to his mom on the other end. "Well, that's good. It must just be this side of town." Again, he listens, his eyes meeting mine through the darkness. That sexy smirk crosses his lips. "I'll be sure to knock on the door and make sure she's okay."

My hand covers my mouth to muffle my giggle.

"No, we'll be fine. I'm going to light the fireplace. I'll make sure Hollis stays warm," he tells her, but there's something in his eyes that says his plan involves something dirty. "All right, Mom. Love you too. Give my boy a kiss for me."

When he hangs up the phone, he pulls me into his arms. "My mom is worried about you. She wants to make sure you're warm. My mind is suddenly conjuring up all sorts of different ways to make sure you're... *hot* and bothered."

Feeling bold once more, I lean up on my tiptoes, pressing my lips to his. When our eyes connect, I whisper, "Prove it."

CHAPTER 9

Colton

Prove it. She has no idea what she's saying. I've imagined my hands on her body hundreds of times. I'm also a man of many talents. I'll make damn sure I'm utilizing my every talent, including those of my tongue and my cock. I have so many ways to keep her hot and bothered. She isn't aware that she's just given me permission to unleash the beast.

"I need to start a fire, and I need you completely naked." I kiss her lips once more before forcing myself to step away from her. "We're moving this party to the living room."

"What can I do?"

"Blankets and pillows. There are extras in the hall closet." I lean in for another kiss, just a quick peck. I can't seem to help myself when it comes to her. Now that I know her lips are as soft and as sweet as I imagined them to be, I need them. All the time, I need them. "You have your phone for light?"

"Yes." Her reply is breathless and has my cock making himself known in my black boxer briefs and it's making it really fucking diffi-cult to walk away from her right now.

"Pillows, blankets, and nothing against this flawless skin," I remind her. I have to force myself to step back and turn away from her. I need to get a fire started, so we can extinguish the one coursing through my veins. I detour to the nightstand and grab my new, never opened box of condoms and walk past her to the living room. If I touch her again, we'll freeze to death.

Ten minutes later, the fire is blazing, and the flames are already starting to warm up the room. The chill in the air was starting to set in; it's well below freezing outside, so I knew it wouldn't take long. The homeowner in me hopes they can get it back on quickly. You know, frozen pipes and all that. The man in me, well, he likes the idea of cuddling by the fire with a beautiful woman to stay warm. When I bought this place, I wasn't sure I'd ever use the fireplace, but, in this moment, I've never been more grateful for its existence. Even more so, the firewood the previous owners left on the back porch. It's as if all the stars are aligning tonight, and Hollis and I are destined to quell this ache we're both feeling.

"I think this is good," Hollis says.

I turn to face her, and she looks even more beautiful in the light of the fire. "Let me help you." I stand and move the coffee table to the side of the room, and together we start laying out blankets on the floor, layer after layer, and then the pillows. I save an old quilt to cover us up with.

"Looks cozy," Hollis comments as our eyes meet.

Instead of reminding her she's supposed to be ridding herself of the small scraps of material adorning her skin, I stand here, watching her. Waiting for her to bare herself to me. She doesn't disappoint as she reaches behind her and unhooks her bra. Arms at her sides, her hands are in fists as she stands before me in nothing but a pair of panties.

"You okay?" I ask, my voice gritty.

"Yes. It's just... been a while for me."

"Hollis, we don't have to do this," I say the words as my body screams for me to shut the hell up. I ignore my need for her. "I never want you to do anything that you don't feel comfortable with."

My words seem to relax her. "I want this, Colt. I want you."

I nod. Sliding my hands into the waistband of my boxer briefs, I pull them off, letting them pool at my feet. No point in delaying the inevitable. Kicking them to the side, away from our makeshift bed, I stand here, stark naked in front of her. My cock bobs against my abdomen, and twitches when she takes me in for the first time. I stroke myself root to tip while she watches. It's not until her tongue peeks out and licks her lips that I move this party along.

"Hollis, babe, you're killing me here. I need you fucking naked. Now." My voice is a growl, not one of anger but of lust. She must be able to sense it because she offers me a sweet smile before she wiggles out of her yoga panties.

Boy shorts—at least I think that's what they're called—have never looked so good. I watch her, and even though there is a slight tremble in her hands, she continues to step out of them, tossing them to the side.

We're naked.

Finally.

With my hand still tightly fisted around my cock, I take small steps, allowing me time to rake my eyes over her naked body. She's flawless. Her tits look to be a perfect handful, and the softness of her belly leads me to a small landing strip that disappears between her thighs. My mouth waters at the thought of tasting her.

"Colt?" Her voice is soft. My eyes snap to hers, and she looks worried. "W-What are you doing?"

"I've wanted this," I tell her as I give my cock another long stroke. "From the minute I laid eyes on you, I wished I could see you like this. Bare to me. I finally get the chance, and I'm going to take full advantage of it. I want to make sure that when I need to, I can pull this moment up in my mind and relive it."

"Oh." Her lips form the perfect circle, and I can't help but think that's how she would look with my cock in her mouth.

Hollis Taylor is my new obsession.

I can't fight it.

I don't want to fight it.

Not anymore.

She bites down on her lip, something I've noticed she does when she's nervous or unsure. I need to loosen her up. A few more steps and I'm standing so close I can feel the heat from her naked body seep into my own. The room is bathed in a soft glow from the fire, and although unplanned, it's pretty epic as far as romance goes. I'm rusty as hell when it comes to wooing women. Hell, I don't know that I ever have. Maybe in high school? Once I enlisted, picking up women was easy. All I had to do was tell them I was in the Army, and just like that, panties were dropping everywhere. I used that to my advantage. Of course, I also had the good fortune of the Callahan genes running through my veins.

"Come here." Placing my hands on her hips, I pull her close. I'm now the one biting down on my bottom lip as her naked body, all that soft, silky skin, presses against mine. "Dance with me," I murmur.

"T-There's no music."

She's right. I'd use my phone, but without power, I need to save my battery in case my parents or Milo needs me. "Of course there is." My voice is low and husky, and I try to fight off the physical need that's taking over my body as I hold her tight. "Listen to the fire."

Her hands lock behind my neck, her tits showcasing her hard nipples as they mold to my chest. Other than the first moment I held my son, nothing has ever felt this right. I pull her as close as I can get her, our naked bodies aligned perfectly, and with more restraint than I knew I was capable of, we begin to casually sway to the sound of the crackling fire.

My eyes are closed because I know once I see her, those plump lips, and the shimmer of need in her green eyes, I'm a goner. Instead, I bury my face in her neck, and her smell surrounds me. Just a taste.

Just a little nibble to tide me over. My tongue peeks out and traces her skin.

"Oh, God," she moans.

That's all the green light I need. I nip and suck at her neck, grinding my hard cock into her belly. It was my intention to just sample what the night before us holds, but instead, I'm driving us both crazy.

When she reaches down and wraps her hand around my cock, all bets are off. "Hollisss," I hiss. Fuck, I can't have her hands on me just yet or this is going to be over before we get started. And that is going to be disappointing for both of us. "Lie down." With Herculean effort, I pull away from her and settle onto the bed of blankets and pillows on the living room floor.

"Lie back, beautiful," I say when she takes a seat next to me. She does as I ask, and a shiver races through her body. I'm not sure if it's the chill in the room or the anticipation, but I'm not willing to risk it. I move to sit on my knees, facing her. Slowly, my hand travels up her silky-smooth thighs. I don't stop until I reach the promised land. "All this for me?" I ask, and even I can hear the awe in my voice at finding her pussy soaking wet.

My mouth waters.

"Open for me." She doesn't hesitate to spread her legs apart. I maneuver myself so that I'm resting between her thighs before reaching over and grabbing a blanket. Pulling the blanket over my shoulders, I lower my body and pull it over my head and over her body. Part of me wishes I could see her, that I could watch her as I taste her, but there will be time for that. This isn't a one and done for me. I already know she's under my skin, and tonight, that just makes me crave her even more.

Tired of waiting, I suck her clit into my mouth while my hands travel up her body under the blanket. With a plump breast in each hand, I roll her nipples between my thumb and forefinger, all while my mouth is devouring her. Her legs tighten around my head, which only fuels my desire to devour her. I'm relentless, and when her legs begin to quiver, I get my hands involved. One finger then two, I slide them inside her, gently pumping while taking turns massaging her clit with my tongue and my thumb. My cock painfully presses against the blankets we're lying on.

I need to be inside her.

Now.

My hand pumps faster, and that's all it takes. Her legs squeeze me, her back arches off the floor, and she cries out my name. I don't stop until her legs relax. Pulling away from her, I wipe my mouth on the blanket and move my way up her body, kissing everywhere my lips will reach on my way. When my head pops out of the blanket, her eyes are closed, and she has a small, satisfied smile on her lips. My heart skips not just from how beautiful she looks in this moment, but because I did that.

Me.

Colton Callahan.

"You're stunning," I say once again, memorizing everything about this moment.

Her eyes flutter open, and the small smile grows. Her hand slides between us, and she again has my cock in her hand. I close my eyes as she slowly strokes me. "My turn."

"No." I shake my head as a rough sputter of laughter leaves my chest. "I'm not coming in your mouth. I need to be inside you."

"We have all night," she counters.

"Exactly." Snaking my arm out underneath the covers, I grab the box of condoms. I end up having to sit up as I tear open the box and retrieve a small foil packet. I have the pack ripped open and us protected within seconds before pulling the blanket back up over my shoulders and I'm settled between her thighs.

Elbows resting on the floor on either side of her head, I brush the hair back from her face. My eyes hold hers for four heartbeats before she reaches between us and helps guide my steel length inside her. Slowly, inch after inch, I push forward until I'm fully seated. Eyes closed, I tilt my head back and absorb this feeling. The warmth of her body surrounding mine. I can't explain it, and I know it sounds crazy as hell, but this feels different. Unlike anytime before her, before this moment. It's incredible, and I need just a minute to reel it in. Deep even breaths in. Slowly release.

"I-I wasn't sure you would fit" is her whispered confession that causes me to open my eyes.

"Like you were made for me." I press my lips to hers, taking my time, letting my tongue duel with hers. Her body instantly relaxes, and I slide in a little deeper. Something I didn't think was possible. Her eyes widen. "You okay?"

"So okay." She gives me a shy smile.

Leisurely, I begin the slow dance of push and pull. Her hands slide under my arms, and her nails dig into my back. I'm taking my time. We've got all night, and I plan to take full advantage of the fact.

"There," she instructs as I push in deep. Her legs lift, and she locks them behind my back, crossing her ankles.

Pulling out, I go deep again, causing her to moan. That's the gratification I'm looking for, so I continue on. Each thrust develops faster and becomes more intense as the walls of her pussy clamp around my cock. Biting down on my bottom lip, I hold off my orgasm. I don't go until she does.

Faster and faster, I rock into her until she cries out, something I don't understand, and like a vise, her pussy squeezes me, and no matter how hard I try to fight it, I lose control, spilling over inside her. Spent, I manage to rest my forehead against hers as I try and catch my breath. Her chest is rapidly rising and falling, mimicking my own.

When I can finally pull away, I miss the warmth of her being wrapped around me. "I'm just going to go handle this. Don't move." Climbing to my feet, I find my legs are a little shaky. Not that the revelation should come as a surprise to me; I've never come that hard in my entire life.

I find my way to the bathroom in the dark and dispose of the condom. At least I think I did. It's hard to tell, and I didn't bring my phone with me. This side of the house is chilly, but not freezing.

Hopefully, the fire will keep the pipes from freezing. Speaking of pipes, mine is already frozen, missing her warmth. Carefully, I navigate my way back to her and drop to the floor, sliding under the covers. She wastes no time moving into my arms that are waiting to hold her.

I run my hands through her hair as we lie here by the fire. We're both quiet, and while I know why I'm lost in my thoughts, I don't know why she is. "Regrets?" I force the word past my lips. Part of me doesn't want to know, but then there's the other part of me that wants nothing more than for her to be happy. The thought of her regretting this night has my stomach in knots.

"No. No regrets," she finally answers. "You?"

"How could I regret something that changed my life?"

Tilting her head up, she furrows her brow. Reaching over, I soothe it with my thumb.

"Changed your life? That's a pretty big statement, Callahan."

"I'd say life-altering deserves a big statement, Taylor." I wink at her.

"Really, no regrets?"

"None." I pull her a little tighter, willing her to believe me. "Tell me something. Anything."

"What do you want to know?"

"Tell me about you. About your life, your friends, your family. I feel like I barely know anything about you at all."

"Well, I was born and raised in Southern California, and I'm an only child."

"What made you move here? Why Missouri of all places?"

"I needed a change. I wanted to experience all four seasons. My best friend, Tina, works crazy hours, so I decided why not. It sounded like an adventure."

"An adventure, huh?" Her answer seems too canned for me to not think there is something else lying beneath the surface. I can only hope that one day she'll trust me enough to let me in. I know we're virtually strangers who have lived together for a short amount of time, and now we've just complicated things by sleeping together. However, I meant what I said. I don't regret it, and it was life-changing. In so many ways. Not only was it the best sex of my life, but it's opened my eyes to see what I've been missing all these years. A home of my own, a woman to not only keep me warm at night but to share my life with. The hardships of parenting, my hopes, and dreams. I see Chase and Gabby, and I've been envious, but tonight, it's put things in a new perspective for me. If Hollis were not here, I'd be alone in the dark. Sure, I could have gone to my parents' place, but still, I'd be alone. My bed would be cold, and my heart, still surrounded by self-imposed walls that are there for no reason.

It's not some tragic story of having my heart broken. No, when I enlisted and witnessed how upset my mother, father, and brother were when I was thousands of miles away and could hear the worry in their voice over a cracking connection, I knew I could never do that to someone else. I vowed to keep my distance and never get too close. The Army was where I felt I was supposed to be, and I refused to bring that pain and worry onto anyone else.

The day I found out about Milo, there was no other choice to make. I was a father, and my son wouldn't have to worry if Daddy was coming home.

"Why graphic design?"

"I don't know really. I took a class my first year of college and enjoyed it. I caught on quickly, and we are living in the digital age. I liked the fact that I could make a living anywhere. I can have clients from all over the world and never have to leave my living room. And I can work in my pajamas all day."

"Great. Now all I'm going to think about is what skimpy little number you're wearing while your door is closed."

"All you have to do is knock, and I'll show you."

"Hollis," I warn. "You can't tease a man like that. Not after I've just been inside you and still have your warm naked body in my arms."

"I'm not teasing. I don't know what happens next. If this was us just... scratching an itch, or what, but I'm keeping an open mind."

"And an open door?" I tease."I'm crazy about you. I want to spend more time with you. Not just between the sheets, but us together, doing couple things. Although there is something that we need to discuss."

"I'm listening."

"I'm a single dad. I know Milo is still a baby, but he's getting bigger every single day. He recognizes faces and voices, and well, if that's too much for you, if being with me and my son is too much, I'd like for you to tell me now. Tell me before I fall any harder for you." My hand is trailing up and down her back, enjoying the softness of her skin beneath my fingertips.

Pushing up on her elbow, her hand rests against my cheek. "You're an amazing man, Colton Callahan. I've said that before, and I'll continue to do so. The fact that you're a single father and proud of it warms my heart. You love that little boy to the ends of the earth, and that shines through in everything that you do. You're not just Colton, the retired Army hero, you're Colton, the brother, the son, and the father. That little boy is the best part of you, and I'm honored you allow me to be a small piece of your lives."

Lifting my head, I kiss her. We roll to our sides, and we kiss. Our hands roam each other's bodies as we explore on an intimate level. I don't know how long, minutes, hours pass us by, but it's been one of the best nights of my entire life.

"I should put more wood on the fire." It's starting to fade quickly, and the chill in the room, even under the blankets and with our body heat, is noticeable.

"Yeah." She yawns.

"I'm stoking the fire, and then we're sleeping." I kiss the tip of her nose. "I'm sorry for keeping you up."

"Don't apologize. I've enjoyed every second of our time together."

Nodding, I throw off the covers and yelp. "Fuck, it's cold." I rush to the fireplace, thankful I brought in enough wood to get us through the night. "Babe, as bad as I want to hold you skin to skin while we sleep, I think we better get dressed. I don't want you getting sick."

She sighs. "On one condition."

"What's that?" I ask, tossing logs onto the fire.

"Raincheck?"

I stop and turn to look at her over my shoulder. "Raincheck?"

"I want another night that I get to sleep skin to skin with you."

"You want that?" I ask, ready to say fuck the fire, douse it with water, and drive through the fucking blizzard outside to the nearest hotel just to make it happen.

"More than anything."

"Done. Now get dressed before I change my mind and we run off to the nearest hotel."

"The roads sucked hours ago, and the temperature is only dropping," she says as if I'm crazy for wanting to leave.

"I know," I sigh. "That's why you need to get dressed, but I promise you we will get our raincheck." I turn back to the fire and pile as many logs on as I can to keep it going while we sleep. I replace the glass to keep sparks from flying and rush to find my clothes. I forgo the boxer briefs, and slide into my sweats, pulling my T-shirt on over my head. "You good? Need something warmer?"

"Just you, Colton. Just you."

"I'm going to grab a drink of water, you want one?"

"Yes, that actually would be great."

I make my way to the kitchen from memory and the light of the fire, and grab two glasses from the cabinet, filling them with water. I down mine, then fill it again before carrying them both into the living room. Once we're done, I set them on the end table, so we don't knock them over while we sleep. Taking my spot on the blankets, I burrow under and pull her into me. It's noticeably warmer with clothes on. It's a sacrifice I've made, but I would feel terrible if she were to get sick just to appease my desire to be next to her.

As we lie here next to the warmth and the glow of the fire on our bed of blankets, I realize that I want more than just a raincheck. I want every night she's willing to give me. I want to learn more about her, what she loves, what she hates. I want to know it all.

"Hollis?"

"Yeah?"

"What's your favorite color?"

"Blue."

I snuggle in deeper, burying my face in her neck as I make a silent vow to learn it all. I want to get to know all of her, and I won't stop until I do.

This night has been more than I ever could have imagined, and we owe it to ourselves to see where this goes. I just pray that she knows what she's signing up for being with a single father. There will be times when Milo will need all of me. From what I know of her, she's going to be right there by my side. It's that image that I see, the three of us together, as I drift off to sleep.

CHAPTER 10

Hollis

When I wake in the morning, I'm smothered in heat. From head to toe, warmth envelopes me, making it damn near impossible to fully wake up. But I do, and when I open my eyes, I find nothing but smoldering ash in the fireplace, and a big, muscular arm stretched around me.

Oh. Yeah. Last night.

I can't help but smile as I stretch. A delicious soreness tingles my thighs and lady parts. Last night comes back in bright Technicolor. The sexual tension stretched over the evening, from the moment we got to the gym to the second we pulled in the driveway. It burned with anticipation so thick you could practically cut it with a knife.

And the makeshift bed in front of a fireplace? Well, that was just the icing on top of the orgasm-laced cake.

Now, as the sun slowly peeks through the curtains, a bubble of uncertainty lodges in my stomach. Am I supposed to go home? Tell him thanks for the good time and then leave, returning to my side of the wall and to our landlord-renter relationship? Is it still a walk of shame if it's only a matter of yards, and you're the only one to see you?

God, this is why I don't do this.

This is why I don't sleep with random guys, especially ones who I see on practically a daily basis.

But then his words, his actions come back to me. He told me he was tired of fighting it. He led me to believe this wasn't just an isolated in-the-moment occasion. The way he held me and touched me felt like it was the start of something. Something new.

Something great.

"You're thinking awfully hard," he mumbles, adjusting his arms and pulling me even closer. My ass comes in contact with his already hard cock, and I can feel myself getting wet with anticipation.

"I was just noticing it's warm in here, even though the fire's almost out," I tell him, completely avoiding the "other" thoughts in my head.

"The power came back on about three, which is good because I let the fire burn too low. I was too nice and warm here with you," he tells me, nuzzling my neck and rocking his hips.

A noise croaks from my dry throat, sort of a hum and sort of a moan. Colton seems to take my sound as a positive and runs his lips along the back of my neck as his hand slips up my shirt and splays against my stomach.

"I have an idea," he whispers, licking and kissing my skin and basically sending me into a hyper-aware sexual frenzy.

Pushing back gently and grinding my ass against his erection, I say, "I can't wait to hear it."

He grunts, gripping my hip and holding me tightly against him. "Breakfast. Shower. Get Milo." His words are clipped, edgy as he continues to hold me perfectly still, as if having me pressed to him is causing him pain.

Not the bad kind of pain, mind you.

Oh, no. The good kind.

Ignoring his silent pleas, I wrap my palm around the hand he's gripping my hip with and press back with my ass. He moans in my ear, nipping at the lobe, and sending me orbiting into a frenzy of desire and need. Lifting my leg, I sling it back and over his outer thigh. He takes his hand and mine with it, and slips them under the waistband of my pants. Big thick fingers slide against my clit, teasing until I'm practically riding his hand.

"Colt," I moan, "I need you. *Please.*" I recognize the fact that I'm begging.

"I've got you, Holls," he grunts, my heart skipping a beat at the sound of the nickname. With deft fingers, he discards my pants, and rips my panties tossing them to the side. "No. Inside me. Now."

He stops the assault with his fingers, which is both heaven and hell. I need more. More Colton. He's able to turn slightly and grab the open box of condoms on the coffee table. One handed, he pulls one out and rips the package with his teeth. He has to pull his other hand out from under my neck so he can sheath himself, but the moment the protection is secure, Colton slides his arm back underneath me.

"Come here," he whispers, hitching my leg over his thigh. He presses against my entrance from behind, lining our bodies up as best he can. Then he pushes forward. That delicious tightness and subtle burn sweep through my blood as a sigh slips through my parted lips. "Is this what you wanted?" he asks when he's completely buried inside me from behind.

"God, yes. That."

Colton slowly eases out before thrusting forward, filling me completely. As his pelvis starts to move, his hand comes around and rubs my clit. Sparks of need ignite through my blood as he drives me closer to release. His lips are everywhere: my neck, my shoulder, my ear. His cock moves easily within me, guiding me, step-by-step, to the orgasm he's promising.

"I want to feel you come, Hollis. Come on my cock," he demands, as if he has complete control of my release. I detonate, blinding white light filling my vision as I cry out his name.

Colton grunts and presses his mouth to my shoulder. He shudders before flexing his hips and stilling, filling the protection with his release. "Christ," he whispers, his warm breath tickling my neck.

"Mmhmm." I can't seem to form words.

He gently eases out of me, my body missing him already, and holds me against his chest. "I have an idea. Why don't you go take a shower and get ready for the day while I make us some breakfast?"

My heart cries a little with happiness. Mostly because I wasn't quite sure where this would really go afterward, but breakfast is good, right? I mean, I know we talked about moving forward last night—err, early this morning—but I know a lot can be said in the heat of the moment. Maybe he didn't really mean to advance so quickly now. A change of heart would be normal, right?

"You're thinking again," he whispers, kissing that place between my shoulder and my neck.

"I'm sorry."

"What are you thinking about?" he asks, his right hand moving to cradle my head as he holds me.

"Ummm," I start, but stop. I know I just need to say it. Rip off the Band-Aid. "I wasn't sure what's next. I mean, we had fun, but is that it?"

"Is that it?" he parrots, his body stilling against mine, a touch of panic on his gorgeous face. "Is that what you want? Last night when we talked—"

Swallowing, I realize I already know the answer. I place my finger on his lips, cutting off his words. "No."

Colton seems to relax instantly. "Good. Tell me what you want."

Sighing, I turn so I'm facing him. His jaw is covered in a thick stubble, even thicker than it was coming in yesterday. Something tells me this man could really grow a beard if he wanted. I can't help but run my fingers over his jaw as I lock my eyes on his. "I still want to see where this could go."

My words are barely out, and he's smiling that breathtaking grin I've come to love. "Yeah? Good, because I'd really like to see where this goes too." He places a chaste kiss to my lips. "I meant it last night, Hollis, I like you. I've wanted you from the moment I laid eyes on you."

"But now you've had me," I tell him.

He turns me and moves so he's hovering over me. "And I just want more," he says softly, before claiming my lips with his own.

*****

Tina:I miss you.

Me:I miss you too. How's work?

Tina: Busy, which is the only reason why I haven't flown there to see you. I can't believe you've been gone a few weeks already. How's the weather in Missouri?

Me: It snowed last night. We lost power.

Tina: Yikes! What did you do?

Ummm... things I probably shouldn't spell out in a text message. I decide to go with the PG version of last evening.

· · ·

Me: Well, I ended up hanging out with Colton.

Tina: The former military, single-dad thing is hot. You know that, right?

Uhhh, yeah! I'm not dumb or blind.

Tina: Seriously, please tell me you're banging the hot guy next door!

Me: Tina! I can't believe you said that.

Tina: Yes, you can. That's why you love me. My inappropriate dirty talk.

Me: That's it exactly.

Truth be told, I miss the hell out of my best friend. I've always been more of a loner, working from home, and enjoying my quiet time. When I met Tina, she barreled into my life at a coffee shop, insulted the book I was reading and hasn't left my side since. She's the most loyal, trustworthy person I've known. Well, until Colton. That's why it pains me that she doesn't know everything. That I'm holding out one big piece of my life from her.

Colton too.

Tina: Anyway, I gotta jet. I'll text you tomorrow.

. . .

Me: Sounds good.

Tina: Make sure you suit up before you go to the races, Hollis. *insert devil emoji* *insert eggplant emoji*

Me: You're horrible.

Tina: Don't think I didn't notice how you didn't deny it. Hooker.

Me:*insert shocked face emoji*

Tina: Hey, don't feel bad. It takes a hooker to know a hooker. Tootles! *insert heart emoji*

Me:*insert kissy face emoji*

Just as I set my phone on the chair, a knock sounds at the door separating my place and his. After breakfast, we both got ready for the day, and since the gym is closed because of the weather, he left to go get Milo. He invited me to come with, but I used the work excuse to stay behind. I really do have to work on the gym's new site, but I also received two more inquiries via my own website. I wanted to pull as much information on their businesses as I could before offering them my package details.

One time, when I first went out on my own, I received an inquiry and sent them all my information. I found out after I started digging that the company didn't exist. The email address was a dummy account, and my correspondences went unanswered. The next week, Arrow Media, my biggest rival in the web design business, went viral with their brand-new packages and rates. Turns out, they were the exact services I offer, just a few dollars cheaper. To a small business, a few dollars adds up, and while I saw a steady increase in inquiries, I saw a decline in the ones who actually purchased a package.

The result was a complete overhaul of my services and the costs associated with them, as well as a better system for dealing with customer inquiries.

"Hey," I reply as I open the door, a smile instantly spreading across my face.

"Hello. So, after Milo's nap, he reminded me he hasn't played in the snow, and well, he's ready to go make baby snow angels. He also told me he'd rather you go out with us, since you're much prettier to look at than I am."

I smirk back at the sexy man who's wearing winter weather gear and holding a baby in a snowsuit. "He said all that, huh?"

"Word for word," he confirms. "My dad bought him a baby sled with a little seat, and I'm thinking since the sun's out and it's about thirty degrees warmer than it was yesterday, today would be a great day to go for a ride on the sled. You in?"

The rest of my work is completely forgotten after that invitation. I reach forward and tap Milo's little nose. "I wish I could, but I don't have any snow boots yet."

"I have some extra ones. They'll be big, but if you double up on socks, I'm sure it'll work."

I squint my eyes and glance down at his feet. He's wearing camo snow boots and thick, insulated overalls. "Umm, Colton, I don't know if that'll work. What size of shoe do you wear?"

"Eleven."

A bubble of laughter spills from my lips, which makes Milo smile and start to kick. "Eleven? Colton, I wear a seven. There's no way your shoes will fit me. I'll probably walk right out of them."

"No way are you getting out of this, Holls. Milo would be very disappointed if you weren't to come outside with us."

Rolling my eyes, I smile in defeat. "Fine, I'll wear your too-big boots. For Milo."

"Did you hear that, buddy? Hollis is gonna come outside and play with us." He bounces his son in his arms as if to cheer. "I'm going to head outside now, so we don't get too hot in all these layers. My extra boots are by the back door, and there's a few extra pairs of insulated gloves on the washing machine. Grab whatever you need," he says before leaning in and kissing my cheek.

I feel a blush tinge my skin where his lips grazed and have to fight from breaking out into a full-fledge crazy grin. You know, the kind that makes people look at you like you're utterly batshit nutty? The kind that actually hurts your cheeks from smiling so hard.

"See you in a few minutes," he says, before turning and heading out the back door.

Exhaling, I glance at the gloves he left on the washer, which is right next to a hoodie sweatshirt with Army printed in green and another pair of Carhartt overalls. I grab the warm clothes he left and slip back into my apartment. I throw on a pair of looser jeans over leggings and then slide my legs into the overalls. They're way too big, but they're definitely warm, so I don't complain. Next, I throw on the hoodie over my long-sleeved T-shirt, which is really big, yet comfy, and smells just like Colton. I add a second pair of socks and stuff my feet into the too-big boots. It's actually a bit hard to walk in them, but it'll work until I get my own boots. I finish off my outfit with gloves, hat, scarf, and coat, and turn to take in my appearance in the mirror.

I immediately burst into laughter.

I look like a five-year-old wearing her dad's clothes.

But I'm warm, and that's the point.

Shuffling my heavy feet, I make my way to the laundry room and out the back door. It's not nearly as cold as it was last night, with the sun warming the air and slowly melting the snow. A bubble of laughter catches my attention, and I'm suddenly smiling beneath the scarf wrapped around my jaw as I watch Colton pull his son on a little red sled. It has a seat in the middle with a buckle, and with the help of blankets for positioning, he's reclined in the seat to keep from falling over. His nose is red, but the smile on his face says everything as he reaches for the fluffy white stuff just out of his reach.

I make my way to them, Colton's eyes dancing with humor. "You look..."

"Like I'm wearing clothes three sizes too big?"

"Amazing," he answers with a grin as he reaches over and adjusts my hat, pulling it down on my forehead. I'm ready to throw my hands around his neck and plaster my marshmallow man body against his when Milo lets out a screech. "Okay, buddy." He looks at me and reaches for my hand. "Care to take a walk around the backyard with me?"

And we do.

I walk beside Colton as he pulls Milo on the sled. I fumble with my phone, but I manage to pull it from my pocket and snap a few pictures of Colton and Milo. I'll have to send them to him later. We walk slowly around the large yard, making new tracks with each pass, but when we reach thirty minutes, Milo is at his max with sitting. He lets out a squeal of annoyance and tries to slip from the seat. "All right, buddy. Let's try something new."

Colton unclips the belt and helps Milo sit in the snow. The little guy instantly reaches for it, shrieks of laughter filling the air as he whacks his hands down into the fluffy snow repeatedly. I plop down in the white stuff beside him, fall back and stretch out, moving my arms and legs to make a snow angel. I've never made one before, and I feel like a kid on Christmas morning. I wave my arms and legs, just like I've seen done on television or the internet.

When I open my eyes, I realize I'm smiling so wide, my face hurts. Okay, it could hurt from the frigid air, but I'd like to think it has something to do with how happy and free I feel lying in the snow, making my very first snow angel.

My eyes connect with Colton's, and it takes a few seconds before I realize what he has in his hand. He's holding his cell phone, angling it down and tapping on the screen. But it's not at Milo that it's pointed. No, it's at me. Something passes between us. Understanding, maybe. Acceptance. Joy. Probably a good mixture of it all.

When I turn my head, I burst into laughter. Milo is lying beside me in the snow, kicking his little legs like he's running a race. "Milo, are you making a snow angel too?" I ask, crouching carefully next to him and moving his legs and hands until we've made a small baby snow angel.

"Buddy, look here," Colton says as he snaps a few more pictures of us making the angel.

I stand Milo up in the snow and laugh at his eager little shrieks of delight. Glancing up at Colton, I see him still snapping photos. With my right hand, I hold Milo upright, but with my left, I reach for the phone. "Give it to me. I'll take some of you two."

His entire face lights up as he hands me the phone and gets down on the ground with his son. For the next several minutes, I take photo after photo of father and son frolicking in the snow. Colton demonstrates the building of the perfect snowball, to which Milo tries to eat. They build a few more and toss them off into the yard. When I slip Colton's phone into my pocket, and the boys stand up, there's a gleam in their eyes that gives me pause. Well, to be honest, I'm pretty sure the look in Milo's blue eyes is because he's trying to grab the snowball, but the one in his father's eyes...?

That has trouble written all over it.

Carefully, I take a retreating step backward, followed by another, but Colton advances. I have about a half-second warning before the snowball hits me square in the chest. "What the..."

"It slipped!" he insists, though the sparkle in his eyes betrays him.

"Slipped? Seriously?" I ask, bending down and gathering up a wet ball of snow in my hand.

"I'm holding a baby," Colton notes, moving Milo and using him as a human baby shield.

"I see that," I reply, patting my snowball to keep it from falling apart.

"You wouldn't," he adds, dancing to the left.

I shrug. "Not while you're holding Milo."

Slowly, he crouches down and sets his son back against the backrest of the sled and straps him in securely. Then, he stands up and locks eyes with mine as a seductive smile spreads across his gorgeous face. Suddenly, he moves, throwing his arms around my waist and putting his shoulder into my chest. It's not hard, but it catches me off guard, especially when he hoists me up in the air, throwing me over his shoulder like a sack of potatoes.

I wail his name, which sounds odd considering I'm giggling too.

"Any final words you'd like to share, Holls?" he asks, dramatically spinning me around.

"Don't you dare," I start, but the rest of the sentence is lost when I start to fall. No, not fall, per se, because I'm still in Colton's arms, but we do fall. Together. His body taking the brunt of the weight as we land and roll.

When we stop moving, he's lying directly on top of me, my head cradled in his gloved hands as our bodies align so perfectly from head to toe. I shiver, but not from the cold snow pressed against my back. I shiver from the desire laced in his eyes, and the warmth of his breath tickling my dry lips.

"That wasn't very nice," I whisper, gripping the back of his coat.

"You were going to throw a snowball at me."

"Allegedly."

Colton smiles and presses his lips to my own, the heat of his skin against mine a welcome jolt to my senses. He sweeps his tongue inside my mouth, tasting and savoring our connection. A jolt of lightning strikes through my veins as his thumb grazes across the apple of my cheek, his teeth nipping at my full bottom lip.

Milo starts to cry. We both look over as the baby rubs his eyes, a sign he's done with the great outdoors. With a chaste kiss to my lips, Colton rolls over and gets up, unbuckling the belt and taking his son in his arms. Together, the three of us make our way to the house.

"I have an idea," Colton says as he shuts the door behind us. "I'm going to get this guy a bottle and down for a nap. When you get warm and dry, come back over here, and I'll make dinner."

"Dinner, huh?" I ask, taking off my wet gloves and throwing them on the dryer.

"Steak and baked potatoes," he confirms as he starts to strip Milo's winter snowsuit and layers.

"Sounds delicious. Can I bring anything?"

He shrugs out of his own coat while juggling a baby who's getting more upset by the second. "Just yourself," he replies, kicking off his boots. He seems to forgo the removal of his overalls, choosing to take care of his son first. "I'm going to get him some food," he says just before he places a kiss on my lips and turns to leave the laundry room.

I stay behind, laying out our wet clothes so they can dry. When that's done, I slip quietly into my apartment and shut the door. In the kitchen, I warm some milk in the microwave and pour a packet of powdered hot cocoa into a mug. When the drink is ready, I take my favorite unicorn mug and head to my chair. Heat spreads through me as I sip the chocolaty treat and catch the familiar scent of Colton's detergent still clinging to his sweatshirt. Like a lunatic, I bring the shirt to my nose and inhale deeply.

I may have to keep this.

Smiling, I reach for my laptop and fire it up. I have a few more hours of work on my current job, with a few new ones waiting in the wings. Plus, I need to meet with Gabby soon to finalize the All Fit Gym website for publication. I'm excited for it to go live.

My email has five new messages since I last checked, two of which are junk phishing messages. One is from my website host for my annual renewal and another a notification from my bank about a payment to hit my account. That makes me happy. I'll be able to pick up a few more things for my apartment soon, including a small two-seater table for the kitchenette.

Smiling, I click on the fifth email, a contact from my website, and find myself unable to pull oxygen into my lungs. Tears burn my eyes as I stare at the words marring my screen.

Contact: iwillfindyou@gmail.com
Message: I'm getting closer, Hollis. Soon. I'll see you soon.

I'm not sure what's more unsettling: the fact he's still sending me messages after I disappeared a few months ago or that he's actually getting close.

CHAPTER 11

Colton

I'm jolted awake from my son's cries through the monitor. I scramble out of bed, and turn off the monitor, so it doesn't wake Hollis, and rush down the hall. Milo doesn't cry. My heart is pounding in my chest as I make my way to his room.

"Hey, bud," I coo, lifting him from his crib. I immediately notice he's burning up. His cries begin to quiet as I rock him in my arms, running my hands up and down his back. "Daddy's got you. You feeling bad?" I ask him. Not that I expect him to answer, that's just what we do. I talk, and he listens. It's our thing. "I wish I knew what was wrong," I say, rocking from side to side. "Let's go get you some Tylenol." Grabbing his blanket and binky from his bed, I carry him to the kitchen. I'm struggling with getting the Tylenol and the dropper filled with one hand, so I carry him into the living room and lay him on the couch sitting in front of him to keep him from rolling off. As soon as I lay him down, he begins to cry. Not just any cry. No, this one is loud, a piercing wail. It's a mix between I'm pissed off and Daddy it hurts.

"I'm sorry, buddy. Daddy has to get your medicine." I try to keep my voice soothing, even though I'm nervous as hell. I hate it when he cries, and it puts me on edge. "It's okay," I tell him, but I don't even think he can hear me over his cries. I fumble with the Tylenol bottle, and I'm finally able to get the lid off. My hands are shaking. What if there is something really wrong with him?

"Colt?"

I look up to find Hollis standing in the kitchen. Her hair is a mess, she's wearing my T-shirt from yesterday, and her eyes are sleepy but soft. Somehow through my son's tears, I was still able to hear her. I don't have time to figure out what that means. "I'm so sorry," I tell her, continuing to work to get the dropper full of medicine. Milo's little arms and legs are flailing, and he hits my arm, and I drop the bottle, spilling it all over my lap.

"Hey." Her soothing voice is next to me. Before I know what's happening, she reaches around me and lifts Milo into her arms. He shudders a breath, and his cries quiet. "I've got you, handsome. What's going on, huh? Are you not feeling well?" She continues to talk to him in a calm, soothing voice, and his cries stop completely. Shuddered breaths and whimpers are all that you hear.

"Thank you. I'm sorry we woke you." I stand and grab the bottle and rush to the kitchen to clean up the mess and start over.

"It's not a problem. What's going on with him?"

"I'm not sure. He woke me up screaming, and he's burning up. I'm trying to give him some medicine, but as you can see, that's not working out too well."

"Let's go change your diaper while Daddy gets you some medicine." She breezes past me and down the hall to his room. I wait for Milo's cries, but they never come. Instead, all I hear is the low hum of Hollis's voice as she talks to him.

Bracing my hands on the counter, I let out a slow breath. This single-dad thing is hard. I'm so thankful she's here right now. I grab a towel from the counter and wipe off my lap, but it's no use, the sticky medicine has already soaked into the material of my boxer briefs. Tossing the towel back on the counter, I fill the dropper to the correct amount and go in search of my girl and my son.

"That's better," Hollis says softly, lifting Milo into her arms. He's no longer crying, as he stares up at her. "I'm sorry, buddy. I wish I could make it better for you," she tells him, and he shudders a deep breath.

"Looks like you already have," I say, stepping into his room.

"There's Daddy." She smiles down at Milo. "Nah, he's still feeling bad. You can see it in his eyes, then there's the fever."

Her words strike me in my gut. This woman, so new to our lives, yet she knows my son. She pays attention to know he looks ill in his eyes. She cares enough to pay attention. I'm falling hard and fast for her. Seeing her like this, comforting Milo, getting up with us in the middle of the night. That's sexier to me than anything else she could have done, any seduction she could have offered. A year ago, I would have told you that you were crazy if you said that's how I would feel someday. Today, however, that's just not the case. She's never looked more beautiful to me than she does right now. In my clothes, hair a mess from our lovemaking before bed, holding my son.

"Do you mind holding him while I give him this? He's not really a fan." I hold up the dropper of medicine.

"Sure." She shifts him from her shoulder to cradle him in her arms. "Okay, buddy. Daddy has some medicine that's going to make you feel better. I need you to work with us, okay?" Her voice is soft and soothing and has a calming effect on my baby boy.

Moving in close, I place my hand under his chin and stick the dropper in his mouth. He tries to spit it out, but the gentle hold of my fingers under his chin helps him to swallow. Pulling out the dropper, he lets out a cry, but it's short-lived as Hollis once again cuddles him to her chest. She rubs his back and sways side to side, and his cries stop.

"You don't think it was us playing in the snow last week, do you?" she asks. I can hear the worry in her voice.

"No. It could be anything. He's been cutting teeth, so that's my guess. I'll call the doctor in the morning and see what they think I should do. Let me wash my hands, and I'll take him."

"He's fine." She follows me back to the kitchen and heads straight for the rocker recliner I bought two days ago. She settles into the chair and wraps Milo's soft blanket around him and begins to rock.

"You sure you don't want me to take him?" I feel guilty that she's missing out on her sleep.

"No. We're good, aren't we, buddy," she says softly, smiling down at Milo. His eyes are already shut, unable to resist the pull of the rocking of the chair and being snuggled up with Hollis. *Like father like son.* I can't resist her either.

With the dim lighting of the lamp, I take a seat on the couch and watch her. Watch them. My relationship with Hollis has developed fast, but I wouldn't change it. I'm crazy about her, and seeing her like this, so loving and caring toward Milo, well, it's hard to separate the sex and the emotions. I sound like a fucking chick, even to my own ears, but it's the truth. I can't help but wonder what it would be like to have her by my side all the time. Sure, that's how things have been this past week, but I mean more permanently. As in, her room is no longer hers. Maybe we'll have more kids? Move to a bigger place? My mind is all over the place. All because of the beautiful woman, sitting on my chair, in my clothes, holding my son.

All because of Hollis.

I can't tell you how long I've been sitting here just watching her with him. I know it's not polite to stare, but I couldn't pull my eyes from them even if I tried.

"He's out," she whispers.

"Okay." I nod but make no effort to move. I'm not ready for this time to observe her, observe them together to be over. I imagine this is what it's supposed to be like. When there are two parents, and this parenting gig isn't being done solo. This is how it's supposed to feel. "I'll take him," I finally say, standing from my place on the couch.

"No, I can do it. We don't want to jostle him too much and wake him up." I nod and follow her down the hall to his room. I watch intently as she lays him back in his bed. When she kisses the tips of her fingers and places them to his forehead, I'm a goner. Reaching out, I link my fingers through hers and guide her back to my room. I make quick work of stripping us both of our clothes before snagging a condom from the nightstand and pulling back the covers. There are no words spoken. We don't need them. Our bodies are talking for us.

We're both giving.

We're both taking.

I'm falling in love with you.

That last one, that's all me, but I'd like to think she feels the same way. The way she looks at me, the way she looks at my son. It has to be true, right? Together, we fall over the cliff of ecstasy. When I've caught my breath, I handle the condom and slide back into bed, pulling her into my arms. I hold her tight, and don't let go. I don't ever want to let go.

* * *

"What did the doctor say?" Hollis asks when I walk through the door. She's sitting on the couch with her computer on her lap. She's still wearing my shirt, and her hair is still a mess. I love her like this.

"Teething." I look down at my son, who is all bundled up in his snowsuit and trying to rest his head on my shoulder.

"Poor guy." She moves her laptop to the couch beside her then stands to greet us. "Those teeth are meanies, huh, buddy?" she asks Milo.

"I guess I'll call Chase and see if he can watch him for me while I do my classes tonight. Mom and Dad are out of town, and Gwen offered, but he's clingy and doesn't feel good. She's pregnant, and she has Sophia, and Harrison to deal with."

Hollis laughs. "I'll keep him."

"No. We already deprived you of sleep. I can't ask you to do that."

"You didn't. I volunteered. Besides, when he sleeps, I'll work. I got some work in while you were gone too."

"Are you sure?"

"Positive. Hand me the cuteness." She holds out her hands, waiting for me to hand my son to her.

I hand him over, and she turns her back to me, carrying him to the couch and lays him down, stripping him out of his snowsuit. "There, now you don't look like a marshmallow man." She lifts him into her arms and kisses his cheek. "What are we going to do today?" she asks as if he's going to reply. Just like I do.

"You sure about this, Hollis?"

"Absolutely. We're going to hang out, play, nap, eat, and make a mess of the house." She smiles over at me, and I find myself smiling back.

"I don't have to go in until two."

"Go take a nap. You didn't get much sleep last night."

"I can't do that. You go work until I have to leave."

She reaches down and closes her laptop. "Stop trying to steal my thunder, Colton Callahan. Today, I get to be the hero. Go." She shoos me away with a swing of her arm. "We've got this, Daddy."

Sliding my hand behind her neck, I pull her into a kiss. My hand slides around her waist, as I deepen the kiss, needing more of her when a tiny hand lands on my cheek, and a cry comes from my son. I chuckle and pull away, and he stops crying. "Looks like I'm not the only Callahan man falling for your charms," I say, bopping my son on the nose with my index finger.

Hollis throws her head back and laughs. "Go call Gwen. Let her know that you won't be bringing Milo today and get some rest." She shakes her head as if she can't believe my words. She doesn't see herself like we see her. I'm going to change that. She needs to believe how incredible she is.

"Thank you." I lean in for another kiss before heading to my room. It's going to be hard to sleep knowing they're out there, but it could be another long night of Milo not sleeping, so I need to take this opportunity while I can. Pulling my phone out of my pocket, I strip down and climb under the covers before dialing Gwen.

"Good morning," she greets. I can hear Sophia babbling in the background.

"Hey, Gwen. Milo's teething and running a fever, and just overly fussy, so I'm not going to bring him today. He's been pretty clingy."

"So, what you're telling me is my sister talked you into letting her keep him?" she asks, amused.

"No. Actually, Hollis is going to keep him for me. I don't have to be at the gym until

two, and I have two classes, one at three and one at five." I don't know why I told her my schedule. She knows it. Hell, she has a copy of it since she is my babysitter.

"Hollis, huh?"

"Yep," I say, popping the P.

"Nice. Well, if something changes and you need me, you know where to find me."

"I do. Thanks, Gwen."

"You're welcome. Tell Hollis and Milo I said hi." I can hear the smile in her voice.

"You got it," I agree and end the call. I'm not going to hide the fact that Hollis is in my life as more than just a tenant. She's important to me, important to Milo. She's not a dirty little secret. No, she's more like a prized trophy you want proudly on display. Not because of her looks, although she is beautiful, but because of the person she is. She's kind, loving, and fun to be around. I'm honored to have her in our lives for those reasons alone.

Knowing that Milo is in good hands, I place my phone on the nightstand and close my eyes.

A few hours later, I wake feeling a lot less exhausted. Glancing at the clock, I see it's just after noon. I need to get up and get moving.

Grabbing some clothes, I hit the shower, which does wonders to wake me up. Once I'm showered and dressed, I go in search of my son and my girl. She doesn't know it yet, but that's a title I hope she keeps.

I find Hollis sitting at the kitchen table with her laptop. The house smells like she's cooking something amazing. Peeking in the living room, I see Milo asleep in his Pack 'n Play. My eyes dart back to Hollis, who doesn't see me standing here. No, her eyes are glued to the screen of her phone, and she looks... worried.

"Hollis."

She jumps, knocking over the bottle of water that thankfully has a lid on it. It rolls to the floor, and she rushes to pick it up. "Sorry, you scared me."

"What's wrong?"

"Nothing. I was just lost in thought." She sets the bottle on the table, and her hands are trembling. She sits back down in her seat, her eyes darting around, looking everywhere but at me.

Bracing one hand on the table and the other on the back of her chair, I lean down and kiss her. At first, she's resistant, but her shoulders fall, and she begins to kiss me back. That's when my hand that's on the table moves until I find her phone. Once I have it in my hand, I pull away from the kiss. Standing at my full height, I hold the phone in front of my face. It unlocks, and I look at what's on the screen.

Contact: iwillfindyou@gmail.com

Message: I'm coming for you.

What. The. Fuck. "Hollis." My voice is hard. "Who is this?"

"I-I don't know. It's nothing." She reaches for her phone, but I lift my hand in the air, evading her. "Hollis."

Those beautiful green eyes fill with tears and have me dropping to my knees. I toss her phone back on the table, and I cup her face in my hands. "You can talk to me. Tell me what's going on."

"I can't."

"Yes. You can," I say firmly.

She shakes her head. "I don't know. I just... I can't talk about it."

"Hollis. You are living in my home. With my son. Sleeping in my bed. I'm about to leave this house, and you will be in charge of making sure my son is safe. I need something more than I can't talk about it."

"I'm sorry," she cries. "I don't even know where to start. And Milo, I would never let anything happen to him. Never. Colton, you have to believe me."

"I don't know what to believe. You're obviously hiding something from me. I have a child to think about, Hollis."

"I know." Her cries grow louder. "I know that. I'm sorry. I'm so sorry."

"Sorry for what, Hollis. You have got to give me something." She shakes her head again as tears flood her cheeks. As much as I want to trust her, I just can't put my son in danger like that. I can't leave him alone with her until I know what's going on. Pulling my phone out of my pocket, I call my sister-in-law. "Hey, Gabs. Can you do me a huge favor? Can you watch Milo this afternoon? My last class is at five, so I should be there a little after six to pick him up."

"Yeah, I'll just bring him with me. He's been fussy and is teething." I listen to her ask about Gwen. "I canceled on her. Hollis was going to watch him, but something came up." Again, I listen. "Thanks, Gabs. I owe you one." I end the call and stand.

"Colton." Sad green eyes peer up at me. They're pleading, and although I want to comfort her, I can't. Not until she opens up to me.

"Get ready. We're leaving in thirty minutes."

"What?" She wipes at her eyes. "Where are we going?"

"I'm going to work, and I can't leave you alone." I point at her phone. "Not after reading that. You can come with me or go home with Chase and Gabby. Take your pick."

"I can take care of myself," she counters, standing and placing her hands on her hips.

"That's great, Hollis. Truly, and if I knew what you were taking care of, I might be inclined to believe you."

"It's a long story."

"Then you can tell me tonight. Get ready." I turn and walk back down the hall to Milo's room and begin packing the diaper bag. I make sure there are plenty of diapers, a binky, some toys, and bibs. In the kitchen, I toss in a can of formula, some bottles, and the bottle of Tylenol and the teething gel the doctor gave me samples of. Carrying the overstuffed diaper bag into the living room, I shove in his favorite blanket and zip it up.

"Colton," her soft, sad voice says from behind me. I turn to look at her over my shoulder. "I'm sorry."

"You're not leaving my sight unless you're with my brother. Do you hear me? Not until I know you're safe." My voice is gruff as the reality of the situation lies heavy on my chest. I care about her. Not just "hey, she's a good friend, a nice neighbor," no, I'm falling for her. Hell, I'm already half in love with her, and she's in danger. Someone is coming for her, and I don't know why. She won't tell me why. It's fucking eating me up inside.

"I think it's best if I go," she says as more tears flood her cheeks.

"No." My voice is hard and stern. "You don't get to do that. You don't get to make me want you. You don't get to come in here and wrap your fucking hands around my heart and then just walk out the door taking it with you. You don't get to do that," I say again.

"I'm sorry." Her voice cracks.

Pulling her into my arms, I hug her tight to my chest, burying my face in her neck. "Talk to me, Hollis. Let me help you. I don't know what we're up against, but I promise you, baby, you are not in this alone. I can protect you, but I need to know what I'm protecting you from."

Her tear-filled eyes peer up at me. "I can't ask you to do that, Colt."

"You didn't ask me." I move her hair out of her eyes, tucking it behind her ears. "You didn't ask, and you don't need to. I'm in this with you, Hollis. I want you in my life. I want you in Milo's life, but we need to handle whatever this is. Whoever sent that message, are they fucking with you? Is this a real threat? I need to know."

"It's real."

Fuck. That's what I was afraid of. "Okay. Tonight, after we get home, we're going to have dinner, spend time with Milo, give him his bath, and put him to bed. Then, you are going to tell me everything. I want to know it all. I can't protect you if I don't know."

"I can stay?"

"Damn right, you're staying. I never want you to leave. Fuck me, but I never want to let you go. Let me help you, Hollis. Let me get you through this so that we can move forward."

"Forward?"

"Me, you, and Milo." I want the three of us to be a family. I know enough to realize that I want her in my life. There is nothing she can tell me that will change that. I just need to know, so I'm aware of what we're up against. I have to keep them both safe. That's my main priority. To keep them both safe.

"Okay. Tonight," she agrees. "I made dinner. It's in the Crock-Pot."

"Thank you. Go get ready. I'm going to start the truck and get Milo suited up."

"I can stay here," she tries.

"No. You come with me to the gym. If you don't want to be there, you go to Chase's with Milo. Those are your choices. At least until I know what we're dealing with."

She looks behind her, where Milo is still sleeping peacefully, unaware of the turmoil going on around him. "I want to be with both of you."

That right there. That's why I know this woman is worth fighting for. "I guess we can keep him with us at the gym. We have a ton of baby stuff there from Sophia. How was he before he went down? Still fussy?"

"No, he was fine. I think the Tylenol helps and the teething gel."

"Okay. As long as he's in a good mood, the two of you can stay at the gym with me. You can hang out in the office that's set up for the kids."

"You have an office for the kids?"

"Harrison knows no bounds when it comes to his wife and kids. Chase is going to be the same with Gabby. So, yeah. We have an office for the kids. There's a bed, changing table, and rocking chair. A TV for cartoons and lots of toys."

"Okay. I want to do that."

Leaning in, I kiss her softly. I don't know what I'm up against. I don't know who is sending her those messages or why. What I do know is I'll do everything in my power to make it go away.

CHAPTER 12

Hollis

There's a weird tension in the truck that wasn't there the last time I rode shotgun. Hell, it wasn't present an hour ago. Damn that website notification. Damn the asshole who has been sending them to me.

A cold shudder of dread runs through my veins.

I should leave. Just the thought of endangering Colton and Milo makes me want to vomit. I thought the creep was just trying to scare me. I never believed he'd actually find me, but now, the messages are getting more and more frequent, and I can't help but feel like maybe he's actually getting closer.

Closer to me, means closer to Colton.

And Milo.

My eyes fill with tears again. I try to wipe them away without drawing any attention. Milo has been snoozing since he was bundled up and put in his car seat, the medicine doing wonders for his discomfort. If only a little Tylenol would help my own discomfort right now, but I know that won't help. Nothing will help.

Except the warmth of Colton's hand. He reaches over and takes mine, seeming to understand and offering a little bit of comfort. He doesn't speak, yet holds my hand on top of the console, his coarse thumb gently stroking over my knuckles in a way that brings both solace and an unspoken reminder of the mess I've made and the problems I'm causing.

We pull into the lot easily, the piled remnants of last week's big snowfall turned an ugly shade of brown. It's a bit reminiscent of my mood. What once was white and bright is now dull and drab. A little sludge mixed in too.

Colton parks his truck in the back and only lets go of my hand when he has to turn off the ignition. We sit in the quiet, the only sound Milo's even breathing and a thousand thoughts and unsaid words. I can feel his eyes on me, and while I'd much rather hide my head in the sand, it's what got me into this mess in the first place.

Slowly, I turn and face the man I find myself falling for a little more every day. There's a mix of emotions swept up in those blue eyes. Hurt. Fear. Resolve. And maybe even a little of that love I find myself experiencing. It's the same look he gave me last night when he was sinking inside me, the muscles in his neck tight with tension and the lines around his eyes soft. It's the same look he probably sees in my own eyes after he kisses me goodnight.

Something he may never do again after we talk.

It's like he knows I'm on the verge of losing it. Colton leans over and takes my cheek in his big hand. He leans forward and places his lips gently against mine. The kiss is soft, yet full of meaning. He's letting me know he's beside me, ready to figure this out. That he's not letting me go.

At least not yet.

"Come on, I have a few things to set up for the class," he says, sliding his full lips along mine one final time before he slips out of the driver's seat. His first stop is to release the latch on Milo's car seat. He throws the blanket over the top of the handle to protect him from the elements, and before I can even shut the passenger door, he's there, taking my hand in his and leading me to the gym.

Inside, the music is pumping, and the echo of weights clanking fills the hallway. We used the back entrance so we can slip inside the room Harrison designated for the kids. It's warm and bright, the lights already turned on in a welcome fashion. Colton sets the car seat down and pulls off the blanket. We're greeted with a smiley, toothless Milo, who seems to have enjoyed his catnap. He instantly starts to babble, and even grins ear to ear the moment his dad unhooks the buckles and picks him up.

"Hey, little buddy, I'm going to work for a couple hours. You're going to play in here with Hollis." Milo's eyes instantly turn to me as if he knew exactly what his dad was saying. In fact, he reaches for me at that moment, and I swear my heart is going to leap from my chest. It's a mixture of elation and love for the little guy, and as I snuggle his little body into my chest, more tears fill my eyes.

Colton pulls me into his arms and kisses my forehead. "We'll figure this out, Hollis. I promise," he whispers. He kisses my lips once more before bending down and kissing Milo's forehead. "I'll be in the large matted room if you need me, or Gabby and Chase are floating around here, okay?"

I nod, unable to form words. Colton hesitates, but it doesn't really seem like it's because he's leaving me with his son. It has more of a protective way about it, as if he doesn't want to leave me, period.

When the door closes, I glance around and take in the room. It's exactly as Colton said, and exactly as I'd expect from a man like Harrison Drake. I can't imagine too many guys have an office set up for the owner's kids, but this one does, and it says a lot about the guy who runs this place. A lot about Chase and Colton too.

I pull an activity mat from the shelf and set it out on the floor. The moment I lay Milo down, he starts kicking and reaching for the animals that dangle. Each one makes a noise, which seems to keep him entertained, at least for now. I take a seat on the floor next to him. Sure, I could sit on the couch, but I'd rather be close to him. I'm not exactly sure how this talk is going to go tonight, so I'd rather soak up as much of his sweet smiles and scents while I can.

Just in case.

I spend the afternoon playing with the baby. We have a quick snack and diaper change, and he goes right back to playing. He's currently sitting in a Bumpo seat, trying to eat a cold teether, his little gums gnawing on the plastic as if it were his job. It seems to bring him a little relief, though, so I don't care. Even if his shirt is completely soaked with slobber. I'd gladly change his outfit four more times if it meant he was happy and content.

The door behind me opens. I expect to see Colton there but am pleasantly surprised to find Gabby at the entrance. "Hey," she whispers, instantly smiling when she sees her nephew sitting on the floor. "He's sitting up," she observes.

"I hope it's okay. I saw the Bumpo seat along the wall and thought he might like to try it. I'm right here and watching him closely to make sure nothing happens to him," I tell her, my heart starting to pound in my chest. I guess I'm not sure if he's supposed to be sitting up or not in this thing, but I've seen him sit on the couch with Colton before, so I thought it wouldn't hurt anything.

Gabby waves her hand. "Oh, it's fine. He's the perfect age for it," she observes, that smile still on her pretty face. Her belly is getting bigger every time I see her, but that doesn't stop her from coming over and squatting beside Milo. "Hey, little man. How are you?"

Milo grins at his aunt, waving his teether in her direction.

"Aww, I heard those nasty toothies are being mean to you," she coos in a voice meant for babies. Gabby takes a seat on the opposite side of him and helps hold the teething toy. The baby continues to chomp on it, big wads of drool hanging from his chin.

I reach for the cloth and wipe his face, which irritates him a little, but he keeps moving that toy against his gums. "He's having a tough time with that first tooth, aren't you, buddy?" I say, the smile instantaneous on my lips.

"He seems to be doing better today," she notices.

"He had a dose of Tylenol before we left, so he's feeling better right now." When I glance up, she's staring at me, the hint of a smile on her face. "What?" I ask.

Gabby smiles even wider now. "Nothing. Well, it's just you look... different."

Feeling a little uncomfortable under the sister-in-law microscope, I chuckle awkwardly and ask, "Different how?"

"Not bad," she quickly replies. "It's kinda hard to put into words, but I guess I'd say you look... happy." She takes a long pause before she adds, "Colt too."

Those stupid tears that seem to never want to stop today prickle my eyeballs and make me blink unnaturally. "I don't know about that." I avoid eye contact and fuss over Milo's bib, making sure it's absorbing as much of his drool as possible.

"I do," she says, drawing my attention back to her. "Colt, when he came home, he was sort of lost. He was thrust into this new life he didn't expect, and it was really hard on him. He hid it well, but we could see it. He was a career military man, and all of a sudden, he was a single dad and working a nine-to-five. Now, don't get me wrong, he's amazing with Milo, but that doesn't mean it wasn't a hard adjustment for him."

"I couldn't imagine," I tell her, knowing he had a tough transition. I am so thankful he had his family to help him. It makes my own chest fill with longing for my own family. My dad passed away when I was a young girl, and my mom moved to Florida a few years back. She works for the Hilton Hotels and Resorts and was offered a job overseeing a region in sunny Florida. It was a great opportunity for her, and you can't beat the weather.

"My point is, he's different recently. He smiles more and seems to be eager to leave the gym and head home. I think it has a lot to do with you," she says, that knowing look in her eyes.

I'm saved from having to reply just yet when Milo decides he's had enough sitting. He hollers his displeasure and brings on the waterworks.

"Oh, Milo," Gabby sings, glancing over at me. "Do you mind?"

"Of course not. He's your nephew. I'm just the sitter," I tell her, swallowing over the thickness in my throat. Just saying that, making light of what Colt and I share as if I'm nothing more than someone who watches the baby, doesn't sit well with me, because we've become so much more than that.

At least it feels like we have.

"Come to Auntie Gabs," she coos, picking up the squirmy baby. Milo gazes up at her, but the tears continue to fall. He rubs his eyes, letting us know he's getting sleepy again. She takes him over to the changing table, grabbing a diaper on her way, and sets out to change his pants. I grab a bottle of water and the formula from the bag and mix up his next meal.

When she heads my way, Milo is still not happy, even with clean britches. She heads over to the rocking chair and takes a seat. I hand her the bottle right away, which she places in his mouth. He drinks for a few seconds, but then spits it out and cries. Gabby rocks gently, trying to get Milo to settle down, but he's just not having it.

I'm on the other side of the room, trying to keep quiet so he can fall asleep, but the whole time, my heart is screaming at me to go to him. To hold him. To comfort him.

"He's not a happy little boy," she says, her eyes holding just the slightest hint of worry.

"No, those teeth are really bothering him," I say.

The moment Milo hears my voice, he turns and looks for me. He's fussing more, his hands reaching out blindly. He's reaching... for me. Gabby seems to realize it at the same time I do and offers me a smile. She carefully sits up, holding Milo to her chest as she does, and meets me in the middle of the room. He turns, his hands extended for me. The moment he's against my chest, he snuggles in, his cheek resting just over my heart.

"Awww, he just wanted you," she whispers as I rub his back.

"We uh, we snuggle a lot at home."

Gabby smiles. "I think that's great," she adds, popping his pacifier in his mouth and rubbing his arm.

The silence extends for several long minutes as Milo's eyes finally start to droop. I bounce lightly, swaying back and forth as he drifts off to sleep. Ignoring the burn in my arms, I hold him against my chest and hum a song. I can't sing the way his dad can, but I can at least hum a little tune to give him a sense of normalcy.

"Look at you. He's out," she says.

"He's had a long day," I tell her, my heart soaring with happiness as I hold him in my arms.

"He's not the only one." Her observation strikes a little too close to home as I gaze down at the wonder in my arms.

"It was a long night, but Colton was able to catch a catnap today. Tonight should be better," I whisper.

I can feel her eyes on me. "That's not exactly what I meant."

My heart pounds fast and furious in my chest.

"I'm not sure what's going on, but I can tell something is bothering you. You don't have to tell me, but if you ever need a friend, I'm here. I'm sure it's not easy moving to a new town and not knowing anyone." Gabby shrugs. "All I'm saying is if you want to talk, I'll listen. And I promise not to tell Chase. Whatever you say stays between us."

Again with the damn tears.

Movement catches out of the corner of my eye, and we both turn to find Colton and Chase in the hallway. They're standing in front of the window, chatting and watching us. Colton's eyes drop to his son and then back to my face, the softest smile on his full lips.

I glance over at Gabby, who's smiling like the cat that ate the canary. "Thank you for the offer," I tell her, "but I'd never expect you to keep anything from Chase. I wouldn't want to put you in any position that you can't talk to him."

"Well, if it involves Colt or his family and it's alarming, I'd probably have to tell Chase, but if it's good, you know... like he gave you four Os last night and you're still not walking right, well, that would totally be between us girls." Then she giggles.

I giggle.

And feel lighter than I have since that notification appeared on my phone.

I have a friend. Yes, I have Tina, but she's a call or a text away. Gabby is standing in front of me, offering me something I've been desperate to find since my life was turned upside down. Yes, I found something similar with Colton, yet that's completely different. With Colton, I found solace and passion with his friendship. Gabby is offering comradery and a sense of belonging. Girlfriends.

"Thank you," I whisper, trying not to wake the baby, but also because it's the only word I can choke out over the lump in my throat. She wraps her arms around me and hugs tightly just as the door opens.

"Everything okay?" Chase asks, instantly alarmed.

"Everything is just fine, Mr. Callahan," she barks as she releases me with a wink.

Chase instantly pulls his wife into his arms, hugging her close and rubbing a hand over the belly. "Ready to go home?"

"Yep. I'm starving," she says, heading over to pick up the few things I got out for Milo.

"I can grab that stuff," I insist, swaying with Milo against my chest.

Gabby waves me off. "There's like two things."

Chase helps bag up the garbage, which only consisted of a diaper and a few wipes, and takes it to the door. I can feel Colton's presence beside me, but I don't look his way. I keep my eyes trained on the sleeping baby in my arms. I catch a whiff of sweat and detergent as he bends down and kisses his son's forehead, rubbing a big hand over the fuzzy top of his head. Our eyes meet for only a second, but a thousand words pass in that time. He places his hand on my lower back and bends down to kiss me on the forehead too. My heart dances in my chest with elation, knowing he still feels the same as before.

At least for now.

Until I tell him what's going on.

And then he may ask me to leave.

Chase and Gabby seem oblivious to the war raging inside me. They both kiss Milo's sleeping head before heading to the door, hand-in-hand. "See you tomorrow," Chase says to his older brother before exiting the room, leaving us alone with our thoughts.

"You ready?" he asks, clearing his throat and glancing around.

"Yes," I whisper as he heads over to retrieve the diaper bag and gather up the few things left. I move to the car seat and crouch in front of it. I move his snowsuit to the floor, but before I set him down to get him ready to go, I run my nose against his soft forehead, letting the peach fuzz on his head tickle my nose. He smells like baby shampoo and his daddy.

God, I'm going to miss this if I'm asked to leave.

I push that thought away, not wanting to start crying again, and work on getting Milo in his suit. He wakes up and hollers his disap-proval, but his pacifier does wonders to calm him down. I get him situated in the car seat, buckled in tight, and ready to go. When I stand and glance to the right, I find Colton there, watching us. A look in his eyes that resembles love. Love for his son, sure, but maybe even love for me.

I slip on my coat as Colton does the same, takes the car seat, and throws the diaper bag over his shoulder. When he reaches the door, he extends his hand, which I readily take. We walk together down the hall and out the back door. I can't help but wonder if this will be the last time I'm here. If things go south with Colton and me tonight, I'm sure I won't be welcomed back inside, let alone back to watch Milo.

That thought is soul-shattering.

Milo babbles in the back seat of the truck, swatting at the toys that hang from the seat handle. There are no other words spoken, just the sounds of a happy baby playing. I soak up every ounce of it, committing every second of his noises to memory. Just in case.

Back home, I grab the diaper bag from the back and get the door unlocked for Colton. Even though he's carrying his son, he still insists I enter the house first. I set the bag down on the kitchen table as he removes the blanket from the carrier and smiles down at his son. "You about ready to eat, little man?"

Milo smiles and kicks, letting his dad know he's more than ready.

"I'm going to feed him some peas and carrots for dinner. What time will the Crock-Pot be done?" he asks hesitantly. There's that feeling we're both walking on glass, and I hate it. I hate that we've come to this.

"Thirty minutes," I tell him after glancing at the clock.

Colton nods and heads to the cabinet to get jars of baby food.

"Why don't I go take a shower while you feed him. I'll come back and get the dinner dished up," I say, wringing my hands together in front of me. "Unless you'd rather not eat together."

Once Milo is secured in his high chair, he turns my way. "I want you here," he states. "I want to be able to see you, to know you're safe. I want you to help me give my son a bath and help put him to bed tonight. I want to pull you in my arms and snuggle under the blankets, only to fall asleep with you in my arms after I've made you come no less than twice. I want to wake up with you, and maybe even make love to you again before Milo wakes up. I want all of that, but I know in order to get it, we have to talk about what is going on."

He takes a deep breath. "So, go to your place and take your shower. Then come back here and have dinner with me. After we put Milo to bed, we're going to figure out what is going on so we can move forward. Together."

God, the confidence in his voice, that conviction that everything is going to be okay almost brings me to my knees. I just pray he's right. That once he hears what I say, he won't ask me to leave, that the only way he can protect himself and his son is to ask me to go.

I don't want that.

Not at all.

But I would do it in a heartbeat if it meant they were safe.

Because I love them.

* * *

After my shower, I feel marginally better, but that looming sense of dread still niggles my mind. I slip through my door and into the laundry room, the scent of dinner filling the small space. When I open the kitchen door, I find Milo still in his high chair, orange stains from his dinner on his bib, and Colton standing at the counter. The table is set with two plates and two glasses of water, a basket of rolls sitting in the middle.

"Hey, buddy," I say softly to Milo, who throws a toy on the floor for me to retrieve.

"That's his new favorite game. I've picked that block up twenty times in the last five minutes, and if I don't do it quick enough, he lets me have it."

I smile widely as I bend down and retrieve the wet plastic block. It has raised numbers and shapes on it in bright blue and red colors. When I set it down, he takes the block and tries to shove it in his mouth, only to drop it over the edge of the high chair tray once more. The moment he does, he looks up at me expectantly, and I can't help but laugh.

"See what I mean?" Colton asks as he joins me at the table, setting the dish with pot roast, potatoes, and carrots in the middle.

We eat in comfortable silence, both taking turns to retrieve the block Milo continually throws on the floor. When we're both full, I pick up the dirty dishes, while Colton places the leftovers in lidded containers. After, we go about our nightly routine, as if there isn't this big *thing*, this living, breathing being following us around. Colton gives Milo his bath while I sit on the closed toilet seat and watch. There's something so soothing, so domesticated about the act that makes me want to cry. Instead, I take out my cell phone and snap a few pictures of them together. Their smiles, the tender way Colton washes his son's hair to make sure no soap gets in his eyes, the excitement in Milo's face when he smacks the water and sprinkles droplets all over his daddy's shirt. I document it all with my phone.

Just in case....

After the bath, I trail behind as we head to Milo's room. Immediately, I go to the dresser and pull out a warm footed sleeper with bears. It reminds me of the brown outfit he wore last week with the bear ears on the hood. At the changing table, Colton is trying to wrangle his son into a diaper, but the little one is wiggling all over the place, throwing his head to the side as if he were about to roll over.

"Listen here, little monkey. You need to hold still so I can get this diaper on you before the waterworks start."

I can't help but giggle.

"Oh, it happened a lot when he was an infant. The moment the cold air would hit his boy part, it was like someone flipped on the faucet," he adds, finally securing the diaper into place.

While he sets out to get the child into the sleeper, I head into the kitchen and make his bottle. As I'm shaking the water and formula together, I find Colton and Milo standing in the doorway, watching me. I offer a small smile and follow them back into Milo's room. My gut churns with anxiety as we approach the rocking chair. The one Colton uses to rock his son to sleep.

"May I?" I find myself asking.

He nods in reply and hands me his son. I set my phone down on the small table by the chair and take a seat, positioning him in the crook of my arm. He's getting bigger every day, and I know it won't be long before we'll have to come up with another way to get him to sleep.

We.

Will I be a part of it?

I grin widely when I glance down at the baby. His daddy gave him a baby mohawk, even though his hair isn't very long.

"He gave me permission to style it that way. He said he wanted to look cool for bedtime," Colton says.

"Well, he's definitely the coolest dude here," I confirm, tapping the baby on his nose with my finger. He reaches for it, and the moment he catches my hand, he tries to shove the fingers in his mouth.

"Ouch. I'm being upstaged by a four-month-old."

"I'm sure your ego can handle it."

"Yeah. I mean, he *did* get his good looks from me, after all," he says, smiling from ear to ear as he looks down.

I take my fingers from his mouth and replace them with his bottle. Milo instantly starts to suck it down, his blue eyes never wavering from mine. There's so much trust and gratification in those tiny eyes, as if he knows we'll always take care of him and give him what he needs.

Colton moves away, letting me take care of his son. Gently, I start to rock the chair and hum a song I heard on the radio earlier. It's a country tune about finding love, only to lose it. Probably not the vibe I was going for. Or ever. The thought of losing my new love makes me want to toss my cookies. I just found him. How can he be stripped away so quickly?

As I keep rhythm with my humming and rocking, Milo's eyes start to grow heavy. His bottle is nearly empty, and he spits out the nipple, an indication that he's full. Carefully, I set the bottle to the side and move him to my shoulder. With tender taps, I snuggle him to my chest, inhaling his sweet baby scent. Is there anything better than baby shampoo?

Yes, Colton's body wash.

When I get a nice burp from the sleeping baby, I get up and head to the crib. Colton is there and helps me put him down for the night. He'll still get up at least once, but I'm hoping that the teething part is better, so it won't be multiple times like the night before. Colton tucks the blanket around Milo's abdomen, his little fists resting above his head as he snoozes. With a final kiss to my finger and then to his forehead, I slowly retreat from the room.

I head to the kitchen, my throat suddenly parched. I hear Colton close Milo's door before he joins me, taking the glass from my shaking hand and filling it with water. He holds the glass, grabbing my hand in the other, and leads me back to the living room. He takes a seat on the couch, his arm thrown over the back. It's as if he's giving me the option to sit wherever I want without pressuring me to sit directly beside him. Of course, I take the seat to his right.

There's nowhere else I'd rather be.

Colton doesn't say a word—just waits me out. He watches me as I take the glass once more. After I sip more water, I set it down and lean back against his chest. He's warm and familiar as his arm comes down to rest on my shoulder, holding me close. Taking a deep breath, I begin my story.

"I guess it's best to start at the beginning, right? You know I lived in Southern California before I moved here. I grew up in Costa Mesa. My dad passed away when I was nine from a massive heart attack." I feel Colton tense behind me. "He seemed totally healthy to me. He coached my soccer team in the summer and would take me fishing. He was this big guy, larger than life, and one day he was just... gone."

Deep breath.

"Mom never really recovered, though she tried. She was a good mom, would always bake cookies for class parties, and drive me to and from practice. But she missed him. She worked at a hotel nearby and was excellent at her job. She ended up moving up the ladder, and a few years ago, was offered a regional director position in Florida. I was working, doing well for myself with my design business, so she decided to take it. She wanted a fresh start, you know? And I wanted that for her. I wanted her to be happy again.

"My grandma had always talked about the place she grew up. Fair Lakes, Missouri. She met my grandpa, who was in the Army, and when he moved, she went with him. They ended up in Southern California, where they got married and had my dad. She always would talk about this place, though. Grandma made it sound so wonderful, with that midwestern charm and hospitality."

My heart starts to pound in my chest as I take another quick sip of water.

"That's why, when I needed to leave town quickly, I came here." My voice sounds distant, foreign, even to my own ears.

"Why did you have to leave, Hollis?" Colton asks, his thumb gently stroking my arm in comfort.

I sit up and turn so that we're facing each other. It takes me a few long seconds, but I finally get the words past my lips. "I saw something."

CHAPTER 13

Colton

Her words have my blood running cold in my veins. "What did you see, baby?" I ask, pulling her a little closer. I need the comfort as much as she does. I need her as close as I can get her. A thousand different scenarios are running through my mind. Is she safe? Are we safe? I have my son to think about too. "You can tell me." Fuck, at this point, I need her to tell me. It's no longer a want. I need to know what we're dealing with here.

She nods. "I used to volunteer at a homeless shelter. Just one night a week, I'd go and help cook and serve meals. There was this mom, Charity, and her little girl, Jasmine. They lived there. They were on the run from Jasmine's father. He was abusive to both of them, and they had nowhere else to go. I don't know where they were from—Charity would never talk about it. Anyway, that little girl, she stole my heart. They both did. I thought of Charity as a friend, and Jasmine, she was a perfect example of innocence. She was just happy to have a hot meal and a place to lay her head at night. It breaks my heart still today to think about what they went through to get out. To get to a place where they were safe. One night, she drew me a picture. It was of me, her, and her mom at the park. We'd gone there the week before." She pauses and takes another sip of water. "She was so proud of the picture, and I promised her I would put it on my fridge as soon as I got home."

There is a knot in my gut. Did the abusive ex find her? Did he hurt her? My hold on her tightens yet again at the thought of anyone hurting her.

"Colt?"

"Yeah?"

"I can't breathe," she wheezes.

"Sorry." I loosen my grip and kiss the top of her head. "I see red at the thought of someone hurting you." She's quiet, and I know I've said the wrong thing. "Please keep going, Hollis. I need to know what we're up against so that I can help you." There's a brief silence before she begins again.

"She worked so hard on the picture, I didn't want to bend it, so I decided to just carry it home. I was walking to my car that night, just a block over from the shelter, and a gust of wind blew the picture from my hand. Of course, I chased after it. That drawing meant so much to me, and to her, that I didn't have any other choice. I made her a promise, you know? I told her I would hang it on my fridge, and I didn't want to break my promise to her."

"Because you're the sweetest woman I know." I don't know what higher power brought her to me, but I will forever be grateful to have her not only in my life but my son's.

She laughs lightly. "Have you met your mother, or your sister-in-law or Gwen? You're surrounded by sweet women."

"Maybe," I agree. "But you're the only one who's mine." The tension in her shoulders eases just a little at my declaration.

"Um... your mother?"

"Dad's already claimed her," I tease.

"Fair enough," she says, and I can already hear that she's starting to relax a little. "Anyway, I chased after the picture. It had so much meaning to both of us. The wind blew it down an alley, and as fast as my feet could carry me, I followed. The picture fell to the ground behind a dumpster. I didn't even hesitate to kneel down and reach for it. When I finally had it in my hands, I heard a deep, menacing voice that had me freezing."

She pulls out of my arms and turns to face me. "I should have run. I know that now. I never should have stopped moving. I should have just moved on and not stopped until I got to my car. I had the picture, which is all that I wanted. Instead, I froze. Two guys, they were talking about drugs and money, and evidence."

"Fuck," I mutter, running my hands through my hair. "Drug deal?"

"Yeah, I assume so. Only it's a little more complicated than that. I knew I had to get out of there. I knew I was in the wrong place at the wrong time. And it may sound bad of me, but I didn't care what they were doing. I just wanted out of that situation. I wanted to be away from them, and whatever it was that was going down."

"What did you do?"

"I stood, and it was my intention to take off running, but I tripped over my own feet. My legs were shaking so bad I lost my footing and fell to the ground. They, of course, heard me and came running. One of them was a cop. He was in uniform. I will never forget his face as he stared down at me." She stops and takes a deep breath. "He looked so angry, and there was a hint of panic in his eyes."

Fuck, this is not good. Who knows what was really going on and a crooked cop takes this to an all-new level. "You're doing great, babe," I encourage her. I need to know the rest of the story.

She nods. "I scrambled to my feet and was walking backward when he started following me. I turned to run and ran into a body. Looking up, it was another cop, this time a woman. She could see the fear on my face and immediately pushed me behind her. She recognized the other cop and asked him if she needed to call for backup. That's when a gunshot went off, and all hell broke loose. I didn't stick around to see what the end result would be. The female cop got distracted, and I took off running. I didn't stop until I got to my car and locked the doors. I sped out of my parking spot and drove around for over an hour. Just in case they were following me, I didn't want them to know where I lived."

"Were they? Following you?" I ask, holding my breath, waiting for her reply.

"No." She shakes her head. "There wasn't a car in sight the last twenty minutes or so of my drive."

"Good." I exhale.

"I was scared out of my mind, didn't sleep that night, and I was mad at myself for losing the picture that Jasmine has worked so hard on for me. If I'd had a better hold on it, I wouldn't have been in that alley, and I wouldn't have had to run."

"I get that, but you were safe. That's what's important. And although I hate that this happened to you, it still brought you here to me and Milo. I can't be upset about that."

"Yeah," she agrees. She turns to look at me, and a soft smile pulls at her lips. "I didn't go back to the shelter for a month. I missed everyone terribly, especially Charity and Jasmine. I thought that was enough time, but it turns out I was wrong. I was in line serving when the cop, the guy presented a plate in front of me." She shivers. "I can still hear the menacing sound of his voice when he said my name."

"How did he find you?"

"I don't know. He's a cop and has connections, I guess. He asked around, I'm sure, and I'd been volunteering at the shelter for years. He got a good look at me, so he had my description."

"What happened next?" I prompt her. I know this is hard for her to tell me, but I need all the information. I can't protect my family. I can't protect her without it.

"He said he had been looking for me all over the city. I was scared out of my mind. Jasper, the older man who runs the homeless shelter, could tell there was something wrong. I asked him if I could stay there that night. Without a single question, he told me I was welcome anytime. He even went out of his way to set me up in his office, on the couch, where the door had a lock. The next morning, I drove home, constantly looking over my shoulder and packed my bags. I called my mom and told her it was time for a change of scenery. I told her that I wanted to see where Grandma grew up, and she believed me. My best friend, Tina, however, wasn't buying it. I eventually confessed it all to her and swore her to secrecy. She wanted me to go to the cops, but he is the cops. I came here instead. I stayed with Tina for a couple of days. Canceled my lease on my apartment that was thankfully only month to month, I saw your ad, and here I am."

"You didn't tell anyone else? No one else knows why you left town?"

She shrugs. "No one else to tell really. My mom moved to Florida, I worked from home, so there were no nosey coworkers. Tina is it, and I trust her."

"And the messages?"

She takes a sip of her water. "They all have the same tone. I'm coming for you. You can't hide forever, those kinds of things. There is no way he can find me. I canceled all of my credit cards, and I have no loans in my name."

"You're a business, Hollis. He can find your business."

"It's still registered in California, as is my bank account. I have automatic withdrawals set up monthly to go to an account in Texas. That account has a withdrawal from a bank in Arkansas, which has a withdrawal to my bank here in Missouri."

She's really put some thought into this. "He can still trace you."

"Yeah," she agrees. "I see that now. I don't know if he actually knows where I am, or if he's just trying to scare me. The emails came from my website."

"So, he knows your name, where you used to volunteer, and the name of your business," I state the facts.

"Yes."

"Hollis, we need to go to the police about this. You can't live in fear every single day, constantly looking over your shoulder. You can't run forever."

"I know, but I'm scared, Colt. He is the cops. How do I know who I can trust?" A single tear slides down over her cheek. She's finally lost the composure she managed to hold onto while telling me her story.

"Do you trust me?"

She wipes at her cheek and looks me in the eye. "With my life."

I nod. "Come here." She moves closer, and I lift her to sit on my lap. I wrap my arms around her and remind myself that she's safe. Here, with me, she's safe. "Let's start with I want you here. We have to be careful, especially with Milo, but I want you with me. I want you to be a part of our lives."

"I want that too, Colton. More than anything, but I also can't stand the thought of someone hurting Milo, or you or your family. I won't let that happen."

"Hey." I place my hand on her cheek. "That's not going to happen. We're going to handle this so we can move forward with our lives together."

She nods, then asks, "What does that mean exactly?"

"I know some people I can trust. Ex-military, remember?" I wink.

"And the other part?" Her voice is soft, and I can hear the uncertainty there.

"I hope that means that you'll stay. Not as my tenant. I want you here as mine. No more paying rent and no more sleeping in your room. I want you in my bed next to me every night."

I watch her closely as she absorbs my words. Her eyes well with tears, and she shakes her head. "I never thought I would find someone here. I thought I would lay low until he had a chance to forget about me and move on with my life. I didn't expect to meet a little boy who stole my heart. I couldn't love him more if he were my own." She whispers her confession.

"I love that about you. I love how good you are with him. How much you care. That's all I could ask for. Someone who will be there for both of us." It's true. I've never really thought much about finding a mother for Milo. I was thrust into this single-parent gig, and leaving the Army, buying this house, and finding a tenant to help lighten the load, it was a lot to take on in a short amount of time. Worrying about my dating life, falling in love, that wasn't even on my radar.

"They say that you find love when you least expect it."

"I didn't expect you," I whisper. Leaning in, I press my lips to hers. "I love you, Hollis Taylor. We're in this together, and I promise you that I won't let him near you."

"Milo." My son's name is said with so much reverence.

"It's all going to work out." I say the words and will them to be true. I do have some connections, favors I can call in, but will they be enough? We don't even know this guy's name, just the general location, and that he's on the force. We're going to have to lure him to us, and that has danger written all over it. Maybe I'm wrong, maybe there is another way.

She nods. "I love you too. So much that if I think for one minute that you or that precious little boy is in harm's way, I'll leave. I would never risk either of you."

"Hey, now. None of that. You said that you trusted me."

"I do trust you, Colt. I also know that if something ever happened to either of you, I would never forgive myself."

"It's not going to come to that," I assure her.

"So, what do we do now?"

"It's late. We should get to bed. Milo will be up bright and early, and we need to get some sleep. Tomorrow, I'll take what I know and make some calls. We'll see where that leads us and take it from there." Tapping her leg, I smile as she climbs off my lap, and I follow her. In my room, we strip out of our clothes, and she grabs a T-shirt from my drawer to sleep in. Together, we climb under the covers, and she snuggles up to my side.

"I love you," I say, kissing the top of her head. It feels good to say those words to her. I've never felt this way about a woman, and I'll be damned if some crooked fucking cop is going to take her away from me.

"I love you too," she says over a yawn.

I hold her until her breathing changes, and I know she's asleep before I let myself drift off too.

It's been four days since Hollis told me her story. Four days since I told her I was in love with her. Four days of restless nights as I analyze every angle and every option to keep her safe. I made a few calls to a few military connections, but there is mandatory training for them through this weekend. So, really all we can do is wait. I want to go to the local police, but this is Missouri, not California, and so far, there have been no real threats made. I've replayed the story over and over in my mind, and I don't understand why they didn't have someone watching the shelter. They obviously knew she slept there that night. Something is not adding up. Do they know where she is? Is he just trying to scare her to keep her away? Are they just biding their time? I have so many questions. I've been on high alert, making sure the alarm is set at night when we sleep, and all the doors and windows are secure. Not that I didn't do that before, but I'm vigilant about double and triple-checking.

"You know, you don't have to do this," I tell Hollis as she puts on her coat.

"Do what? Spend the day with Milo, Gabby, and your mom? That's not exactly a hardship, Colton."

"I know, but you could come with me. Both of you."

"Let's see. Hang out at a sweaty gym all day or hang out with two women who are a joy to be around and this little guy." She taps Milo on the nose with her index finger, and he grins, kicking his arms and legs where he sits on the kitchen table, all strapped into his car seat.

"I didn't tell them, but we need to. It's not fair to them to not know what's going on."

"Okay." My face must show my shocked expression. She continues, "What? It's nice to not have to keep it in, to have to hide it. Besides, I already told you if I have to leave to keep you all safe, I will. I agree that they need to know and to be alert. They need to be aware of their surroundings. I hate that I brought this to you and your family. It wouldn't be fair of me to keep it from them at this point."

My chest constricts at the thought of her leaving us. "We said no more leaving talk," I remind her.

"We did." She's quick to agree. "You know my position." She pretends to be zipping up her lips. "My lips are sealed on the topic from here on out, but I won't stand by and let you all be in danger."

"We're already in this, Hollis. If they know where you are, they know who we are. We're facing this together. There is no other option." I give her a pointed look. "Right?"

She sighs. "Right. I hate this, Colt. I hate worrying all the time. I just want to... enjoy life with you and whatever that looks like."

"That looks like forever." I pull her into me and kiss her. Milo lets out a squeal. "I know, son, I know," I tell him, making Hollis laugh. "Text me when you get to Mom's." I lean in for another kiss. "I love you."

"I love you too."

I help her carry Milo out to her car and get his seat strapped in and watch them leave. Jogging back into the house, I grab my bag and lock up, heading to All Fit. I call Chase on the way.

"What's up? Am I not going to see you in like ten minutes?" he asks.

"You are. Is Harrison coming in today too?"

"Yeah, we're both here."

"Good. I need to talk to both of you before we get started."

"What's going on?"

"I'll explain when I get there."

"Milo?" he asks.

"Is perfectly fine. He's with Hollis heading to Mom and Dad's."

"All right, bro. I'll see you when you get here."

Eleven minutes later, I'm walking into the back door at All Fit. I head straight to the office that Harrison and Chase share. They both stare at me expectantly, waiting to hear what I have to say.

"There's something I need to tell you." I go on to tell them about Hollis. I explain the events of that night just as she had to me. Chase and Harrison sit quietly and listen, but I can tell from the expressions on their faces they are just as concerned as I am. "So, yeah," I say when I'm finished. "That's what's been going on."

"So, there have been no actual threats?" Harrison clarifies.

"No. Just messages through her website saying he found her, and he's coming for her, those kinds of things. No physical threats of harm. Not yet."

"Fucking dirty cop," Chase mutters.

"I made a call to my old command sergeant. I had to leave him a message. They're out in field training until Monday."

"You called in the Army?" Harrison asks, eyes wide.

"Damn right, I did. I gave years of my life to this country, and if my family is in trouble, I'm calling in the best."

"Can you do that?" Harrison asks, surprised.

"I don't know," I admit. I run my fingers through my hair in frustration. "I don't know if they can help, but maybe they can give me the contact of a person we know we can trust that can. Honestly, I'm reaching, and I know it. It's the best I can do. The local police won't do anything. There is no imminent threat, and the incident in question happened states away. There is really nothing to go on unless she goes back."

"She might have to, Colt. How else are we going to lure this guy out?"

"Fuck, I don't know. I don't know. I've been wracking my brain trying to figure this out, and I'm coming up empty."

"Our wives and kids?" Harrison asks.

"Safe. Just be on alert. Check the doors at night, all those things." I stop and take a deep breath. "Look, if this is too much, I can step away from the gym for a while. I don't want to bring this asshole down on you and your families, but Hollis, she's my family now. I protect those I love."

"What can we do?" Chase asks.

"Nothing. Not right now. Just be aware. Talk to Gabby and Gwen, make them aware. Hollis might tell them today at Mom and Dad's. I'm not sure."

"When you know, you let us know," Harrison says. "We'll do whatever we can to keep her safe."

"Thank you. I just hate not really knowing what we're dealing with. Her best friend, Tina, still lives there. I might have Hollis reach out to her, maybe have her visit the shelter, and see if anyone has been asking around about Hollis. I just don't know where to start."

"Has she received anymore messages?" Chase asks.

"No. Not in the last few days, which is a good thing. At least I hope it is." I really don't know what to think at this point. I feel like we're going to be looking for a needle in a haystack unless this guy has found her and makes himself known, or if we put her in plain sight, making her easy to find. I'm not okay with either scenario. I just hope Sergeant Jones can give me some insight and guidance or a contact. Something.

My phone rings, and it's Hollis. I hit Accept and place the phone to my ear. "Hollis," I greet her. Chase and Harrison freeze to listen to my conversation.

"Hey, I just wanted to let you know we made it. Milo fell asleep on the way over. He's sleeping in his room here at your mom's place now."

"Good." I nod and give Chase and Harrison a thumbs up, letting them know everything is okay. "Have a good day."

"You too. I'll see you at home?"

"Yeah. Text me before you leave?"

"Oh, wait." I hear her pull the phone away from her ear and talk, but I can't make out what she's saying or who she's talking to. "Colt, your mom says that the three of you need to come here once you're finished today. She's going to have dinner ready."

I chuckle. My mother is one of a kind. "Okay. I'll let the guys know. I'll call you when we're on our way."

"Sounds good." The line goes dead.

"Well, it looks like we've all been summoned by Mom. Once we finish the staff education training today, she wants us all there. She told Hollis she would have dinner ready."

"I'm in. My wife and daughter are there, and no way am I going to pass up your mother's cooking," Harrison says, rubbing his stomach.

"Let's get this over with. I'm ready for some good eating." Chase smacks his hand down on my shoulder and grins.

Together the three of us head toward the room where I hold my classes. Harrison thought it would be a good idea to have all the staff trained in the basics of self-defense. You can never be too careful. So, we chose today as a mandatory training day. Chase volunteered to help out, and since Harrison is following us to the room, it looks like he is going to help as well. Good. The sooner we finish this class, the sooner we can get home to our families.

Damn, do I love the sound of that.

CHAPTER 14

Hollis

This is what I've been missing.

It was me, my mom, and sometimes my grandma for the longest time. Small gatherings, intimate meals, no big celebrations, even though we always celebrated our accomplishments. But I've never had this. I've missed the big, boisterous family that's too loud and too nosey, but that's what I'm dealing with as I sit around the Callahans' dining room table and listen to them share stories of when Chase and Colton were younger.

"Of course it was about a girl!" Chase hollers. "He knew she liked me!"

"She thought you were cute, like a puppy. Ellie Jacobs was interested in a man, not a boy," Colton boasts proudly, rubbing his chest.

"Man? You were sixteen. The other one hadn't even dropped yet," Chase argues, making everyone laugh.

Colton leans back, his arm extended over the backrest of my chair. His thumb lazily draws circles below my shoulder blade, spreading awareness through my blood. Although, I'm always aware of Colton. "But you were fourteen. What were you going to do, give her a ride on the handlebars of your bike?" he teases.

"You're a dick," Chase mumbles, taking a drink of his iced tea, and again, drawing laughter from everyone at the table.

"You boys were always fighting over girls back then," Connie says, shaking her head.

"It's not my fault they all wanted the younger Callahan," Chase tells his mom.

"They wanted you like they wanted a rash," Colton mumbles.

"Speaking of rashes," Harrison says, glancing over at Colton with an evil gleam in his eyes.

"Uh, no. We're not going there," Colton states, drawing a line on the table.

Harrison and Chase burst out laughing. "How did you get the chickenpox again?" Harrison asks, ignoring that invisible line Colton just laid down.

"Fuck you," he whispers, making everyone giggle.

"I don't think I've heard this one," Gabby says, her hand rubbing circles on her belly.

"And you're not going to," Colton replies, turning and looking at me. "You ready to go?"

I glance over at his younger brother and have to admit, I'm really curious. "Actually..."

Chase and Harrison laugh, while Colton just closes his eyes and groans. "I'm not getting out of this, am I?"

"Nope. Just tell the story, big brother. Tell your girlfriend all about how you got chickenpox in high school."

"What was her name again? Cori? Candy? Clarissa?" Harrison asks.

Colton is silent for a second before he confirms, "Calena."

"Ahh, yes, that's it. Calena," Harrison says, proudly bouncing his daughter on his knee.

"Calena gave my brother the chickenpox," Chase tells me, a wide smile on his face. "Tell her where, Colt."

"Yeah, Colt, tell her where," Harrison chimes in as if they're a comedic duo telling a big joke.

"Mom doesn't want to hear this," Colton insists.

Connie laughs. "Mom's already figured this out, Colton."

Colton's dad, Wes, sets his tea glass down and adds, "Besides, it wasn't that hard to figure out. I mean, you had chickenpox on your peter...."

I gasp and glance at a mortified Colton. "Seriously?"

Gabby giggles. "She gave you chickenpox down under?"

Colton holds up his hands. "I can't believe we're talking about this at the dinner table. And in front of my son," he argues, glancing over at Milo, who's sitting in the high chair, happily gnawing on a cold teether.

"Leave him out of it," Chase contends, "and just tell your girlfriend about your itchy peter."

"You have to tell the story now, Colt. These two will never let it go. Or worse, they'll tell the story how they want to," Gwen says, a knowing grin on her face. She knows her husband and his best friend well. Even I know they'll tell the story with tons of embellishments, all not very flattering to Colton. That's what little brothers do, right?

"Fine," he grumbles, looking down at his empty glass—anywhere but at us around the table. "I was seventeen and dating a girl name Calena. She didn't know yet she had chickenpox," he says, glancing my way.

"And I take it, she gave them to you," I deduce, not wanting to draw out his misery anymore.

"On his little willy," Chase bellows with a laugh.

"It's not so little. I got all the good Callahan genes," Colton argues, giving his brother a smug grin.

"I'm not so sure about that," Gabby chimes in as she fights her own smile. The way she looks at her husband tells me all I need to know about something I really don't want to know anything about.

"That's right, baby," Chase croons at his wife and nods.

"Tell them," Colton says, and I realize he's talking to me.

"What?" I gasp, my eyes surely bugging out of my head.

"Tell them who clearly is packing the heat below the belt," Colton instructs, leaning back with his own smug grin.

"I will not!" I insist, my eyes connecting with his parents. I can feel the blush already taking over my face.

"The blush says it all," Colton tells his brother as he pulls me into his side and kisses my forehead.

"Anyway," Chase interrupts, "as my delusional brother was saying, he got itchy dick from his girlfriend, but didn't realize it was the pox until Mom had to take him to the doctor."

Colton groans. "We're back on this?"

Chase just looks at his brother. "We never left it, Colt. You just tried to distract us with talk about your little dick."

"Wait, you went to the doctor?" Gabby asks, her eyes dancing with humor.

"Oh, I had to take him. It was about three or four days later when he started a rash," Connie says, telling the rest of the story. "I caught him discretely scratching his area several times, and I was afraid it was something else."

"Crabs," Chase adds.

Connie nods. "You never know, and I wasn't going to let my son have a crab infestation."

"Jesus," Colton mumbles, rubbing his forehead. "It wasn't crabs, okay?"

"Well, we know that now, don't we?" she says to her son. Then, she looks at me and adds, "We didn't know it at the time. I suspected he had something going on down below because he started to get a rash on his thighs and lower stomach, so I took him to the doctor to get a prescription. I didn't want him spreading crabs to the family through the toilet seat."

"It was chickenpox! I had it everywhere, not just on my groin!" Colton hollers, startling Milo in his high chair. The baby starts to fuss, but when Colton goes to take him out, he starts to reach for me. Colton just glances my way, a small smile playing on his lips as he nods for me to step in and take the fussy baby.

"Anyway, it turns out it was just chickenpox," Connie confirms, "and they just had to run its course, but they appeared all over his chest and arms pretty quickly too."

"I kept him home for three days," Wes adds. "It was horrible watching your son scratch all day long."

"And Calena was out too since she had them all over her body," Chase chimes in.

I start to stand and gently sway with Milo against my chest. He reaches up and grabs my hair but doesn't pull it. He just wraps his little hand around a strand and holds it.

"Now that we've discussed how I got chickenpox in high school, I think I'll take my son and my girlfriend—if she doesn't leave me because of my inappropriate family—home." He gives me a look with a silent smile, letting me know he doesn't think I'll actually leave him. At least not for something like this.

"Actually, you didn't really say *how* you got them," Gabby says, her tiny little devil horns popping up from her head, making me grin from ear to ear. Chase laughs.

It wouldn't take much imagination to guess how he got chickenpox in high school.

"And we're not going to," Colton says as he heads over to retrieve the diaper bag.

"Next time," Harrison adds, glancing down at his daughter. "We're out too. This one needs a bath and a bottle."

"Oh, Harrison, I made you up a little to-go bag. I had some extra chocolate chip cookies, so I threw those in there too," Connie says, heading over to the counter and grabbing the grocery sack.

"What the hell?" Chase says, glancing at his brother.

"Seriously? You're sending all the cookies with Harrison? He's not even a son," Colton argues.

Connie just rolls her eyes. "I have some for you two as well."

"But we all know who her favorite is," Harrison says, heading over to give Connie a hug. "Thanks, Mama Callahan."

"You're welcome, my boy."

I can see the love between them, and it pings my heart with sadness. I was close to Tina's mom too. Often, I'd be invited over to their house for dinners or celebrations. After my own Mom moved away, and Grandma was put in the nursing home, her family sort of became my family. I've missed Tina these last few weeks, but now I'm missing her little family too. They weren't as big and loud as the Callahans, but it was nice to belong.

We all say goodbye, and I help get Milo situated in his seat. We throw the blanket over his head and make our way to Colton's truck, the cold winds blowing in more snow.

"Oh, Colt, we're having Christmas dinner here. Will that work for you and Hollis?" Connie asks from the front porch.

He glances my way, and if he notices the tears swimming in my eyes, he doesn't say anything. "Will that work for you?" he whispers, squeezing my hand in comfort.

"Yeah," I croak over the lump in my throat. "That would be fine."

"Sounds good, Mom. Just text me what you want us to bring," Colton says as he leads me the rest of the way to his truck.

Inside, the cab is already warm as I slip inside and rub my hands on my jeans. After Colton gets the car seat secured, he jumps in the driver's seat and glances my way. "You okay?"

I nod instantly. "Yeah."

"I know my family can be a lot. If you're not ready for something like Christmas—" he starts, but I cut him off.

"No, it's not that. I'm honored they'd invite me along," I assure him.

"Well, you're part of the family now," he whispers, bringing my hand to his mouth and running his lips over my knuckles. "They want you here, but if it's too much, too soon for you, all you have to do is say so."

"It's not, Colt, I swear." I take a deep breath. "It just reminds me of Tina and her parents. She has an older brother too, who wasn't always at dinners, but they usually tried to include me after my mom moved to Florida. Tonight just made me miss them a little more."

He gazes at me from across the seat, his eyes full of compassion and understanding. "Have you talked to Tina much?"

I nod. "We text all the time."

"But it's not the same," he concludes.

"No," I whisper, hating the emotions that are suddenly bubbling up, as if from out of nowhere.

"I can't replace your best friend, sweetheart, but I'm here for you. My family too," he tells me as he pulls me across the console and wraps his arms around my neck. "I love you."

"I love you too," I whisper, absorbing all his heat and support as I cling around his neck. "Thank you."

He kisses me on the forehead again as Milo lets out a holler, letting us know he's not happy to just be sitting here. Colton straightens and buckles up. "You don't ever have to thank me for loving you, Hollis. Ever. That's the easiest thing in the world to do."

And with that, he backs out of his parents' driveway and heads for home.

* * *

With Christmas in a week, I start to panic. I've completed a handful of jobs in the last few weeks, including All Fit's website and branding package, as well as other site designs and restructures. My bank account is comfortable, which is why I'm heading out today to go Christmas shopping. I've already sent Tina a package, but still have Mom and Grandma to take care of, as well as Milo, Colton, and a hostess gift for his parents, Connie and Wes.

I got this.

It'll be fun, especially with my little sidekick, Milo, in tow.

"Are you sure you'll be okay today? It's supposed to snow again later," Colton says as he fills up his water bottle in the kitchen.

Milo's on my hip, holding my hair, as he does most nights as he tries to fall asleep, babbling as if he's in the conversation with his dad. "We'll be fine. Won't we, Milo?" I ask, bending down and raspberry kissing his chubby cheek.

"How about if you take my truck? I'll drive your car to the gym," he offers, drying his hands on a hand towel and tossing it on the counter.

I want to smile in return. If I've learned anything about Colton Callahan in the last month, it's that he's protective of his son, and me. "If it'll make you feel better, I'll take your truck."

He nods and grabs my car keys off the counter, which are right beside his. After our discussion about what I saw in California, he made sure I have keys to all the doors, including the front one that he uses. He runs outside and starts my car so he can take it, letting it warm up. While the temperature isn't consistent with what I imagine winter in the Midwest to be, it definitely has some very chilly mornings. One thing I've learned is that Mother Nature can be a little whacky. One day she's fifty and beautiful, and the next twenty degrees and snowing.

It's definitely taking some getting used to.

"The truck is ready when you're ready," he insists as he comes back inside and wraps his arms around me and Milo. When he got the garage ready, I insisted he park his truck in there. Not only is he the owner of the house, but it's the usual vehicle to transport Milo. He argued up one side and down the other, but in the end, when I threw his son into the equation, he relented.

"Thank you," I tell him, just as I lean up on my tiptoes and swipe my lips against his. He tastes like mint and coffee, and so very much like Colton. I'm not sure I'll ever get enough.

"Are you sure you even need to leave today?" he asks. He'll be gone most of the day. As Christmas approaches, the gym has been hopping as everyone gets all their sessions and classes in before the holidays. His self-defense classes have been sold out, and Harrison is considering adding another in the new year. I'm excited for him, but I know he's torn. More time at the gym means more time away from Milo.

He still goes to Gwen's, but only three days a week. Any other time, he's home with me. I'm able to get a lot of work done on those three days, and then a little when I'm with Milo. But to be completely honest, I'd much rather spend my day with him on the floor, rolling over and sitting up, than working on my computer.

"Yes, Mr. Worry Wart. I have to finish my Christmas shopping. If I don't get my gifts for Mom and Grandma in the mail ASAP, they won't get there in time. Besides, the snow isn't supposed to start until this afternoon. We'll head out soon, get our shopping done, and be home before the first flake falls," I reassure him.

Colton sighs. "Okay, but be careful. People are crazy this time of year. I don't need you getting hurt over a toaster."

"First off, that's Black Friday that brings out the crazies. And second, I wasn't going to get you a toaster. I was thinking about a blender," I tease, fighting to contain my smile.

Strong arms wrap around my torso as he pulls me against his chest. "A blender, huh? I do like to blend things."

Milo bellows, before reaching up and smacking Colton in the face.

"Hey, little buddy, we don't hit. No, no," he tells his son sternly. Milo brings on the waterworks, ducking his head into my neck and holding on tight. "Awww," Colton grumbles, reaching down and taking his son from my arms. Milo tries to hang on tight but is no match for his dad. "Listen, little man, I love you with all my heart, but you can't hit. That's not a good boy," Colton instructs. Milo's tear-filled eyes widen as he listens to his dad.

Milo leans into his chest and grabs his shirt.

"I'm Dada. Can you say Dada?" Colton asks, and I can hear the emotion in his voice.

The boy stares intently at his daddy's lips and opens his mouth, like he's mimicking Colton, but doesn't make the right sound.

"I love you," he adds as he hugs his son to his chest. When he pulls back, he looks down at Milo and says, "Now, you be a good boy for Hollis, okay? Make sure no boys mess with her."

I know he means it goodheartedly, but I don't miss the hint of worry in his voice too. Ever since I told him about California, he's always very observant of our surroundings and watches me closely. Even though I haven't received a message since that one he saw, Colton is always mindful of where I am and who's nearby. His brother put him in contact with a police officer friend who helped him track down Laura when all that went down this summer, but so far, they've come up empty in finding who sent me those messages. Maybe since I haven't received any lately, they've finally let it go.

Let me go.

"All right, I need to go, or I'll be late for my first session," Colton says, kissing his son on the forehead and handing him back to me.

"We'll see you when you get home. I'll have dinner ready," I tell him, propping Milo on my hip and giving Colton a kiss.

"Love you," he says, those blue eyes so full of conviction. He smiles down at his son and adds, "Love you too."

"We love you more," I tell him, taking Milo's hand and waving it goodbye.

"I'll be back soon!" he hollers before he slips out the door to head to work.

"Well, Mr. Milo, let's get ready to go. We have tons of shopping to do today. I hope you're ready," I announce as I gather the diaper bag and snacks for our shopping excursion.

Thirty minutes later, I'm walking into the first department store. I'm armed with my list and the baby, as we set out to grab the few things I need. I'm able to find a gorgeous lightweight sweater for my mom, which will be perfect for those cooler Florida nights, as well as some fancy lotions and body sprays. I find an adorable little shirt and bowtie set for Milo, and a Henley shirt in a smoky gray for Colton.

Not very personal gifts, but it's a start.

My next stop is a gourmet candy shop. I find some fresh salted caramels I know my mom will love and some sugar-free mint and chocolate drops for Grandma. They even have a large sampler box with a variety of sweet treats, which I grab for Colton's mom and dad.

As we head down the corridor of the shopping center, Milo hollers from his stroller seat. When I pull over to the side of the walkway, I grab the bottle of formula. "Need a drink, little man?" I ask, crouching down in front of the stroller. He reaches for it, instantly shoving the cup in his mouth.

Standing back up, I glance in the window of the store I'm in front of. It's a photography shop. Inside, I see a woman on her hands and knees, posing a newborn on a cloud of white fluff. The baby is naked, except for a blue ribbon wrapped around his abdomen. The sign on the ribbon reads, "Heaven sent."

I glance around at the sample photos on the walls. Most are large portraits, beautifully framed, and displaying the photographer's work. Two catch my eye right away. It's a little girl posing on an All Fit T-shirt. I realize I've seen that photo before. At the gym. It's little Sophia on her daddy's shirt.

But the photo next to that one is the one I study now. It's Milo, only a month old, and sleeping on an Army jacket. My heart clenches as it rises to my throat. I've seen this one too. It's on Colton's living room wall. The gift Gabby and Chase gave him when he moved in.

Suddenly, I know what I need to do.

I slip inside the studio, the photographer giving me a wide smile. "I'll be with you in just a minute," she says as she finishes snapping pictures of the sleeping angel on the cloud.

Milo and I have a seat in the sitting area. He's anxious to get out of the stroller, so I unhook his belt and hold him on my lap. He's super chatty, now that he's had some juice, and is giving big cheesy grins.

"Oh, that's the smile I want to catch," the photographer says as she approaches. "How can I help you?"

"I don't have an appointment," I start. "I was hoping you had an appointment available this morning?"

"While I take appointments, I also love walk-ins, sweetie, so you're next! Do you have a set in mind?" she asks, as she reaches her finger out, Milo grabbing on.

"Not really, but he's the little one in that photo over there," I say, pointing to the wall. "The one with the Army jacket."

The photographer smiles widely. "I remember him. His daddy was away in the Army, right?"

I nod, that familiar lump in my throat returning. "He's home now, but I'd love to get an updated version of Milo for his wall."

She agrees. "Yes, I can picture it now. I still have the jacket too. Let me get the set ready. Give me two minutes," she says as she turns, heading toward her studio. "I'm Helena, by the way."

"Hollis," I reply, following slowly as Helena removes the white cloud and the sky backdrop. She pulls a brown version down, stretching it out over the floor.

"How about you strip him down to his diaper? I think that'll be a cute picture." Helena goes to the clothing rack and pulls the Army jacket off the hanger. She pulls a small wooden crate from the stack and flips it over in the middle of the set. Then, she drapes the jacket over the crate, arranging it so it covers the wood and displays the branch of the military's name across the floor.

"What do you think of this?" she asks.

"I love it," I tell her, my heart galloping in my chest with excitement.

"Will he be able to sit on the crate? You can stay close," she says.

"He should be okay. He's practically a little monkey all of a sudden."

When I set him down on the crate, his pudgy little legs on the floor, Helena brings over a helmet. "What do you think of this? I can set it on the floor, or it might be really cute if he's wearing it."

I can't help but smile. "I'll leave it up to you," I say as the scene starts to come together perfectly.

"You hold it, and I'll get my camera ready." It only takes her a few seconds. Helena snaps a couple of pictures and checks the screen. "I'm ready to go."

For the next ten minutes, she takes photo after photo of Milo. The little guy is all smiles as he looks at the funny lady making silly noises and faces at him. Tears fill my eyes as I watch, unable to hold in the emotion any longer. Unable to hide what this little boy and his dad mean to me.

"How about you stand behind him, Mommy? Kick off your socks and shoes first and slip back on his little blue jeans, but keep his shirt off. See if you can get him to stand up, holding onto your fingers," she directs.

That's when my heart basically explodes with love.

"Oh, I'm not...." But I can't seem to get the rest of the words out.

Because in my mind, I *want* to be his mom.

I *am* his mom.

So I do as the photographer instructs. I stand behind him, my blue painted toes on display as I stand him up. Milo takes my fingers immediately, looks up at me, and smiles. I hear the shutter snapping, but I don't pay it any attention. My eyes are cast down on the little boy who owns my heart.

"I think we got some amazing pictures," Helena says, setting her camera down beside her. "I'm assuming these are gifts?"

Picking up Milo, I nod.

"I'll have them ready Christmas Eve. I'm offering a framing special too right now for the holidays. Frames are forty percent off with the purchase of photos. You can get him dressed and throw your shoes back on. I'll pull these up on my computer so you can pick which ones you want."

I spend the next fifteen minutes placing my order. I've never spent money on professional photos before, and I'm a little surprised at the price, but they're worth it. I order an eleven by fourteen of the Army jacket photo for Colton. Milo's holding the helmet on his head and smiling a big grin at the camera, his first two front teeth on full display. I order a bunch of smaller ones too to give to family, as well as an eight by ten for Connie and Wes.

Then, I look at the one of Milo and me. You can't see my face in the photo, only my legs from just above my knees and my hands. I'm not the focal point of the picture, though. That's Milo. He's standing in front of me, his little Buddha belly on full display. He's smiling, but not at the camera. This time, he's looking up. He's grinning at me. And even though you can't see my face, I know I'm smiling down at him too.

That's why I order it and have it framed.

For me.

To remind me of the love and adoration I have for this little boy, who clearly adores me too.

We finish up our shopping, stop in the food court for a quick bite to eat, which includes jarred sweet potatoes and Hawaiian delight for Milo, and head for home. The snow is falling, sooner than anticipated, so I take my time. Even in Colton's truck, I drive a little under the speed limit, careful to slow to a stop at all intersections. When we pull into the driveway, I finally feel like I can breathe. I didn't realize I was practically holding my breath and completely tense until I'm parked safely in the garage.

I leave my bags and the stroller, for now, anxious to get Milo inside and to bed for a nap. He's been a trooper today, but I can tell the crash is coming. With my keys already in hand, as Colton keeps instructing, I head toward the back door, Milo's car seat in hand. I'm barely inside and have him released from the buckles of his seat when the front doorbell rings.

"Who could that be?" I ask, picking up Milo and positioning him on my hip.

When I glance out the peephole, I don't see anyone. Did I imagine it?

I turn around just as the doorbell rings a second time. My heartrate escalates as I glance through the peephole again. This time, I see a woman standing there. I don't recognize her. Against my better judgment, I release the lock and pull open the door. A burst of cold air hits me, and I try to adjust Milo, so he's shielded from the frigid temperatures.

"Can I help you?" I ask through the glass screen door.

"Actually, yes. Hollis Taylor?" she asks politely, a friendly smile on her face.

"Ummm, yes," I confirm, my hand on the door. It would only take one second for me to step back and close it quickly.

But I'm unable to move.

I have no time to react.

Behind the woman stands a man.

One I recognize.

A face that's haunted my dreams for months.

The one from the alley.

The one I'm running from.

He steps completely into view, his hands stuffed in his pockets as he says, "I've been looking for you."

CHAPTER 15

Colton

With the snow starting to fall, the calls and cancellations begin to roll in. Normally, I would be irritated because that makes the day drag by, but Chase and Harrison have decided to close the gym. For the safety of the employees and the members. We're all going home. I can't be mad about that. Hollis and Milo should be home from shopping by now. An early day with my two favorite people sounds like exactly what I need.

"You going to make it home in that?" Chase asks, pointing out the window to Hollis's car.

"Yeah, I should be fine. It'll just take me a little longer."

"You want me to drop you off?" he offers.

"No. I'm good." It's going to take me a little longer to get home, but that's a small price to pay knowing that Hollis and Milo were safer today in my truck. I need to talk to her about maybe getting an SUV. She needs something with four-wheel drive or at least all-wheel drive for these Missouri winters.

"Can't believe you let her take your truck," Chase comments.

He's grinning, so I know he's giving me shit. "So, you're telling me that you would let Gabby go out with your baby when you knew the weather was getting bad in that"—I point out the window to Hollis's car—"instead of your truck."

"Nope." His reply is immediate.

"That's what I thought," I fire back, and he laughs as my phone rings. Glancing at the screen, I see Hollis's name, and I smile. "Hey, babe, we were just talking about you."

"Colt."

The way she says my name has fear racing down my spine. "What is it? What happened?" My voice is steady and stern, with a hint of fear that my brother picks up on immediately.

"Everything is fine." She tries to reassure me, but I can hear it in her voice that everything is not fine.

"Hollis," I warn. I hear her words, but I also hear her voice, and I can't describe it. Is it fear? Is it pain?

"Are you on your way home?" she asks, her voice soft.

"Yes. Tell me what happened," I say, pulling her keys out of my pocket and heading for the door. I'm stopped when Chase's hand lands on my shoulder. He holds up his keys and points to his chest. I get what he's saying. He's driving. I nod, and he turns off the lights and locks up before we climb into his truck and head toward my place.

"I'm fine. Milo is fine," she says, her voice cracking.

"That's good, baby. I need you to tell me," I say, glancing over at Chase. He has a worried expression on his face, but he keeps his eyes on the road. Focused on getting us to them. To my entire fucking world.

"It's a lot to explain. I promise you that we're both fine."

"What's a lot to explain?" I question her. Trying like hell to pull something out of her. Any morsel of information to know what I'm walking into.

"It's over. It's finally over," she says, and now I know she's crying.

"What's over, Hollis?"

"I'm safe. We're safe."

The tension I was feeling lessens. "Can you tell me what that means?" I ask her.

"I will when you get home. I just... needed you."

My chest tightens. I never in my life thought hearing a woman tell me that she needed me could cause my heart to swell as it tries to beat out of my chest, but that's exactly what's happening right here in the passenger seat of my brother's truck. "Chase is bringing me home. We're in his truck so we can get there faster. We're maybe ten minutes away," I tell her.

"Okay. I'll talk to you when you get here." She pauses. "Colt?"

"Yeah?"

"I love you."

Damn this woman, and what she does to me. "I love you too. I'll be there soon."

"Okay." The line goes dead, and I drop my phone to my lap.

"Well?" Chase asks.

"I don't know, man. All she managed to tell me was that she was safe. That we're safe. I don't know what that means, but I can only assume the guy has been caught? I hope to hell he's either dead or rotting in jail. I hate looking over my shoulder, and what's worse is the worry and fear for Hollis and all of you. My son, you and Gabby, and Mom and Dad. Everyone who is close to us."

"She's all right? Milo..." He swallows hard. "He's all right?"

"Yeah. She assured me they were both fine."

Chase nods. He loves his nephew, their bond is... special. Chase thought he was Milo's father for a while, and he fell in love with him only as a father can. Then, he learned that he wasn't the father, but the uncle. It was hard for him. I think the fact that he and Gabby are so close to the delivery of their own baby helps. I also know it's a bond that I will never be able to explain, and I don't want to. It's special between the two of them. My brother, although younger, he's the true hero. He stepped up, and even after he found out Milo wasn't his son but his nephew, he loved and cared for him until I could. I'll never be able to repay him for that.

"Seems like my little brother is always bailing me out," I say, trying to lighten the mood. I'm still scared as hell, but I trust Hollis.

"Nah, you would do the same for me."

"I would. I appreciate you driving me. I'm sure you'd much rather be home with Gabby."

"She'll understand. I'll call her when we get to your place."

"Thank you, Chase. For stepping up with Milo, for loving him and taking care of him. For being here with me now."

"That's what family does."

"I don't know how I'll ever repay you."

"Your thanks is enough. I mean, you can throw in some babysitting when my little girl gets here. Give Mommy and Daddy some alone time," he says, smiling, his eyes still on the road.

"Definitely," I say, and then his words register with me. "Little girl?" I ask. He's so blissed out over the thought of his wife and daughter he doesn't even realize what he just said.

"Fuck," he mutters under his breath. "Did I say little girl? I mean, when my girl delivers." He tries to cover up his slip and does a terrible job at it.

"No, that's not what you said." I'm grinning from ear to ear. "I'm getting a niece," I say. "Don't worry, Uncle Colt and Cousin Milo will help you scare off all the boys."

"Let's not talk about my daughter and boys," he says, his voice stern.

His grip tightens on the wheel, and I hold in my laughter. That could be any of us, and the thought of a daughter, and all the dicks out there... that shit is scary.

"There!" I point at him. "You admit it."

"Fuck, don't tell Gabs. She'd kill me if she knew that I let the gender slip. She has this big reveal planned when we're all together for Christmas."

"I won't say a word," I assure him as he pulls into my driveway. "You recognize that SUV?" I ask Chase. It's all black with tinted windows. I know before I ask the question that he's not going to know who it is.

"No," he says, putting his truck in Park, but I'm already reaching for the handle and climbing out. "He's here. He found her, and her call was her way of getting me here. Fuck!" I run into the house, slipping and sliding on the snow and ice. I almost bust my ass, but I get my footing under me and keep running. I don't stop until I reach the front door, and bust through, not knowing what I'm walking into, but knowing that my entire fucking life is behind these four walls.

Twisting the handle, I push through the door and survey what I see. Hollis is sitting on the loveseat with Milo asleep in her arms. She's holding him close, but she doesn't seem to be afraid or in distress.

"Colt." She smiles as tears shimmer in her eyes.

I rush to her, taking the seat next to her. Leaning over, I kiss her softly on the lips, running my hands down Milo's back. I then look at the man and woman sitting on the couch. "What's going on?" I ask, keeping my eyes on them.

"Who are they?" Chase asks, joining us. He walks over to the loveseat and perches on the arm on the other side of Hollis, crossing his arms over his chest.

"This is Nancy Dawson and Tom Lane."

"LAPD, special task force," Tom offers.

"Why are you in our home?"

"Tom is the cop, Colt. He's the one I saw that night," Hollis tells me.

"Leave," I say, my voice deadly calm.

"No," Hollis speaks up. "I'm sorry I'm not doing very well at explaining. I'm just relieved that it's all over."

"Okay, baby." I kiss her temple, resting my hand on her thigh. I then turn my gaze to Tom. "Start talking."

He nods. "Special Task Force also means undercover. I was undercover the night Hollis ran into us in the alley. We had to stay in part. I wanted to tell her that she was safe, my partner Hannah too, but Hannah couldn't leave what looked like a drug bust to chase after an innocent bystander."

"You were dealing?"

He nods. "Yeah. We had been working on this bust for months. I was playing the part of the crooked cop, stealing drugs from the evidence room."

"It wasn't real drugs," Nancy speaks up. "It was manufactured to look that way. That night was the big bust. Hollis just happened to be at the wrong place at the wrong time."

"The messages?" I ask them. "She's been getting messages." I look over at Hollis. "Did you tell them?"

She nods. "I did."

"I can explain," Nancy says. "That night, Hollis being in the alley wasn't all that went wrong. There were supposed to be two men meeting Tom that night. One of them didn't show up. One was arrested, and Tom got away. Obviously, we let him. However, they knew he was a cop and insisted on a copy of the police report. Hollis was mentioned. Not her name, but a woman. They were insistent that we, the police, knew who she was. We didn't know that night, but we found her."

"That's why I went to the shelter. I had a note." Tom reaches into his pocket and pulls out a piece of paper. "I was going to hand you this, but you ran." He holds out his hand, and I reach for the note. "I was being followed, so I had to sound menacing. When you're undercover, you never know who is lurking in the shadows. You never know who you can and can't trust. That note was the only way for us to let you know that you were safe. He didn't see you that night, Hollis. It was only me," Tom says reassuringly.

"Here." I hand Hollis the note, but she shakes her head.

"You read it." She places a kiss on Milo's head, making my heart leap out of my chest. I love how she loves my son.

Nodding, I unfold the small piece of paper and begin to read.

Hollis,

My name is Tom Lane. I am an undercover cop. You ran into me and my partner,

Hannah, a few weeks ago. You're safe. They didn't see you. If you have any questions,

call this number and ask for my partner, Hannah. She can explain everything.

Tom

"There's a number for you to call." I hold it up to show it to Hollis.

"So, this all could have been avoided. I was afraid, so I ran. I'm so sorry," she says, her voice cracking.

"You did what anyone would do in your situation," Nancy tells her.

"What about the messages from her website? Nothing you've told us this far explains those," I tell them.

Nancy nods. "We mentioned an unidentified woman in the police report. That wasn't good enough for them. They wanted to find her. We had to prove we were working on it."

"A few times I'd been working on my computer, and they would walk in. I was on your website looking for clues as to how to find you, so I flipped over to your contact page and sent the message. Luckily, I scrolled so that the name of your business wasn't showing, just the contact form. Me sending those messages, they kept him from looking for you himself."

"So, why didn't you just send her a message explaining all of this?" Chase asks.

"We couldn't do anything that might compromise the bust. We were close to getting the other guy, and him running was the last thing we needed," Nancy explains.

"You put her at risk." I stare him down. "You were careless. They could have easily got your computer and tracked her down. How do we know she's safe? How do we know there are not others coming after her?" Hollis makes a sound but quickly disguises it, hiding her face in the top of my son's head.

"My computer never left my side. We have tracking software on it just in case. We know that my files were not compromised."

"So, this is what? All over?" Chase asks as his phone rings. "My wife," he says, leaving and going to the kitchen to talk to Gabby.

"Is it over?" Hollis asks.

"It's over," Nancy assures her. "You can come home."

"She is home." My voice is stern and leaves no room for discussion, but then it hits me that this wasn't her home. She's been hiding out, and now there is nothing that can keep her here. My shoulders sag as I think about the possibility of losing her. I glance over at her, holding my son, and I know that if she goes back and she's open to it, Milo and I will go with her. I'll miss my parents and my brother, but fuck if I can lose her.

I can't. I won't.

"What did I miss?" Chase asks.

He must not have heard my heart cracking at the thought of losing Hollis. "It's over. She's safe. We're all safe." The words are thick in my throat.

"You good?" he asks me.

"Yeah. We're good here. Thanks for the ride. Let me know when you make it home safe. Tell Gabs I'm sorry for holding you up."

"Not a hold up, brother," he assures me.

I watch as he gives Hollis's shoulder a gentle squeeze and waves at Tom and Nancy before leaving.

"We're sorry for all that you went through," Nancy tells Hollis. "We have statements here from the LAPD. It ensures your safety. There are numbers there that you can call if you ever need us or feel unsafe in any way."

I want to tell them she'll never need them because she's never going back there, but I can't do that. I don't know what she's going to do.

"Thank you," Hollis says.

"I can take him," I tell her, reaching for my son.

"No. He's fine. He's sleeping peacefully." She glances down at my son in her arms.

"What now?" I ask Tom and Nancy.

"Nothing. Life goes on as normal. Both men will be incarcerated for a very, very long time."

"And their gang or people or whatever you call them?"

"No gang. There are a few other people we have also brought in on minor charges. They will be in jail for at least ten years. They didn't know anything about Hollis, or this situation. They were the pushers of the drugs if you will. We can assure you that you are safe. We wouldn't be here if that wasn't the case."

"Just like that?"

"I know it's hard for you to grasp, especially you, Hollis," Nancy says. "Rest assured, you are safe, and this is over. You are safe to go home."

She gives us a kind smile. It does nothing to ease the knot in my stomach. "Hollis?" I look over at her. "Do you have any questions?"

"No," she says, shaking her head.

Nancy and Tom stand, leaving a manila envelope on the table. "This is your letter and both of our cards. If you ever need anything, don't hesitate to call us."

I stand and see them to the door, making sure to lock it behind them. I have so many conflicting emotions. On the one hand, I'm relieved, so damn relieved that she's safe. That we are all safe from this nightmare. On the other hand, the fear is still there; it's just shifted. The very real possibility that she could leave me, leave us is damn near crippling.

On autopilot, my feet carry me back to the loveseat, back to Hollis and my son. "How are you?" I ask once I'm in my seat next to her.

"I'm glad it's over. It all feels so surreal, the way it all happened."

"Do you feel safe?"

She nods. "I do. I trust them. We talked for a while before I called you, and it all makes sense the way they described it."

"It does. I just hate that he didn't make more of an effort to tell you. You've been living in fear this entire time."

"Yeah," she agrees.

"What's going on in that beautiful head of yours? Talk to me."

"It's over now. Besides, if I hadn't run, I never would have found you." She smiles at me, then looks down at Milo. "Or this little man. I never could have imagined that not one, but two handsome men would steal my heart."

"Stay." The word is out before I can stop it. "This is your home, Hollis. We are your home. I know you have a life back in California, and your best friend, but we need you. I need you," I tell her.

Tears well in her eyes. "I don't want to go back." Milo stirs in her arms, lifting his head. A grin lights up his face when he sees her. "Hello, baby boy." She smiles at him.

"He loves you."

"I love him too."

"Stay."

"There is nowhere else I'd rather be."

Leaning in, I press my lips to hers. "I love you," I whisper just as Milo's tiny hands land on my cheek. "No, hitting," I tell him firmly. His bottom lip juts out, and it breaks my heart, but he has to learn. I take him from Hollis. "Listen, little man, hitting is bad," I tell him.

Big fat tears roll down his cheeks as he reaches for Hollis. "Mama," he mumbles, and a sob breaks free from Hollis's chest.

"Did he just..." Her voice trails off as she pulls Milo into her arms, giving him a hug. "I'm sorry, Colt. I swear I don't tell him to call me that. I don't know where he got it."

"You're the closest thing he has to a mother. Other than the time he spent with Gabby, it's you, Hollis."

"Oh, sweet boy, how you have stolen my heart," she tells my son.

"How do you feel about that, Hollis?"

"How do I feel about what?" she asks, making silly faces at Milo. The tears once in their eyes are now masked by smiles.

"Being his momma?"

She freezes and turns to look at me. "What are you asking me, Colton?"

"Milo here, he told me that he chooses you. He knows that it's special that he gets to choose you, and you're his pick."

"Colt." The tears are back, and this time they slide over her cheeks.

"We both love you, Hollis. We want you in our lives, and I would be honored to have you be the mother of my son and any future children we might have."

"More?" she asks, a beautiful smile pulling at her lips.

"Milo also told me he wants a brother and a sister."

"Two more?"

"At least." I wink.

"Colton, I don't know what to say. I mean, this is huge."

"What does your heart say?"

"Yes." She nods. "My heart and my head say yes. I love you both so very much. I can't... this is the best day of my life."

"Did you hear that, Milo? Mommy said that this is the best day of her life. We're going to have to see if we can top it," I say, leaning in for a kiss where my son again pushes me away from her. "Listen, little man. She might be your mommy, but she's going to be my wife." Hollis gasps, but I keep my eyes on Milo. "So you're going to have to learn to share her with me. Especially if you want those siblings you were telling me about." I bop him on the nose with my index finger making him giggle.

"Wife?" Hollis asks.

"Wife. What do you think, baby? You ready to be a Callahan?"

"More than you ever know." She doesn't hesitate with her reply.

It's the day before Christmas Eve, and here I am in the jewelry store picking out a ring. It's fast, and some might think we need more time before we make this kind of decision. I don't agree with them. Not with this. I know she's the one. In my mind, Hollis and I are together, and we will eventually get married and have more kids, but life is short. I don't want to wait to let her know that's where I see this going. I want my ring on her finger. A sort of misunderstanding brought her to us, and no way are we letting her go. I know I love her. I know my son loves her. There is nothing that is going to change that. Not even time. No, in fact, time will only make us love her more. I want my ring on her finger, and I need her to plan a wedding. Sooner rather than later.

"Colton?" I hear, and turn to see Gwen smiling at me with a grinning Sophia in her stroller. "Are you waiting until the last minute to get Hollis a present?" She tsks at me.

"No, this is... extra."

"Extra?" Her brow furrows in confusion.

The jeweler decides this is the right moment to bring my purchase out to me. "You're in luck." She grins. "We have her size in stock." She holds up the ring to show me.

"Oh my God! Are you going to propose?" Gwen asks. She rotates the stroller and comes closer, getting a better look. "Colton, she's going to love it."

"Please don't tell her."

"Never. I'm so excited for the two of you."

"Thank you. I know it seems soon—" I start, but she holds her hand up, stopping me.

"When you know, you know. You do what's best for you, Colt.

You and the precious baby boy of yours. She loves him like her own."
She waves her hand in the air. "I know you already know that, but I
thought it was worth saying."

"He loves her too. We both do."

"You found a good one. When's the big day?" she asks, handing
Sophia a sippy cup.

"Soon."

She nods. "I figured. You and Chase are a lot alike."

"I'll take that as a compliment."

"You should." Her phone rings. She looks down and then back up
at me with panic in her eyes.

"What's wrong?"

"Nothing. Just Hollis is here in the mall. I told her I was shopping, and she and Milo are here now. She wants to know where
I am."

"Shit. Okay, can you distract her at the other end of the mall?
This is my only purchase. As soon as I get it, I'm leaving."

"Where does she think you are?"

"I told her I had to help Dad with something. He's on board, so is
Mom."

"The things I do for love." She grins. "All right, Soph. Let's go
visit Aunt Hollis and your cousin Milo." She looks up at me. "I've got
this." She starts pushing the stroller with one hand, her phone at her
ear. "Hollis..." I hear her say before she's out of sight.

I make a mental note to do something really nice for Gwen.
Maybe we can watch Sophia for them one night. I'll have to bring
that up to Hollis after I propose, of course. Can't go giving away the
surprise.

I don't know when I'm going to propose. I've gone back and forth
with an elaborate proposal, something intimate, Christmas morning,
and even when we get together with the gang to celebrate the holiday.
My parents are watching Milo on New Year's Eve, so I thought about
doing it then, but that's a week away. I don't know if I can wait that
long.

I thought that if this moment ever came in my life that I would be nervous. I'm not the least bit nervous. I'm excited to start our life together. The three of us. I'm excited for what's yet to come. I know we love each other. I know she loves Milo. What I don't know is when I'm actually going to ask her.

As the jeweler hands me a small black bag and my receipt, one thing is for sure, this ring is going to burn a hole in my pocket.

CHAPTER 16

Hollis

Christmas Eve is here. The morning is bright, the sun shining, and the temperature just over freezing. But I'm not cold. Oh, no. I'm snuggled into Colton's naked chest, the sound of his steady heartbeat echoing against my ear and the scent of his soap tickling my nostrils. God, I love waking up like this.

Free.

Free to live my life under my terms.

Free to be with Colton and Milo and build a life together.

Is it too soon? Possibly. Do I care? Nope. I've dated my share of duds in the last decade, so why shouldn't I grasp onto the good? And Colton is the good. He's the best. We still have a lot to figure out, but being together, falling in love, that's the one thing I know we got right. So as we're working out how to live together in his small house and what foods he doesn't really like, I know our love will still be there on the other side.

My mind focuses on the positives and the negatives. Should I move out? It's too soon to live with someone like this, even if I'm technically in the in-law suite. I mean, it's not like I've actually slept there in the last few weeks. I've awakened every morning in Colton's bed.

"I can hear you thinking," he mumbles in that sexy, sleepy voice I love. He shifts me in his arms and glances down at me. "What's wrong?"

"Nothing," I insist, shaking my head. Yet, I can't stop the tears from prickling my eyes.

Colton gives me a soft, gentle kiss and smiles. "Liar."

I shrug and burrow into his shoulder. "I was just thinking."

"I gathered that part. About what?" His hand lazily strokes my upper arm, shockwaves of lust mix with that sense of calmness he provides.

"About us. Maybe I should move out, you know, so we can date properly."

Suddenly, I'm moving. Colton has me flat on my back and is hovering over me in the blink of an eye. I'm wearing a tank top and a pair of his boxers that are way too big yet are the most comfortable thing in the world to sleep in, but they're both quickly gone. Colton's own boxers vanish moments later, and he's sheathed in protection.

Painstakingly slow, he presses into my body. Sparks of heat race through me as I hitch my legs on his hips. He makes long, fluid strokes, my lungs forgetting how to pull oxygen, and my brain practically explodes.

"Now, let's have a little talk about you moving out," he whispers as he runs his nose along my jaw and presses into my body, all the way to the root.

"What?" I gasp, trying to grasp onto what he's saying. "You want to talk? Now?"

"Yes, right now, Hollis. It's important," he mumbles just before nipping at my earlobe.

Seriously?

"I don't think I can talk," I inform him, my nails digging into the flesh in the middle of his back.

"No?" Long stroke. "Then, you can listen." Grind against my clit. "I don't want you to go anywhere. I want you to stay here, even if it's in your own room." Pull out and press inside with a little force. "We're going to figure this out. Together."

My heart starts to pound, and my eyes connect with his.

"Do you hear me, angel? I don't want you anywhere but here. With me. With Milo." He stops moving completely. "I love you."

He blurs from the tears in my eyes, but I'm able to still give him a smile. "I love you too."

And then he moves, with passion and abandon. His hips flex as his lips claim mine in a bruising kiss that steals my breath. It takes no time at all before I'm teetering on the edge of oblivion, my orgasm right there within my grasp.

Colton reaches between us, his thumb sliding easily over my clit, and like a bomb, I detonate. Blinding white light fills my vision as I gasp his name over and over again. I feel him still under my fingers before he thrusts hard and slams his lips to mine once more, my name both a plea and a salve as his orgasm consumes him.

When the tremors start to subside, he rolls to the side, taking me with him. I'm right back, nestled into my favorite place to be, curled up into his chest, his arm holding me close. I can feel the strong, rapid beat of his heart against my cheek, and can't help the sigh that slides past my lips.

"I know what I said to you, Hollis, might've come across a little stern. I want you to know that if you want to leave, I understand. No, correct that. I don't understand, but I won't stop you. I wouldn't want you to stay here if that's not what you want, okay? But I *will* try to change your mind."

I can't help but smile against his chest. "I don't want to leave, Colt. I was just thinking, if we're going to try this whole dating thing, maybe, it would be best if we weren't already living together."

He turns so we're facing each other and brings his big, warm hand up to cradle my cheek. "First off, we *are* dating. There's no *going to try*. It's already happening. You're my girlfriend. I'm not dating anyone else, haven't even had the urge to do so since I've been home. Hell, even before that, I didn't date. With my Army schedule, it was just too difficult. And second, we may be living together, but only under the same roof. You still have your space, and me, mine. It's the same as if you had an apartment or a house somewhere else, except better. You don't have to drive home after spending the night in my bed, but you still have your own space."

I feel that slight tension ease in my chest. He's right. We're living together, but... not. I could go back to my space anytime, and I know he wouldn't question it. But I also know I love waking up here, in his bed and his arms. I love slipping across the hall and peeking in on Milo. I love getting up and starting breakfast while he hops in the shower. And then I slip into my own place to get ready for the day. It works for us, and I think he's right.

There's no reason to change it.

As he gently takes my lips with his, a loud wail echoes across the hall. Colton groans as he pulls his mouth from mine and rests his forehead against mine. "Cockblocker," he mumbles good-naturedly.

I can't help but smile. "Why don't you go take care of the condom and shower. Milo and I will start some French toast," I tell him, patting his round, hard ass.

"Or you could join me in the shower," he suggests.

Milo decides he's done waiting on us and cries louder, making us both laugh. "That's a nice thought, but we both know that's not going to happen. Go shower, and then you can come help us in the kitchen," I suggest as we both slip from the warmth of the bed.

I toss on one of his T-shirts and those soft, discarded boxers, as he heads toward the bathroom. When I slip across the hall, I'm already smiling as I find Milo sitting up in his crib. His arms are already extended my way, a toothy grin spread across his chubby little face.

And there goes the rest of my heart.

* * *

"Merry Christmas, Hollis." Colton's warm breath tickles my ear as I slowly start to wake. When I glance to the side, it's not his familiar face I see, but that of his son's. Milo is there, reaching for me.

"This is the best wake-up call ever," I announce as I take the happy baby boy and snuggle him into the bed. Milo has other ideas, however, and tries to squirm away, ready to play.

"Milo insisted on waking you up himself," Colton says, grinning widely.

"He did, did he?" I ask, rolling into my side and sitting up the baby so he can see. Milo instantly grabs the blankets and tries shoving them in his mouth.

Colton nods. "We have a Christmas morning surprise for you," he tells me as he reaches over and swipes a strand of hair off my forehead.

"I've never really been a fan of surprises," I confess, keeping a close watch on Milo, as he tries to move to the other side of the bed.

"Well, Milo and I were talking about that while I was making his bottle and your coffee."

I can't help but smile at how cute he's being right now.

"Anyway, I told him that since it was his first Christmas, and your first Christmas with us, I wanted to start a few new traditions."

Again, I'm smiling. "Yeah?"

"Yep," he replies as he stands up. "Grab the little guy, and let's go."

Happily, I take Milo from the bed and get up, thankful to be wearing pants. When we reach the doorway, Colton stops and reaches for his son. "Go do your thing in the bathroom and then come meet us in the living room." He gives me a quick peck on the cheek and turns and leaves me standing here.

I detour to the bathroom to pee and brush my teeth. When I glance at my reflection in the mirror, I'm already smiling. It's been awhile since I've woke up on Christmas morning and had someone to share those joys with. In fact, I've gotten so used to being alone until it was time to visit Grandma at the assisted living complex or go to

Tina's parents' house that I almost forgot what it's like to feel excitement and anticipation in the early morning on Christmas.

With a little more spring in my step, I head to the living room to find Colton and Milo. The first thing I see is the big tree. Colton insisted on a real one for Milo's first Christmas, and in true male fashion, we had to get the biggest one he could find. It barely fits the space, and there's no star on top because there was no room, but that's okay. It's kinda fitting of Colton and his personality.

The next thing I notice is the coffee. He has two mugs of steaming coffee sitting on the table, waiting. Colton reaches for the mug he deemed mine and hands it to me. He's added the perfect amount of creamer, and I can't help but smile as I enjoy my first sip.

Colton waves to the floor, and I take a seat in the middle of the room. "Okay, so first, we enjoy coffee together, and maybe someday, we'll watch the snow fall too. That's tradition number one. Plus, Milo and I already have breakfast warming in the oven. That's tradition number two."

My God, could I smile any wider?

"Tradition number three is music." Colton turns on the satellite radio, and a bubble of laughter spills from my lips as I hear a classic rock version of "Jingle Bells." He shrugs and sets the remote down. "I mean, it's still holiday music, right?"

"Right."

He then takes a seat in front of the tree, beside his son, and pulls out a few presents, sliding them our way. Milo's eyes are fixed on the bright red bow as he reaches for the gift just out of his reach. "And number four is sitting around the tree, watching those we love open their gifts."

With that, he pushes that gift with the big red bow on top to Milo and an even smaller one to me. It's a jewelry-box-shaped gift. My heart starts to pound, and my breath hitches in my throat as I gaze down at it, almost too afraid to open it.

"You won't know what's in it until it's opened," he says smoothly, giving me a small grin as he helps Milo rip open the Santa Claus paper.

I reach over and snatch a piece of paper from his tiny little grip before he can shove it in his mouth, and Milo takes a moment to let me know he doesn't approve. "I bet what's in the package is much better than the paper," I tell him, a wide grin on my face.

With my small box in my hand, I watch as Milo opens his first gift. I spy Colton's phone sitting on the couch, so I quickly grab it to take a few pictures. He should definitely have his son's first Christmas documented with photos. When I slide my finger across the screen and enter his passcode, my eyes instantly start to water when I see the photo he has as his home screen. It's Milo sitting in the bath, a little baby mohawk with bubbles, and me. I'm kneeling beside the tub, laughing at the boy who has completely stolen my heart. The joy and love are written all over my face.

When I look up, Colton is watching me, that same look on his face that I have in the picture. His hands have stopped ripping open the box in his hand, and Milo isn't too happy about it. We both glance at him and smile.

We spend the next fifteen minutes slowly helping Milo open gift after gift. New clothes, some bath toys that squirt water, and a bunch of little toys for his young age. He seems completely fascinated with the red tractor I found. When you pull it back, it rolls forward. Every time his dad pulls it back and lets it go, he laughs.

I realize I'm still holding onto my gift, and Colton does too. One eyebrow rises as he glances my way and down at the box. "Are you going to open it?"

Nodding, I reply, "Yes, I just wanted to see Milo open his stuff first." Then, I quickly get up and pull the three gifts I stuffed behind the tree out for Colton.

"You didn't have to get me anything," he says when he spies the presents.

"I could have told you the same thing."

"Fine, but you have to open yours first."

With a smile, I slowly pull the ribbon off the small box and lift the lid. It's hard to see the necklace through my watery eyes, but I manage. There, nestled against the ivory lining, is the most beautiful necklace I've ever seen. "Colt—" I start but can't seem to get anymore words out.

He's moving, kneeling beside me, and takes the box from my shaking hands. "This is a dual gift from both Milo and me." He holds up the piece of jewelry, giving me a closer look at the two items dangling from the white gold chain. "This heart, that's for Milo. When we went shopping, he picked it out because he said he loves you with all his heart."

There's no stopping the tears as they slide down my cheeks now. The heart is small but surrounded in gorgeous diamonds that shimmer under the sunlight filtering through the window. "I don't know what to say," I whisper, my hand covering his as I clutch onto that tiny little heart as if I were clutching the one in Milo's chest.

He moves my hand and carefully clasps the necklace around my neck, kissing the tender skin behind my ear. "Well, there's more to this necklace," he starts, holding up the other charm. It's a key in white gold, a single heart diamond in the middle. "This key represents me. My heart. And I give you the key." He smirks just a little as he adds, "Hell, I think you've owned it since I opened the door and found you standing on my porch."

My arms wrap around his neck as I hold on tighter than I may ever have before. "It's amazing. It's the best gift I've ever received," I whisper.

He turns me and places his lips against mine. "I mean it, Hollis. You own me."

"I love you," I murmur, right before he starts to deepen the kiss. His tongue slides in my mouth as his hands move to my back and then up to the back of my neck. Prickles of awareness slide up my skin with each stroke of his tongue, every touch of his hand.

We're unable to take the kiss further, though. Milo can't reach his new toys and takes the opportunity to tell us about it. Colton and I laugh as we separate and retrieve all the new goodies that fell just out of reach for Milo's short arms.

"Oh! It's your turn to open your gifts," I tell him, wiping the remaining tears from my face as my right hand touches the necklace around my neck once more.

Colton settles back on the floor and reaches for the first box. It's a shirt-box-shaped gift, so I'm pretty sure he already knows what's inside. He pulls out the gray Henley and smiles. "Thank you."

Shrugging, I tell him, "It's not anything really personal. I just saw it and thought the gray would look amazing with your eyes."

Those hypnotic orbs are focused solely on me as he smiles. "Thank you."

"There's more," I say, brushing off the compliment and pushing the smaller package his way. I watch as he opens the travel coffee mug that reads Best Daddy Ever and offers me the biggest grin.

"Thank you. This is the best," he says, glancing back down at the mug and then over to his son, who's happily chewing on a teether shaped like a chicken drumstick.

Finally, he looks at the last gift. The big one. My heart starts to skip a little bit in my chest. He unwraps the paper and opens the box. There's a large envelope inside, which he sets aside. Colton moves the tissue paper and reveals the image I purchased and had framed earlier in the week.

"Hollis." My name is barely audible as he looks down at the picture of his son sitting with the Army jacket and smiling a big cheesy grin at the camera while holding the helmet on his head. He doesn't say anything else, just stares down at the framed photograph.

After what feels like minutes, I start to worry he doesn't like it. He still hasn't said anything. Maybe I overstepped on this gift. It's personal, yes, but maybe he doesn't want the reminder of his previous world clashing with his current one.

"If you don't like it," I start, trying to find the right words.

When he glances up, his eyes hold something I wasn't expecting.

Tears. "Don't like it? It's amazing." He looks back down at the image and smiles.

I swallow over the lump in my throat. "I thought maybe you could hang it with the one from Chase and Gabby," I tell him unnecessarily.

Colton's gaze lands on the portrait of Milo from when he was only a month old. Before he knew the boy was his son, not his nephew. He nods and smiles. Even though the tears don't fall, they're there, nonetheless.

Without saying a word, he reaches down for the envelope and pulls out the stack of photos. "There should be plenty there for your family to have," I tell him as he thumbs through different poses and sizes. When he gets to the last one, a look of what can only be described as pure contentment passes across his handsome face. He holds it up for me to see.

I shrug. "I hope you don't mind. She suggested the photo, and it sounded cute, so I went with it. I bought one. For my room," I stammer, referring to that final photo where I'm helping Milo stand, his little belly sticking out over his jeans.

He's moving before I realize it, hauling me up and onto my feet. Suddenly, I'm wrapped in his arms, in his familiar scent, and hugged so tightly I'm not sure I could breathe, even if I tried. "I love it. I want one for *our* room too."

Then his lips are pressed to mine in a fierce, bruising kiss that melts my bones and robs me of the ability to think of anything other than him. Thank God I'm in his arms, or I wouldn't be able to stand.

"And I love you," he adds against my lips.

"I love you too. Thank you for my necklace."

"Thank you for these, for everything," he says, pointing to the stack of photos left on the floor. "Merry Christmas, Hollis," he whispers as he swipes his lips across mine once more.

Milo chooses that moment to yell, his bottom lip jutting out as he gets ready for a fit. I'm there, though, scooping him up and in my arms before the first tear even has a chance to fall. "Are you getting hungry?" I ask, bouncing him on my hip as the doorbell rings. "Are you expecting someone?"

Guilt flashes through Colton's eyes before it's quickly replaced with excitement. "Uh, yeah. Actually," he starts, reaching over and taking Milo from my arms, "it's for you."

I give him a look of confusion. "For me?"

"Yeah, it's for you. The rest of your Christmas present."

I don't move right away, not until I feel his hand on my back. "Go ahead. Open the door."

My legs are a little wobbly as I head to the door and turn the lock. When the chain is released, I slowly open the door, not really sure what to expect. What I do know is I wasn't expecting this.

Her.

"Tina!"

CHAPTER 17

Colton

The smile on my girl's face tells me that even though she doesn't like surprises, she's happy with this one. It took some sneaking around in her phone to find Tina's number, and then I had to wait until I was at the gym to call her. It almost felt as if I was cheating the way I was keeping my phone on vibrate and quickly deleting our text messages. Although it was a job to sneak, I couldn't think of a better gift for Christmas than time with her best friend. I know she's been missing her, and now that she's free, now that she doesn't have the fear hanging over her head, I thought my girl could use some girl time.

She and Tina are sitting on the couch, with Milo between them. My little man has been soaking up all the attention like a sponge. He's been flashing that new bottom tooth and his dimple of his all afternoon. As for me, I've just been sitting here, listening to the two of them catch up. The way Hollis smiles makes me happy to see her this way. She's so relaxed and carefree. I wasn't certain that bringing Tina here was the best move, but within seconds of her opening the door, I knew it was the right choice. There was a long hug, and lots of tears, but the good kind of tears. Happiness, relief, and joy of getting to see each other again.

Milo squirms and begins to fuss. Hollis stands and pats his back, swaying from side to side, never missing a beat in her conversation with Tina. It's as if taking care of my son comes second nature to her. "I'll take him, babe," I say, standing and taking Milo from her arms. "You ready for a bottle and a nap, little man?" I ask my son, kissing his head.

"Have a good nap, sweet boy," Hollis says, waving at him.

In the kitchen, I make him a bottle, and instead of going back and sitting with Hollis and Tina, I opt for the rocking chair in his room. That will give the ladies some time to catch up without me looming around them. I feel like an outsider as I sit and listen to them talk about old times and people they know. There is a jealousy that comes to life when I think about her life before Milo and me. It's irrational, but I can't seem to stop it.

"We have her future, buddy," I whisper to my son as he sucks down his bottle. "The three of us, we're going to make some new memories. And maybe if we're lucky, give you a brother or sister. Maybe both," I muse. He reaches up and rests his hand on my chin, capturing my heart.

I can't believe I could have missed all of this. I stayed away for so long, giving my life to the Army that I missed these connections. Sure, I had them with my parents and Chase, but this. This feeling of my son's tiny fist wrapped around my heart. Every man should experience this. There is nothing like the love you have for your child. I never could have dreamed I'd get excited over a grin, a wave, a first word. It's all magical, witnessing all of his firsts.

Then there's Hollis. She's everything I never knew I wanted. To know that she loves me makes me feel ten feet tall and bulletproof. Even more to know that she loves my son, as if he were hers, that shit goes deep. Soul capturing. Life-changing.

"We're going to make her ours, buddy. Daddy just needs to find the right time." I've been carrying her ring in my pocket. I almost wrapped it and gave it to her for Christmas, but I don't want it to be a gift for a holiday. I want it to be its own occasion. A moment we will never forget.

Milo sighs heavily as the bottle falls from his mouth. He's getting so big so fast. It won't be long, and I won't be able to hold him like this. It's sad, but at the same time thrilling. I can't wait until he's walking and talking more. I'm excited to watch him grow up and see the man that he will become. Moving him to rest on my shoulder, I close my eyes and rock for a while. Life is sometimes fast, and especially these past few weeks, with the holidays and finding out the truth about what Hollis witnessed. It's good to slow down and enjoy life. That's exactly what I am planning to do today.

* * *

"Shh, let's not wake Daddy." I hear Hollis whisper.

"Mmmom," Milo says in his soft baby voice.

"Oh, my sweet boy. I love you. You know that?" she whispers to him as I feel his weight lifted from my arms. "You and your daddy, you mean the world to me," she murmurs.

Slowly, I open my eyes to see her standing with Milo held close to her chest. Her eyes are closed, and my son is clutching her like he never wants her to let go.

This is it.

This is my moment.

"Marry me." My voice is gruff from sleep, but her eyes pop open and lock on mine, telling me she heard me just fine.

"Colt," she whispers.

"We love you, Hollis," I say, standing. I wrap my arms around both of them, and Milo just lays his head against her shoulder. He's watching me closely as if he knows that this is a profound moment for us, and he doesn't want to miss it.

She blinks hard, trying to keep her tears at bay. "This is just a formality," I tell her. "You're already a part of our lives. There is nothing that is going to change that. But we want you to be a Callahan. I want you to know that when you lay your head down at night, you're home. I want you to know that when you walk through that door, this is your home, and we are your family."

"I-I can't believe this is happening." She manages to pull the hand that's not holding Milo free and wipe at her cheeks.

Stepping away from them, I guide her to sit in the rocking chair. Milo lifts his head and smiles at her before resting back against her shoulder. "I told you, buddy. We're going to make her ours."

"Oh my God," she breathes.

I drop to one knee, pulling the ring out of my pocket. Milo takes notices of the sparkle and sits up to reach for it. "This is for Mommy," I tell him, gently moving the ring out of his reach.

"Mama," he says and tries again.

"That's right. This ring is the one that's going to keep Mommy with us forever and ever," I tell my son. I move my gaze to Hollis, and the tears are now a heavy flow running unchecked across her cheeks. "Hollis Taylor, will you do us the incredible honor of becoming a Callahan? Will you be my wife and Milo's mommy? Will you help me fill this house with the pitter-patter of more tiny feet, fill it with love, and with laughter? Will you marry us?" I ask her.

She nods as more tears flood her cheeks. "Y-Yes," she says, her words breaking on a sob.

Milo sits up and tilts his head to look at her. He glances at me, giving me a "what the hell, Dad" look before looking back at Hollis. "Mama," he says, his bottom lip jutting out.

"Oh, no." She smiles through her tears. "I'm happy." A laugh bubbles up. "I'm so happy." She hugs him tight, wiggling around, making him laugh as well.

"Mommy agreed to be ours, Milo. We get to keep her," I say, sliding the ring onto her finger.

"Colt, it's gorgeous."

"You're gorgeous." I climb to my feet and press my lips to hers. Milo reaches for me, and I take him, pulling out of the kiss. "I'm going to change his diaper, and then I'll start dinner. I should have planned better for this, like a turkey or ham or something." I make a mental note to do better next Christmas.

"Lucky for you, I did. We have a spiral ham out in the fridge in the garage. I bought everything we need to have a nice family dinner. Another tradition." She smiles widely.

I lean in for another kiss because I can. "I love that. Let me get our little man changed, and we'll be out to help."

"We're doing this? We're really getting married?"

"You already said yes, and you're wearing my ring. No backing out now."

"Never. When?"

"I'll leave that up to you. As long as you're my wife, at the end of the day, I don't really care."

"I want my mom and Tina there, but other than that, I've never really had big, elaborate wedding dreams."

"Take some time to think about it. I want it to be a day you will never forget."

"We're getting married!" she shouts. Milo squeals because she does, and his baby giggles fill the air.

"What?" I hear Tina cry out and footsteps race down the hall. She stops in the doorway of Milo's room. "Did I hear that right?" she inquires.

Hollis juts her arm out, wiggling her fingers. "Yes! We're getting married."

"Eep!" Tina cheers and rushes into the room, pulling Hollis into a hug.

Milo wiggles to get down, wanting in on the excitement. "It's best we let them do their thing, bud. Trust me on this," I tell him.

"Congratulations." Tina smiles at me once she releases Hollis.

"We're going to go get started on dinner." Hollis rises to her tiptoes and kisses my cheek, then Milo's. I watch her as she links arms with her best friend, both of them wearing smiles a mile wide as they head to the kitchen to make Christmas dinner.

"She's all ours, Milo. Daddy didn't plan to ask her like that, but when an opportunity presents itself in life, you have to take it. Don't let the fear of the unknown or, in this case, rejection keep you from reaching for your dreams. Hollis is my dream, aside from you, of course," I say, tickling his belly, making him laugh. "Let's get that diaper changed."

* * *

"Wow, I'm stuffed," I say, pushing my empty plate that I filled and emptied twice from the table. "You two outdid yourselves."

"We know," Tina says, pretending to brush off her shoulder. The two of them break out into laughter.

"You cooked, so I'll clean up."

"There's not a lot to clean up. We did dishes as we went."

"Regardless, I'll clean up." I stand from the table and start gathering plates. I take Milo's from the high chair, and he grins lazily at me. "Bud, I think those mashed potatoes did you in," I tell him. He just looks at me kind of dazed.

"I think someone could take another nap," Hollis says, removing the tray and lifting him from the chair. "We got up really early this morning, huh? Got you out of your routine." Milo just lays his head on her shoulder, snuggling close. His eyes are heavy, and I know it won't be long. "What time do we have to be at your parents' tonight?" Hollis asks, looking at the clock.

"Seven, but we can be late," I tell her, seeing that it's six now.

"I'm going to try and get him down for a quick nap. I'd hate for him to be cranky when he sees Grandma and Grandpa." She disappears down the hall. I'm sure going to his room.

"Don't hurt her," Tina says, appearing beside me at the sink.

"Never."

She nods. "Thank you for bringing her back to life. Even before that incident in the alley that night, she was just coasting. Her mom had moved away, and all she did was work. It's been a really long time since I've seen her this happy. In fact, I'm not sure I have ever seen her smile this much."

"We love her. Me, Milo, my family. She's one of us now."

She nods. "You better make sure I'm at that wedding." She winks.

"That's all up to your girl. I give her free reign to plan and invite how she sees fit."

"Do you have a brother?" She laughs.

"I do, but he's happily married."

"Figures," she mumbles under her breath. "Are we washing or putting in the dishwasher?" she asks.

"Both. I'll wash the pans, as we transfer everything over to containers and put everything that's left in the dishwasher."

"Point me toward the containers."

"Go relax. I've got this. You helped cook, remember?"

"Yeah, I know, but you flew me out here, you're letting me stay with you and eat your food. This is the least I could do. Besides, you need to get to your parents'."

"You're coming with us."

"Actually, I'm exhausted from the early morning flight. I was thinking about just staying here and calling it a day."

"She's not going to let you get away with that," I tell her.

"You're probably right."

"Go, catch a quick nap. I'll finish up here. Milo will sleep for at least an hour. We'll wake you up when it's time to go."

"You're a good man, Colton. She's lucky to have found you."

"We're the lucky ones."

* * *

We've been at my parents' for about twenty minutes, and no one has noticed her ring yet. On the way over, we decided to see how long it took them. She's not doing anything to hide it, but she's not flaunting it either. I can't believe no one has said anything. Then again, all the focus has been on Milo. Gabby and Chase have a special bond with my son, and they spoiled him rotten. Mom and Dad went overboard as well.

"We're going to need a bigger house," I whisper to Hollis.

She just smiles. "Yeah, one day," she agrees.

"Hollis, will you hand me that pillow?" Gabby asks. She's sitting on the floor playing with Milo and his new toys, but she's pregnant, very pregnant, and I'm certain uncomfortable. Hollis grabs the pillow with her left hand and passes it to Gabby. "Thank you— Wait, what is that?" She pulls on Hollis's hand, almost pulling her off the couch.

"Easy there, tiger," Chase tells his wife.

Gabby ignores him and looks up at us. Her eyes are darting between Hollis and me. "You guys are engaged?"

"What?" my mom exclaims, standing from her spot on the loveseat to come and take a closer look at my girl's hand.

"We are." Hollis beams with excitement. I can't see her face because she's looking at them, but I can hear it in her voice.

"Oh, my goodness! Welcome to the family." Mom pulls Hollis into a hug, as do Dad and Chase.

"You're going to have to come to me, sister of mine," Gabby says, rubbing her very pregnant belly. "I'm not as mobile as I used to be." Hollis settles on the floor next to her, and they hug as best as they can. "Tell me everything," Gabby demands.

"Hey, now," I say, chiming in. "Some things are sacred between a man and his wife."

"Future wife," Gabby corrects. "And we're all family here."

"She's right," Hollis agrees, and goes on to tell them how it all went down.

As if he understands what they're talking about, Milo, who is sitting on Chase's lap, cries out "Mama," and points his little chubby finger at Hollis.

I can see her swallow past the emotions he evokes in her. Chase must see it too. He stands and takes Milo to her. "Here's Mommy," he tells my son, who reaches for Hollis and snuggles up to her chest.

I swear every woman in the room sighs, as the men just smile. There really is nothing else you can do in this situation. You're a cold-hearted bastard if the moment that just passed between mother and son doesn't hit you in the feels. Hollis may not have given birth to him, but she loves him as if she did. Milo doesn't know the difference, and it makes my heart happy to know that he never will. Sure, we'll tell him, but he'll never be able to tell that she's not his birth mother. She loves him that much. You can see it just looking at the two of them together.

The rest of the night is lots of laughter and gifts. In perfect Milo fashion, he soaks up all the love and attention. My mom even had a gift for Tina. I had given her a heads-up earlier this week that she was coming, and she wanted her to feel welcome.

This has been one of the best Christmases I've had since joining the Army. Many of them I was on deployment and not able to come home. I missed my family, but I was serving my country. It was something I was damn proud of and still am to this day. I miss my brothers, and I need to reach out to them more. Make more of an effort, but I can't say that I miss the Army. How could I? That would mean I would be missing all of this. My son, my fiancée, and my family. I've missed out on enough. It's time to start living. For me, and for them.

Chase is flying Milo around the room like an airplane, and he swoops him in toward me. "Dddd!" he cheers, and my heart stops in my chest.

"Milo!" Hollis stands from her seat next to Tina and Gabby on the couch. "Colt, did you hear that?" she asks. I nod because the words won't come. "Are you trying to say Dada?" she asks him.

"Look at that, buddy. You made Daddy speechless." Chase grins, setting him on my lap.

"Dddd!" Milo cheers.

I wrap my arms around my boy and hug his little body tight. "Daddy loves you," I tell him.

"Ddd!" he says again, kickstarting my heart as the room erupts in laughter.

Best Christmas ever.

CHAPTER 18

Hollis

"You excited?" Colton asks from the driver's seat of his truck as he pulls down a long, narrow path.

We haven't been on the road long, maybe fifteen minutes or so, but just long enough to really build the suspense. He's done that since he came home from work yesterday and told me to be ready at five with an overnight bag packed—clothing optional. His lips have been sealed ever since, even though I've begged and pleaded with him to spill the beans. Hell, I even tried to utilize my female wiles last night in a sexy nightgown. Two orgasms later, he still wouldn't tell me what he had planned.

"Anywhere I'm going with you makes me happy," I finally answer, glancing around at the trees and tall grasses. Even though night has fallen, I can see a small building just off to the right. The distant shimmer of water reflects off the headlights as we follow the lane and stop in front of a cabin. "What's this?" I ask, glancing around.

Colton smiles, pulls the keys from the ignition, and exits the truck cab. Before I have a chance to open my door, he's there, helping me out. The New Year's Eve night air is brisk, but not too cold, especially when he throws his arm over my shoulder and pulls me into his side. Colton grabs our bags from the back seat and guides me to the porch.

"Where are we?" I ask again, realizing he didn't answer my previous question.

The moment we step up on the small porch, he turns and smiles. "This is my family's cabin." Colton slips a key into the knob and releases the lock. "Come inside, and I'll show you."

The moment we step inside, I'm hit with the warmth of a fireplace burning in the center of the room. "Uhh, Colton?" I ask, taking in the rustic décor and worn, brown leather furniture.

"Chase was just here and got the fire started," he answers my unspoken question. Setting the bags on the floor, he glances around the cabin before turning back to me. "This was my grandpa's place. Chase and I grew up here, fishing and skipping rocks in the lake out back. When Grandpa passed, he left the cabin to Mom and Dad. I haven't been here much lately, but Chase still uses it. In fact, this is where he and Gabby got married a few months ago."

I'm already grinning, picturing a young Colton and Chase running through the tall grass I saw and jumping into the lake. "That must have been nice," I tell him.

"But I don't want to talk about that now," he says, taking me in his arms and placing his lips against my forehead.

"No? What would you like to talk about?"

His eyes darken as a grin spreads across his face. "We have twenty-one hours together, all by ourselves, so I'm thinking there shouldn't be much talking. At all." He punctuates his statement with a little waggle of his eyebrows.

"I still can't believe you talked your brother into watching Milo. On New Year's Eve, no less."

Colton blows out a huge puff of air. "Are you kidding? There was no talking him into anything. He actually called me and offered."

"Really?"

He nods. "Yep. He was planning a pizza and *Rocky* movie party tonight."

My eyebrows shoot skyward. "Really?"

He shrugs. "Well, that's until Gabs gets a hold of the remote. Come on, let's take a tour."

Together, he shows me the open concept great room and kitchen combo. There are plenty of windows, and even though it's dark out, I can picture the spectacular view of the lake. Down a short hallway to the right are three doors. The first one is a small laundry room with a stacked washer and dryer and a large utility sink. The second door is a bathroom with a four-foot shower unit and small vanity. It's decorated with grizzly bears, and I can picture Colton's mom searching for the perfect décor. The third door is a bedroom. It has a queen-sized bed in the middle of the room with light green bedding. There's an older dresser and a pair of nightstands, and even a rocking chair by the window.

"Even though this is the smaller of the two rooms, Mom and Dad always used this bedroom because it had a door that locked."

"It's nice," I tell him as he takes my hand and leads me back out to the great room.

With the bags in hand, we make our way up the simple wooden staircase with a rustic log handrailing. At the top, we step into the open loft with a slanted ceiling. The room is perfect. There's another queen-sized bed, more aged furniture, and even a small closet. But what has my attention is the small sitting area. The benches look homemade, and the television is the smallest and probably the oldest I've ever seen, with rabbit-ear antennas sticking out of the top.

"Back when I was about nine, we begged our parents to get a TV out here for at night. Dad insisted we come down and sit by the fire, but Chase and I were too cool for that. So, they found that tiny piece of hardware at a yard sale, and when they brought it out on one of our trips, we were so excited to watch it. Little did we know, there was no cable or anything. For two years, that television sat right there on that shelf and mocked us."

A bubble of laughter spills from my lips. "That's funny."

Colton shrugs. "We made do without one, honestly. We had bunk beds at the time, and usually, we'd sit around and tell ghost stories or build a blanket fort. When I was eleven, we brought an old Atari gaming system out here. I think that bad boy is still in the closet," he says with a fond smile.

With a smirk, I look his way. "I had one too when I was little. I was kickass at Donkey Kong."

Colton pulls me into his arms once more. "Really? I was the Tetris king."

I slip my arms around his waist and press my chest against him. "Maybe someday we can play. Together." Oh, there's definitely a little innuendo in my comment.

He just smiles. "No one else I'd rather *play* with. Come on, there's dinner in the oven. We can sit in front of the fire."

Dinner ended up being grilled salmon with vegetables and twice-baked potatoes. Apparently, Chase wasn't the only one in on this little night away. Their mom also left a bottle of sweet white wine chilled in the refrigerator. Together, we dish up two plates on older mismatched plates and head into the living room. When he returns to pour us each a glass of wine, I take the opportunity to look out the sliding glass door to the lake.

"My dad, Chase, and I spent an entire summer remodeling this place when we were in high school," Colton says as he sets two glasses of wine down on the coffee table. "I remember not being very happy about being stuck inside all damn day. There was this girl a few properties down who was a freshman in college. She used to sunbathe beside the water, and if I was stuck inside, I couldn't casually stroll by and check her out," he adds with a chuckle.

"Pervy," I tease.

"I was sixteen. Hell yes, I was pervy. I was just learning what that thing between my legs was for," he states as he waits for me to take my seat and then joins me. We're sitting across from each other, legs crisscrossed under the aged coffee table.

"So, tell me about the remodeling," I encourage as I cut off a piece of flakey salmon.

"Well, the cabin was solid but was in desperate need of some updating. We installed new windows and doors, which helped a lot in the winter. We reinsulated and then added the paneling to the ceiling upstairs and then shingled the roof. Did you know Chase is afraid of heights?" he asks with a chuckle.

"Really?"

"Terrified. He pretended to be big and bad, but every time he was asked to run something up the ladder, he practically pissed his pants," he tells me. Even though he's poking fun at his brother, I can see the love clearly in his eyes.

"Well, I'm not really a fan, either," I confess. "So, if you plan any roofing projects, you'll have to find another helper."

We eat in silence for several minutes, both of us enjoying our food. "This place is great," I finally tell him. "Thank you for bringing me here."

As he stabs an asparagus spear, he says, "I'm hoping to bring you here a lot, Hollis. And Milo. My parents don't use this place as much as they used to. They've taken to sightseeing around the US. Chase used it every once in a while when I was in the Army, but for the most part, this place sits empty a lot."

I give him a smile. "Well, let's use it. You can teach me how to fish."

"You don't know how to fish?"

I shake my head. "I've never been, and I have to be honest, the thought of touching a slimy fish kinda freaks me out."

"I'll help you. You and Milo. I can't wait to bring him here and watch him play. All of us here, together. As a family."

I'm smiling so wide, my face hurts. And my heart? It feels like there's no way I could possibly love this man anymore, yet here I am, falling further and further in love with him every day.

When the food is gone, I reach across the coffee table and take his hand. "So, I was thinking."

"About?" he asks as he brings our joined hands to his mouth and runs his lips over my knuckles.

"The wedding."

Now, he's all ears. "Tell me."

"What if we do what Chase and Gabby did? And got married here?"

His smile is absolutely breathtaking. "To be honest, I don't care where we marry, as long as you're officially mine at the end of the day, but to get married here? Yeah, that's perfect for me, babe." Then his lips are on mine, slightly awkward, since he's leaning across the table.

When I pry my lips from his, I ask, "How about the end of March? That gives us three months to plan. It should be enough time for Mom and Tina to plan their trip too."

Again, his lips brush over mine. "That's perfect. So fucking perfect, Hollis."

"Do you think Gabby and Chase would mind? I mean, we're sort of copying them."

"They won't care, sweetheart. This place means as much to Chase as it does me. I bet they'll be honored," he tells me, again sweeping his lips across mine.

And then he moves, shoving aside the coffee table and sending our drink glasses flying as he lays me back on the large rug. The fire is roaring, just like the blood in my ears. Colton presses his body into mine, covering me from head to toe. His hands are everywhere. My jaw, my hair, my neck. Everywhere he touches, his lips aren't too far behind.

"I think you have a thing for making love in front of a fireplace," I tease, recalling our very first time together.

"I have a thing for Hollis and making love to her anywhere and everywhere," he tells me without removing his lips as they graze across my collarbone. He continues to blaze a trail of hot, open-mouthed kisses to every sliver of exposed skin. When he realizes I'm wearing too many clothes, he slowly pushes my sweater up and over my head, which is quickly followed by the removal of my blue jeans. He also relieves me of my matching bra and panty set, and considering the bottom part was already soaked, they weren't doing me any good anyway. "That's better." He grins a full-watt smile just before his mouth pounces.

First, he starts at my chest, licking and sucking on my nipples. Only after they've both received enough attention, he starts his descent downward. Colton attacks my pussy like a man possessed, and in only a handful of seconds, has me teetering on the edge of release. My fingers grip his hair, and my hips gyrate against his face all on their own.

When he thrusts two thick fingers into my body, my orgasm slams into me like a tsunami. I can barely control my limbs, let alone my voice. "Colton," I groan, riding his tongue and the waves of my release.

He's up and removing his clothes before the tremors subside, his eyes locked on me. "You're so fucking beautiful when you come." He strips off his long-sleeved shirt, jeans, and boxer briefs within seconds. "I love hearing you scream my name," he adds as he pulls a condom from his pocket and sheaths his hard length.

Colton stretches out over the top of me once more, lining us up perfectly. My legs wrap around his hips as he flexes forward, filling me completely. We both sigh. Together.

My hands grip his hard ass, but he refuses to budge. He's taking his time, savoring the feel of our union, and cementing our emotional connection from now to eternity. I don't even know why, but tears burn my eyes. I try to blink them away, but of course, Colton sees them. He stops moving. "What's wrong?"

"Nothing," I reassure him, shaking my head. "I just... love you so much."

His smile is soft as he gazes down at me. He runs his palm up my jaw, caressing my cheek, as he replies, "I love you too. So fucking much."

And then he moves.

Finally.

Not slow and unhurried, but with passion and vigor. A second orgasm starts to build as his cock slides along my G-spot. With each thrust, I see stars, feel the power of the release looming just within grasp. He brings his lips back to mine and kisses me with the same passion his body is displaying.

"Come for me, sweetheart."

So I do. I cry out his name a second time, but I'm not alone. He's there with me, gasping and shaking as he whispers my name. The moment he stops moving, his body sags against mine. I welcome the weight of his body, the heat of his skin, the tenderness of his touch. Colton rolls to the side, taking me with him. I'm tucked securely against his chest, our legs intertwined.

"I was thinking," I start, sighing against his skin.

"If you're thinking, Hollis, I don't think I did a very good job." He chuckles.

I snort. "No, you did *that* perfectly. I was thinking about something else."

"Let me hear it."

"After the wedding, I'd love to go somewhere warm and tropical for our honeymoon."

"Yeah?"

"Maybe Costa Rica or Tahiti. I've always wanted to go to both of those countries, but never really had a reason."

"I think a honeymoon would be the best reason of all," he sighs, his thick fingers lazily stroking my back.

I know we should get up and take care of our mess, but I don't really feel like moving, and I can assume Colton's in the same boat. We lie together for several minutes, just breathing. I'm not sure how my life went from chaos to absolute perfection, but it did. In a matter of weeks, I found the person I'm supposed to spend the rest of my life with.

And his son.

The most spectacular little boy, who just so happens to call me mama. How did I get so lucky?

Snuggling in even closer, I whisper, "I'm ready."

"Ready for what?" he asks through a yawn, even though it's still fairly early in the evening.

I glance up and meet his gaze. "To spend the rest of my life with you."

The smile says it all. "That actually works out perfectly because I'm so fucking ready too." His lips graze softly over mine. "From the moment I saw you, I knew. Every day, I feel it, my love for you. I can't fight it."

"Me either."

After a few more minutes, we finally get up off the floor. Colton takes care of securing the screen in front of the fire while I take all our dirty dishes to the sink. I try to blot the spilled wine and am grateful it was white. At least it won't leave too horrible a stain.

"Leave it until morning," he says, extending his hand toward me.

I can't help but smile. We're both naked. At some point, he got rid of the used protection, but we're both in need of a shower. Taking his offered hand, he leads me up the stairs, flipping off the remaining lights as we go. When we reach the loft, he pulls me toward the tiny bathroom, a mischievous grin on his face.

"You know, when I was younger, I always wondered what it would be like to sneak a girl up here," he whispers, as if his parents downstairs can hear him.

"Oh, really?" I reply, whispering to play along.

"Yeah. I'm pretty sure Chase did when he was eighteen and dating this girl from high school. I was off in the military, and when I called Mom, she told me there was a lot of noise coming from the loft the night before. She thought he was working out up there or something, so she left him alone."

I snort. "Working out. Sure."

"Right? I didn't want to be the one to tell her he was working out all right, but not the way she was thinking. That's not exactly something you want to discuss with your mom, even when you're two thousand miles away."

Sobering, I run my fingers along his hairline. "I know I've said this before, but thank you, Colt, for your service." Then, I go up on my toes and kiss his lips, the slightest burn of his scruff tickling my cheek.

"Have a thing for military men, do ya?" he teases, much like how I teased him downstairs earlier.

"I have a thing for Colton Callahan," I confess, reaching for the knob in the tiny shower stall. When the water is as hot as the man standing beside me, I pull back the curtain and step inside. "Now, let's get back to this whole sneaking a girl in here fantasy."

"You're my fantasy come true."

With a smile on his face and my heart in his hands, he follows me into the shower and proceeds to show me exactly how mind-blowing that fantasy is when brought to life.

EPILOGUE

Colton

I've always loved this place. This cabin holds so many childhood memories for me, and I love that Milo, and now Ella, get to have those same experiences. As our family has grown, we need to talk to Mom and Dad about adding on a couple of bedrooms. I plan on making this place a big part of my son's childhood, and I know that Chase feels the same way about Ella. She might only be a few weeks old, but I know my brother.

"Got you another," Chase says, handing me a beer and taking the lounge chair next to mine. "We're going to need to add on," he says, reading my mind.

"Yeah. Couple of bedrooms, at least."

"I think we need to expand this patio too. That way, we can add more chairs and maybe a covered area to keep the babies out of the sun."

"You already thinking about more?" I ask him. I'm not giving him shit. I really want to know. Having another has been on my mind a lot lately. My wife growing round with our baby is a new fantasy of mine. One, I can't wait to make a reality.

"Yes." There is no hesitation in his answer.

I glance over at him, and he's smiling as he watches his wife and newborn daughter. I know that look, and the feeling deep in his chest all too well. Hollis might not have given birth to Milo, but in every other way, she is his mother. The week after our tropical honeymoon in Costa Rica, we started the process for her to legally adopt him. That night she cried herself to sleep in my arms. I hated to see her tears, but they weren't from pain or heartache, no, they were from happiness.

"What about you?"

"Every fucking day," I admit, placing my bottle to my lips and taking a long pull.

"You know how that works, right? You need some pointers, big brother?" He smirks.

"Nah, I'm all good. Thanks," I say, shaking my head.

"I wish Mom and Dad could have been here."

"Me too, but it's better that they already had that cruise planned. Where would everyone have slept?"

"Good point. We need at least two more bedrooms. One smaller and maybe a huge one with a few sets of bunk beds for the kids."

"How many are we talking?" I ask him.

"As many as she'll give me. You?"

"That about sums it up," I say, making him laugh. Our laughter captures our wives' attention, and they stop their conversation to look at us. They're both smiling with babies in their arms.

"Dada." Milo points to me and wiggles in Hollis's arms.

"No, sweetie. You can't crawl on this concrete. It will hurt your knees," she explains. Well, she tries to explain. He doesn't understand and couldn't care less. He wants to see his daddy.

That's me, Daddy, and seeing his little hands reaching for me as he calls for me, has me on my feet and moving toward them. "Come here, little man." I scoop him up into my arms, and he giggles when I blow a raspberry on his bare Buddha belly.

"I was trying to get him down for a nap," Hollis tells me.

"You giving Mommy a hard time?" I ask my son.

"Mama." He reaches his arms out to go back to Hollis.

"Oh, no, you don't," I tell him. "What do you say, you and I go inside and change your diaper, grab a bottle, and rock a little?"

"And this one," Chase says from behind me. I turn to watch him take a sleeping Ella from Gabby's arms. "Is going to go lie down as well. We'll stay inside with the kids. You ladies enjoy your break."

"And to what do we owe this occasion?" Gabby asks.

"You did all the work," Chase says, glancing down at his daughter. "And I'm hoping I can convince you to do it again and again, so it's my job to make sure you're taken care of."

Gabby physically relaxes at his words, and the smile playing on her lips tells me that my brother definitely knows how to woo his wife and how to have her melting at his words.

"And what's your excuse?" Hollis teases.

"Maybe if you're well-rested, we can work on baby number two," I say, tossing her a wink. I turn to head inside, but not before catching her shocked expression. Take that, Chase. You're not the only Callahan who can turn their wife into a puddle of sweet sticky goo when it comes to hitting them with all the feels.

Inside, I grab a bottle and Milo's favorite blanket. It's a fail-safe, and once he's snuggled up with his belly full, he falls right to sleep. Getting settled in the rocking chair that my parents brought up here a few weeks ago, I settle Milo into the crook of my arm and offer him his bottle. He takes it greedily as he always does. With practiced skill, I tuck the blanket up around his face. The soft plush material against his skin already has him closing his eyes.

"Damn, I need to start that," Chase says, sitting on the couch. He reaches over on the couch and grabs a small pink plush blanket, and places it over Ella, who's sleeping on his chest. "It's chilly in here anyway, right? With the air conditioning?"

"Yes, and can you believe Mom and Dad installed air conditioning? We couldn't even get a working TV when we were kids. Now, they're flipping out that the house might be too hot for their grandbabies."

"Mom swears it's different," Chase tells me. "I called her out on it, not because I'm mad but to just give them shit. She says that when it's your grandkids, you get to spoil them and send them home. She claims that's her job."

"Well, you already know with this little guy that their spoiling game is on point. Get ready." I chuckle.

"We're ready, aren't we, Ella?" he asks his sleeping daughter. "I never thought this would be our lives, Colt."

"Yeah," I agree, glancing down at my son.

"We did good, brother. We did real good."

"I couldn't agree more." I've learned over the years, especially the last year, that life is what you make it. You bring the good, and you work through the bad. I'm well aware of the blessings I've been given in my son and my wife. Both of which, I plan to thank God for every day.

* * *

Hollis

"You going to tell him?"

I glance up at my sister-in-law. She has one of those cat-that-ate-the-canary smiles. "What?" I ask, faking confusion, but I can tell she sees right through me.

She points down. "At the bun in the oven that no one seems to know about yet."

All I can do is gape at Gabby, who seems very proud of herself right now. "How did you— I mean, wow."

Gabby laughs and stretches her legs out in front of her. She's wearing a super cute tank top and shorts, probably the same ones she wore before she was pregnant. In fact, you can barely tell she recently had a baby. I only hope I have that kind of luck with my little one.

Without even realizing it, I have my hand resting on my belly.

"I could just tell. You're glowing. I take it you aren't very far along?"

I shake my head. "I just took the test this morning. The only reason I didn't tell Colton I was taking it was because he wasn't home. I kinda had a feeling, since I've woken up three days in a row nauseous. Plus, to be honest, I was a little nervous about the results."

"To be positive?" she asks, any earlier humor gone from her face.

Again, I shake my head. "For it to be negative," I whisper. "Colt," I start, glancing toward the cabin where he's putting his son—our son—down for a nap. It takes me a second to find the right words. "He's been talking about more kids a lot lately. Hell, ever since we said I do, he's been hinting that he's ready for more. Though he's never pressured me, I guess I was afraid it would be negative. And he'd be disappointed in me."

"He could never be disappointed in you."

That didn't come from Gabby.

My eyes fly back to the doorway, to my husband who's standing there, apparently having heard what I just said. He's moving mere seconds later, dropping to his knees on the rough concrete, his vivid blue eyes so full of hope and love. "Are you saying... Are you pregnant?"

Nodding, I feel the first tear slip from my eye. "Yeah. I just found out."

His hands immediately go to my flat stomach. When his eyes meet mine, I'm shocked to see wetness swimming in his own eyes. "I..." he starts, but seems to choke up a little. Colton closes his eyes for a few minutes, and when he opens them, they're brimming with joy. "I missed everything with Milo, but I won't miss a second of this, Holls. I swear I'm going to be right here beside you the whole time.

We're going to do this together. You, me, and Milo. And this little one."

And then he bends down and kisses my belly. I can hear him whispering, but I don't hear what he's saying. Probably for the best though. I'm already a blubbering mess. When I glance over at Gabby, she's in no better shape. Her hands are covering her mouth as she openly cries.

When Colton is done with whatever conversation he was having, he moves. His arms wrap around my shoulders, and he kisses me. Hard. With so much love and passion, it almost makes me dizzy. "Thank you," he whispers against my lips.

"For what?"

"For completing my life."

I can't help but grin. "I think that's my line."

Colton shakes his head. "No way. It's you, Hollis. You complete the picture. You, Milo, and however many babies I'm fortunate enough for you to give me. I love you."

"And I love you," I tell him, my heart soaring.

"Come on, let's go," he says, standing up and taking my hand.

I start to stutter. "Wh-What? Where are we going?"

"To wake up Milo. I want to tell him he's going to be a big brother," he says, grinning from ear to ear.

I can't help but laugh. "We can tell him later, silly. Let him sleep, or he'll be a total monster for the rest of the afternoon."

He grumbles but finally agrees. "All right. But you know what we could do?"

"What?"

"Ditch these two tagalongs and go celebrate up in the loft," he states, waggling his eyebrows suggestively.

"Gross," Gabby says, keeping her eyes on the lake.

A bubble of laughter erupts from my chest. "I have an idea."

"Does it involve getting naked?"

"No, but maybe while Milo's sleeping, we can sneak away, and you can take me fishing."

His eyes light up. "Yeah?" Colton has been talking about taking me fishing for weeks, but we just haven't found the right circumstances, with Gabby and Chase having Ella, but now, I'm hoping we can sneak away for an hour.

"You guys go. I'm going to go inside and steal an hour or two of sleep, while Chase and Ella nap too. We'll listen for Milo."

"Thank you," I tell my sister-in-law as she gives me a hug before slipping inside.

"Ready?" he asks, extending his hand.

I place mine inside his as I agree, "Ready for fishing."

Colton wiggles his eyebrows once more. "Naked fishing."

* * *

Colton

We're having a baby. My face hurts from smiling. My incredible, sexy as hell, kind and loving wife is pregnant. I don't know if anything will ever top the emotions coursing through me at this moment.

Love. I'm so in love with her. I'm not sure where she ends and I begin.

Happy. I'm not even sure happy says it. Elated is more like it. We're growing and building our family, and nothing is more important to me.

Content. I've never felt this feeling of calm that surrounds me. I know that adding a baby to our trio will change up our routine, and life will be busier and a little more hectic, but the sense of contentment that we're in this together, doing life together, nothing can take that away.

"Are we going to fish, or are you just going to stand there holding your pole wearing a goofy grin?" my wife teases me.

"Actually, I was hoping you could hold my pole," I say, wagging my eyebrows.

"And that is how this little one got here," she says, rubbing her still flat belly.

Dropping my pole to the ground, I place one arm around her waist and one hand on her belly. "We made that," I whisper.

"We did," she says with a happy sigh.

"Do you feel okay?"

"Yeah, a little nauseated in the mornings, which is what prompted me to take a test."

"Milo and I are going to take good care of you. Both of you." I lean down and place a kiss over her belly.

"You and Milo, huh?" she asks, smiling.

"Of course, we are the men of the house."

"Lord, help me if we have another boy." She chuckles.

"I want a little girl. One who looks just like her momma." I take her lips with mine, needing to taste her.

"I don't care what we have," she says when I finally pull away for air. "As long as she or he is healthy, that's more than I could ask for."

"Well, if it's a boy, we have to try again."

"Oh, really? How many little Callahans do you plan on having?" she inquires.

"As many as you'll give me." It's true. I know I'm new at this dad gig, but so far, there is nothing in my life that has ever been better, other than loving Hollis.

"How about we get this little one brought into the world, and we can talk about it."

I nod. "You know, we're going to need a bigger house."

"Why? We have three bedrooms now."

"I know, and it will work for a while, but when baby number three comes along, we're going to need to upgrade," I say, already thinking about a house with a huge backyard for the kids to run and play.

"I thought we just agreed to get this little one here, and we would go from there."

"I'm an optimist." I shrug, making her laugh. My lips trail down her neck, and she tilts her head to the side, giving me full access to her.

"F-Fishing," she murmurs.

"Yeah, I love fishing with you," I say, my lips pressed against her ear.

"I do want to learn one day. I'd like to be able to take Milo and have an idea of what I'm doing."

"Does that have to be today? He's still a little young to know that Mommy doesn't know how to fish. Besides, we need more time, and we should head back soon."

"Yeah," she breathes as my hand slides from her waist to her ass. "Colt," she mumbles. "Not here. Anyone could see us."

"It's just us, baby," I assure her. "We need to celebrate."

"Tonight." She manages to pull away from my lips and step out of my hold. "Once we get Milo in bed, we can celebrate tonight." She nods toward my hard cock that was just rubbing up against her.

"Deal." I concede. Even though there is no one out here right now, that doesn't mean that someone might not walk up on us. The idea of someone seeing her, watching her come undone, it makes me twitchy. That's for my eyes only. The diamond and gold bands on her left hand say it's so.

"I love you, Mr. Callahan," she says, giving me a sexy little smile.

"I love you too, Mrs. Callahan." Quickly, I pack up our two poles and the tackle box in one hand and entwine the other with hers. We make the trek back to the cabin, talking about baby names. I missed all of this with Milo, so it's all new to me. I can't wait to be on every step of this journey with her.

Hollis

"He's out," I whisper, glancing over at the playpen. It's against the far wall of the downstairs bedroom, where Colton and I are bunking. Chase, Gabby, and Ella took the upstairs loft.

"Finally," my husband whispers, beckoning me over to the chair where he sits. He's been sitting there, watching me give our son his bottle and then pat his little back as he drifted off to sleep.

When I approach, he slumps down a little more, and I can already see the hardness of his cock in his pants. I grab the hem of his shirt and pull it up and over his head. His chest, oh his glorious chest, has my heart beating and my panties already wet. I crawl onto his lap, my knees barely fitting between his body and the chair, but he doesn't seem to mind. In fact, his eyes are burning with that unbridled desire I always see.

His hands slide up my outer thighs and around to my ass, his fingers curling up into my cutoffs. The strap of my tank top falls over my shoulder, but instead of replacing it, Colton's lips brush the sensitive skin. They blaze a trail across my collarbone and down to my cleavage.

"You're going to have to be quiet, love," he whispers against my neck.

I mumble a sound that's not really a word, but more of an acknowledgment.

A thump sounds from somewhere in the house, making us both still. "What was that?" I ask, listening intently.

Colton tries to pull my attention back to his task at hand. "That was my little brother," he reassures me without giving it much thought.

"Chase? How do you know?"

His blue eyes stare straight at me, a smile crosses his face. "Because I'm pretty sure that was the sound of either him or Gabby hitting the wall in the shower."

The words register, and a little giggle slips from my lips. "Really?"

"Definitely," he confirms, continuing to slide his lips across my collarbone and up my neck.

"How do you know?"

His eyes hold a hint of laughter. "I was a teenager once with an active imagination. Let's just say I'm well aware of what it sounds like to hit an elbow on the side of that old shower stall while your hands are busy." And just then, like a gunshot in the dead of night, a groan filters down the stairs and slips under the closed door to our bedroom. It's quickly followed by a harsh shush. "See?"

I start to laugh, which only seems to fuel his desire, his need. For me.

For us.

When his warm hand rests on my stomach once more, he gazes into my eyes and smiles. "Thank you."

"For what?"

"For this. Our life. I never expected it. Not Milo or you. The last few months have been the best of my life, and I only want more. More of you. More kids. More love and laughter filling our space."

A smile breaks out across my face. "I like the sound of that."

"Good," he says, carefully holding me against his chest as he stands up and moves me to the bed. He presses me into the bed, his body covering me from head to toe. "Now, let me show you what my favorite sound in the world is."

And then he does.

Twice.

There's no way I can fight it.

THANK YOU

Thank you for taking the time to read and review Can't Fight It.

Be sure to sign-up for our newsletters to receive new release alerts.

Lacey Black
   http://bit.ly/2TVlfGK

Kaylee Ryan
   http://bit.ly/2tIVcrk

Contact Lacey

Facebook: http://bit.ly/2JBssXd
   Reader Group: http://bit.ly/2NWrRU7

Goodreads: http://bit.ly/2Y4Zzuw
BookBub: http://bit.ly/2JJhYnl
Website: http://www.laceyblackbooks.com/

Contact Kaylee

    Facebook: http://bit.ly/2C5DgdF
    Reader Group: http://bit.ly/2o0yWDx
    Goodreads: http://bit.ly/2HodJvx
    BookBub: http://bit.ly/2KulVvH
    Website: http://www.kayleeryan.com/

MORE FROM LACEY

More from Lacey Black

Bound Together Series:
Submerged | *Profited* | *Entwined*

Rivers Edge Series:
Trust Me | *Fight Me* | *Expect Me* | *Promise Me: Novella*
Protect Me | *Boss Me* | *Trust Us*
With Me (Christmas Novella)

Summer Sisters Series:
My Kinda Kisses | *My Kinda Night* | *My Kinda Song*
My Kinda Mess | *My Kinda Player* | *My Kinda Forever*
My Kinda Wedding

Rockland Falls Series:
Love and Pancakes | *Love and Lingerie*
Love and Landscape | *Love and Neckties*

Standalone Titles:
Music Notes | Ex's and Ho, Ho, Ho's
A Place To Call Home | Pants on Fire

Co-written with Kaylee Ryan:
It's Not Over | Just Getting Started
Can't Fight It

MORE FROM KAYLEE

More from Kaylee Ryan

With You Series:
Anywhere with You | *More with You* | *Everything with You*

***Soul Serenade Series*:**
Emphatic | *Assured*
Definite | *Insistent*

Southern Heart Series:
Southern Pleasure | *Southern Desire*
Southern Attraction | *Southern Devotion*

Unexpected Arrivals Series
Unexpected Reality | *Unexpected Fight*
Unexpected Fall | *Unexpected Bond*
Unexpected Odds

Standalone Titles:

Tempting Tatum | Unwrapping Tatum | Levitate
Just Say When | I Just Want You | Reminding Avery
Hey, Whiskey | When Sparks Collide
Pull You Through | Beyond the Bases
Remedy | The Difference
Trust the Push

Cocky Hero Club:
Lucky Bastard

Entangled Hearts Duet:
Agony | Bliss

Co-written with Lacey Black:
It's Not Over | Just Getting Started
Can't Fight It

ACKNOWLEDGEMENTS

ACKNOWLEDGEMENTS

To our Beta readers: Sandra Shipman, Joanne Thompson, Stacy Hahn, Lauren Fields, and Jamie Bourgeois. You ladies are the glue that helps hold us together. Thank you for taking the time from your lives, your families to read our words. Your time and input are invaluable to us. We will be forever grateful.

To our team: There are so many people to thank. We apologize if we've missed anyone. Here goes: Hot Tree Editing (Becky Johnson), Perfect Pear Creative Covers (Sommer Stein), Sara Eirew, Kimberly Anne, Kara Hildebrand, Tempting Illustrations (Gel Yatz), Deaton Author Services (Julie Deaton), and the entire crew at Give Me Books. It truly takes a team and we're glad that you're a part of ours.

Bloggers: Thank you for doing what you do. We know that you take time from your lives and your families to promote our work and we appreciate that more than you will ever know. Thank you for taking a part in the release of Just Getting Started.

Readers: Thank you for taking a chance on us. We are truly thankful to each of you.

To our reader groups: Lacey's Ladies and Kaylee's Kick Ass Crew. You are our tribe! Thank you for your never-ending support.

Made in the USA
Monee, IL
21 August 2020

39259955R00144